THE PRETENDER

Mary Morrissy was born in Dublin in 1957. She has published a collection of stories, *A Lazy Eye* (1993), and a novel, *Mother of Pearl* (1996). She won the Hennessy Award in 1984 and a Lannan Literary Award in 1995.

ALSO BY MARY MORRISSY

A Lazy Eye
Mother of Pearl

Mary Morrissy

THE PRETENDER

V

VINTAGE

Published by Vintage 2001

2 4 6 8 10 9 7 5 3 1

Copyright © Mary Morrissy 2000

Mary Morrissy has asserted her right under the Copyright, Designs and Patents Act 1988 to be identified as the author of this work

First published in Great Britain by
Jonathan Cape 2000

Vintage
Random House, 20 Vauxhall Bridge Road,
London SW1V 2SA

Random House Australia (Pty) Limited
20 Alfred Street, Milsons Point, Sydney
New South Wales 2061, Australia

Random House New Zealand Limited
18 Poland Road, Glenfield,
Auckland 10, New Zealand

Random House (Pty) Limited
Endulini, 5A Jubilee Road, Parktown 2193,
South Africa

The Random House Group Limited Reg. No. 954009
www.randomhouse.co.uk

A CIP catalogue record for this book
is available from the British Library

ISBN 0 09 928367 0

Papers used by Random House are natural, recyclable products made from wood grown in sustainable forests. The manufacturing processes conform to the environmental regulations of the country of origin

Printed and bound in Great Britain by
Bookmarque Ltd, Croydon, Surrey

For Sinéad, sibling without rival

Didn't you once glimpse what seemed your own
inner blazonry in the monarchs, veering
and gliding, in desire, in the middle air?

Galway Kinnell, 'Why Regret'

Charlottesville, Virginia, 1978

'EGGS,' SHE CRIES, 'eggs!'

Jack Manahan stands in the summery doorway, a fat man framed in a lozenge of ferny green light. The voice from inside the purblind house is his wife's. Slowly he steps inside, his bulk eclipsing the sun-bleached portal. The faint shiver of leaves on University Circle and the throbbing purr of an idling car engine are the only other sounds to counter the lazy tick of the high summer afternoon until Anastasia's shrill command.

'Eggs!'

Jack picks through the debris of the living room, an obstacle course he has learned to navigate carefully. Dregtided cups, plates with pools of congealed food, the sour tang of cat piss. There are cats everywhere. Gingers, toms, tabbies, strays all. As he moves towards Anastasia (she is always in the same spot, sunk in a crestfallen yellow armchair near the ivy-shaded window), there is an angry hiss as he treads on Pushkin's tail. Not that he knows the cats by name; in latter years they are all called Pushkin. Their revenge for such anonymity, or so Jack thinks, is to leave their individual claw marks on the furniture. The door jambs are scored so deeply they would feel like the bark of a tree to a blind man. Anastasia loves the cats but is exasperated by them. When they rub up against her legs she swats them away, yet the house has been completely abdicated to them.

'Coming, my dear,' Jack calls out to her as he rummages among the books piled in waist-high, teetering towers. She has of late grown terribly deaf, so even his reassurances have taken on the air of barked caricature. He riffles through the piles of newspapers which lie in a grimy tide at ankle level, then turns to their companions stacked around the room, giving the walls the texture of *mille-feuille*.

Years of Anastasia's imperious shorthand have taught him to anticipate her every whim rather than suffer hours of her cranky displeasure. Most of the time he gets it right. Just now she is thinking of the egg book. An illustrated catalogue of the extant collection of ornamental eggs made for the Russian imperial family by the master jeweller, Fabergé. Fashioned intricately in gold and enamel (some no more than three inches high), each egg contained a surprise, sometimes a singing bird or a music box. The Imperial Trans-Siberian Railway Egg, for example, contained a foot-long model of the royal train, featuring seven carriages made of platinum and gold which ran when wound up with a golden key. The First Imperial Egg is Anastasia's favourite. Perhaps because it was the first. (Jack finds the Imperial Cross of St George Egg more poignant. Dating from 1916, the final one of the series, it features a portrait of the Tsarevich Alexei on its pale green, opalescent surface. Oh doomed child, Jack thinks.) Of all Fabergé's Easter gift creations, the First Imperial was the plainest and the one that most resembled a real egg, being not much larger than life size and finished in unadorned white enamel. Inside, the shell was coated in gold and housed a golden yolk. The yolk opened to reveal a tiny ruby-eyed hen sitting on a nest of golden straw. The hen was also hinged and could be opened. It was said to contain a replica of the imperial crown, but like so much else this surprise, Jack notes sorrowfully, has been lost.

The book is often produced when there are guests. It

pacifies Anastasia and if she is being difficult it provides a welcome diversion. When he bought it, Jack hoped the book would act as an *aide-mémoire* for Anastasia, evoking the long dormant memories of her early, happy years at the Winter Palace. The scenes of his own childhood are so close at hand. This house, the farm in Scottsville, the leafy campus where his father was the dean, these landmarks remain. As do his father's stern landscapes in oil, though now they are eclipsed behind towers of books, while his mother's china figurines are swamped by Anastasia's idiosyncratic memorabilia. (In Anastasia's scheme of things a doughnut carton has as much value as an icon of the Madonna; nothing, *absolut nichts*, must be thrown away.) But Jack feels acutely the loss of Anastasia's childhood trappings. There has been too much upheaval for anything to remain intact; in this way he tries to explain away her fractured memories to people who call at the house. Too many calamities have intervened; too much dirt, as she says herself. And while Anastasia had been awed and fascinated by the book and the demented opulence, the magnificent craftiness of the eggs, there had been no rush of sentimental memory. She had merely pored silently over the colour plates like a forensic child.

'Eggs,' she hollers again, beating the arm of the chair with her hand and eyeing him crossly.

He searches among the papers lapping at her feet. She is shod in a pair of his carpet slippers, which are ridiculously big for her crooked feet. She wears a battered straw hat, a plum-red winter coat over several layers of ill-assorted clothes – there is a grey, pinstriped waistcoat from a suit of Jack's which no longer fits him over a floral print summer dress. Underneath is a brown, cowl-necked sweater and unseen beneath that are a number of vests and slips. She dresses as if she is still on the run. And in a way she still is, Jack thinks. It is this thought which softens his irritation with her.

'I can't seem to find your book, Princess.'

3

Her clenched face opens into an impish smile, showing her teeth, a slightly menacing false set, of which she is inordinately proud. The slangy royal soubriquet, which she would not tolerate from anybody else, never fails to charm. 'Hans,' she says softly.

She has always called him Hans. In the early days he thought it a pet name, the sort of appellation couples late to love might bashfully employ, and it pleased him. Now since Anastasia spends so much of her time steeped in an irretrievable past, he imagines she is mistaking him for some long-dead royal cousin from the house of Hesse.

'Two eggs, sunny side up. And some coffee.'

Wrong again, Hans.

Anastasia has a weakness for coffee, peppering it with four or five sachets of sugar pocketed from the cafeteria where they lunch daily. She is a magpie, always stealing. Plastic spoons from the diner, handfuls of coasters from the Farmington Country Club. Any unwanted food she orders to be wrapped in foil and taken home to the animals. A lifetime of charity has made her thrify in small things, although she is extravagant by nature. After ten years with Anastasia this self-imposed privation still humbles Jack. When he looks at her what he considers absurd is not that this bent-up old woman is a member of the royal house of Romanov, the only surviving daughter of Tsar Nicholas II, but that she is Mrs Jack Manahan.

They always sit at the same booth in the cafeteria. The corner window seat with its red leatherette banquette and spangly Formica table top. Anastasia orders the same bizarre collection of food every day. Cottage cheese and mashed potato followed by an ice-cream sundae. Baby food. As Jack watches her spoon the melting concoction into her mouth, dribbling slightly as she does, he can almost see in her darting blue gaze the mischievous child who earned the nickname *Schwibsik*. Imp! Jack likes to

4

keep an eye on the other diners. It is a watchfulness he has inherited from his wife, this constant fear of ambush as if the past might suddenly and clamorously intrude. He half-expects to look up one day and find a troop of Reds on horseback shattering the plate-glass window and crashing through.

The regulars pay little heed to them. Their indifference is an indulgence, Jack realises, and one that Anastasia welcomes after years of avid scrutiny. But every so often he wants to still the juke-box music. He wants to hush the squealing laughter of the high-school girls who gather in clutches, six to a booth; halt the gloomy mastication of the lightly dusted workmen sitting at the counter; silence the cheery banter of the bustling waitresses. He wants the patrons of this common little diner to rise as one and bow down before her. He knows how foolish this is, but Jack has grown accustomed to his own foolishness; he has spent a decade treading a fine line between devotion and ridicule. He knows how they see Anastasia – a crazy old dame who should be locked up. What he sees is a woman of noble birth stranded in a cheap, democratic modernity that will not recognise her.

He makes his way to the small kitchen and starts to brew the coffee. Anastasia likes it hangover strength and black. Jack stands at the sink and gazes out across the driveway at the large colonial house which they have recently had to abandon. There was not enough room for them, the animals and the junk. (Since they've moved the dogs have been banished to the garden. The garden, he mocks quietly to himself, peering out at the overgrown yard.) He and Anastasia are now in the servant's quarters, where the butler lived until his death. James had been with the Manahans since Jack was a boy, and he treated Anastasia's arrival in their household as a catastrophe. Jack looks around the once spartan and neat quarters of his patient servant. Now it is going the same way as the main house. Outside is a thicket of bramble and creeper. Jack likes the green gloom it lends the house, as if they were living in a medieval castle within which a princess slumbers. The vine has wound its way around the trees and up the walls of the house, weaving towards the gutters, clinging to masonry and timber alike. What the realtors once described as an elegant property has become a rank wilderness littered with dog shit.

Only the kitchen escapes the squalor because Anastasia rarely ventures in there. Here the last vestiges of an ordered life are evident. The ill-stocked fridge of a bachelor, the wipe-down surfaces, the sturdy tubular table. Bare and clean as a monk's cell. Jack fishes out the frying pan from the cupboard beneath the sink. His back locks momentarily as he bends and it takes him some moments to straighten. He chastises his own stiffness. He cannot afford to give in to the indignities of old age with Anastasia to care for. What on earth would she do without him? He rarely asks himself what he would do without her. He cracks the eggs on the skillet rim. They fall with a satisfying splat. As they sizzle he sets out a tray with a plate, napkin and cutlery. He opens the window and plucks a milky trumpet of convolvulus from the green confusion and drops it into a slim-necked vase. He still persists with such gestures though Anastasia barely notices. He does it for himself, a way of counteracting his helplessness in the face of Anastasia's excesses. Alone, he would never have lived like this, but the effort of resisting her is too much. She attracts filth and chaos as if exotic misery was the price exacted for her enormous pride. She almost welcomes it, he suspects; it is somehow proof that she was born for something better but has been reduced to this. It is a lesson to the world.

It is not that he would swap his life with Anastasia for the life he had before. No, he has willingly embraced this ruin. It is an intoxicating and enviable madness. But here in this kitchen he catches glimpses of the old notion of himself, the man who was once a professor of history and political science, a southern gentleman, a respected member of the community. He gazes across at his former home and he can smell it rotting, like his reputation, into the foetid undergrowth.

Under the circumstances their alliance was unlikely to have a fairy-tale ending – plain Jack Manahan marries a princess. He was twenty years her junior for a start and neither of them were spring chicks. There were those who considered him a gold-digger despite the fact that he was doing very nicely, thank you, before the Grand Duchess Anastasia entered his life. He didn't need the whiff of Romanov gold in his nostrils. A mature bachelor (he was forty-nine when he married), Jack had family money to sustain him. What would he have gained by marrying Anastasia? A lot of rumour and innuendo, notoriety certainly. But no loot, as the newspapers had so ungraciously put it. The court case had decided that. After thirty-two years, the German Supreme Court in Karlsruhe finally reached a verdict on Anastasia's identity in 1970. Not proven. By which stage she and Jack were already married.

It was two years before the judgment that Gleb Botkin, Anastasia's childhood friend, first told Jack about his future wife. She was still in Europe then, courtesy of Prince Friedrich, Duke of Saxe-Altenburg at Unterlengenhardt in the Black Forest. Gleb spoke of the crumbling barrack rooms she lived in, her continuing illness, the ongoing legal process and the unwanted attention of the press. She was the 'milch cow of journalists', she had written to Gleb. Jack had been touched. He offered Botkin the price of Anastasia's passage to the United States, appalled that a royal personage of such import should be reduced to filth and penury.

He did not know then Anastasia's propensity for squalor, her appetite for it. She had insisted that the front yard be covered in cardboard, for example, and once he had found a large tree stump she had dragged in, sitting in its pocket of earth in the middle of the drawing-room floor. A stranger, if he didn't know any better, might imagine Anastasia a peasant, with her newspapers laid on the floor for the cats to defecate into and the fermenting stink of the yard. But no, Jack insists to anyone who will listen, it is only the world's refusal to believe that has turned her mind. Here was a woman who had survived the most horrific slaughter of the innocents; had been reviled by her own flesh and blood, and scorned by a sceptical world. Had she not the right to be a little odd? More importantly for Jack, a compulsive genealogist, here was a great-grand-daughter of Queen Victoria.

Botkin had turned up at one of Jack's genealogical society meetings. Jack enjoyed these little soirées, though the matrons of Charlottesville were not as keen as their chairman would have liked. For them it was a social occasion, a chance to sit around Jack's elegantly worn dining room and be served tea and small cakes by James. They paid scant attention to his laboriously constructed charts and only perked up if their own names were mentioned. Gleb Botkin, when he turned up unannounced, was unusual in that he was a man and most of Jack's acolytes were female. It was a warm evening and Gleb lingered after the meeting came to a close and even the most tenacious lady members had reluctantly left for home. James had already started clearing as Jack steered Gleb towards the door. Behind them the testy tinkle of tea-spoons and the irritated clack of plates testified to how late James considered the hour. The tall Russian stood on the threshold smoking furiously. He held the butt delicately like a novice and frowned as he inhaled, as if smoking were a highly skilled activity. The two men stood amidst the thrum of crickets. Botkin seemed uneasy, yet he was reluctant to leave.

'Ah, the Milky Way, laid out for our delectation and how rarely we look up,' Jack said by way of conversation, gazing at the arc of littered stars overhead. The Russian puffed away seriously. He toyed with the pebbles on Jack Manahan's driveway with his foot.

'Tell me, Dr Manahan,' he said, sighing emphatically, 'do you know anything of the name . . .' he paused as if the whole subject wearied him, 'Romanov?'

'You mean the royal Romanovs?'

Gleb sighed again, as if lost in sorrowful thought. It was something Jack would come to know well, Gleb's syncopated conversation. He continued as if Jack had not spoken.

'I have a particular interest in the Romanovs, Dr Manahan. My father was their doctor. He perished with them in Siberia.' Gleb gazed up at the night sky. 'I was a playmate to the imperial children, one of whom still lives. Anastasia.'

Jack felt a shivering tingle of shock. Such were the jangling conjunctions of the world. Standing on his lawn in Charlottesville, Virginia, he was suddenly connected by the word of a stranger to the slaughter of a royal family in a long-ruined empire a half-century before.

If Gleb had not mentioned Anastasia, he might have walked off into the summer's night and the two men would never have met again. It was Jack who cultivated the friendship. He immediately set about drawing up the Romanov family tree and the next time he met Gleb he was able to show off his handiwork. It was both a labour of love and a task coloured by genealogical envy. Jack might have been able to trace Anastasia's ancestry back through three hundred years of Romanov rule, but Gleb had played in the sands of the Crimea with a grand duchess in the summer of 1914. Jack would never be able to compete with that.

An echoing arrivals hall was to be Grand Duchess Anastasia's only audience when she arrived at Dulles Airport. She flew in under an alias – Anna Anderson – the name she had adopted during her previous visit to the United States in 1929 to escape the curious crowds and the phalanx of newspaper reporters who followed her tirelessly. Then, of course, she had looked the part, a frail but imperious young woman bearing the pallor of her recent bout of TB, as she was squired around various well-connected families on Long Island. This time there was only Jack and a chain-smoking Gleb to greet her. Jack could feel his troublesome gut seized by nerves. He had plundered Gleb's store of memories of Anastasia. Now he wanted to see for himself.

When Anastasia finally appeared, on the arm of a steward, Jack had to admit that he was disappointed. In truth she could have been a bag lady with her eccentric combination of clothes – a sleeveless flowered blouse, two silk scarves, maroon slacks, a pair of fluffy white slippers, all topped off by a threadbare fur coat slung around her shoulders. Several plastic bags were crushed into the trolley which the young man accompanying her steered awkwardly. A plume of dyed auburn hair escaped from a punctured hat. Jack watched as she and Gleb embraced, his large bear hug almost crushing her tiny, frail figure. Then Gleb stood back.

'May I present her Imperial Highness, Grand Duchess Anastasia Nikolayevna,' Gleb announced importantly, 'Dr John Manahan.'

The little woman stuck out a gloved hand and Jack, remembering his manners, kissed the rubbed-looking mitt she proffered. Master stroke, Gleb told him later, Anastasia does not hold with shaking hands.

Those first days were a blur of activity. Contrary to Gleb's protestations that she only wanted peace and quiet, Anastasia started giving interviews the day after she arrived. The house was swamped with callers. James was on sentry duty fielding reporters. Jack found himself blinded by the explosion of their flash bulbs when he ventured out. He was alarmed by this unexpected development. Here he was giving shelter and protection to a hunted royal while she was issuing invitations to all and sundry to come to his house and listen to her bizarre stories – she had been abused by her German relatives, who had tried to poison her, the lawyers in the court case had made a fortune out of her, the French press ridiculed her. Jack turned to Gleb for help, but as he was to discover, Gleb and Anastasia would frequently fall out over some perceived slight by one or the other. They were like children in this, long sulks followed by extravagant makings-up.

'What can I say?' Gleb said, shrugging miserably. 'She is crazy sometimes.'

Jack settled her in one of the guest bedrooms at the back of the house. It was a large, airy room. The morning sun streamed through the slatted blinds, although James remarked that their new guest kept the drapes drawn all day, plunging the room into permanent twilight. Jack saw little of her in her first few days in Charlottesville. She stayed in the dark cocoon of her new quarters, where she received a stream of curious callers. James drew her baths, brought her meals on a tray and furnished the various guests with tea. Jack felt a little cheated. The readers of the local newspaper saw more of the 'mystery woman', as they had dubbed her, than he did. He need not have worried. After a week, in a pattern he was to become familiar with, she threw a tantrum, stamping out of her room and down the corridor. She marched into the living room startling Jack, who was taking forty winks.

'*Mach ein Ende*,' she screamed. 'I will see no one else. *Absolut niemand. Nicht mehr!*'

And she stormed out again and into her room, banging the door so hard that a picture in the hall slid from its perch and shattered. So Jack stepped into the breach. He realised then that what Anastasia needed most was to be saved from herself.

Six months later they were married. It was what they called a marriage of convenience. Jack hated the term. Convenience indeed, as if the institution of marriage could be reduced to the status of a public lavatory. He had offered Anastasia hospitality, a civilised haven. Marrying her was merely the logical and chivalrous next step.

It had been Gleb's idea. He had summoned Jack to his sick bed. Recently widowed and ailing, he was barely able to look after himself, not to speak of the exigencies of caring for Anastasia. Jack recognised the power of Gleb's connection with Anastasia – those summers in the Crimea, or towards the end (Jack still considered the imprisonment of the royal family in Siberia as the end) when Gleb, by then a lanky teenager, would stand in the snowy street below Anastasia's prison and wave to her. Now he lay in a high bed propped magisterially on a bank of pillows, an ashtray balanced precariously on his drawn-up knees, nursing a weak heart and wheezing with worry about her. Gleb's room was crowded and brown, steeped in the halo of a bedside lamp which gave off the waxy pallor of candlelight. Icons of the Madonna, large and small, hung around the bed; several more in hinged cases sat on the bedside locker. Gold and blue, they glinted in the low light. It was like entering a medieval chapel. Instead of incense, though, there was a pall of cigarette smoke and the smell of stale nicotine.

'Sit, sit,' Gleb commanded as he lit up.

Jack drew up a hard-backed chair to the high-built bedside. Gleb stroked his white beard pensively.

'Anastasia's visa is almost expired, Jack. She should really go to Washington and see if the German embassy could negotiate an extension. Trouble is, the way she's been bad-mouthing the Germans, they mightn't be in the mood to conciliate . . .'

'Well, perhaps I could go to Washington and plead on her behalf,' Jack offered.

Then he halted. The thought of leaving James alone with Anastasia, even for a couple of hours, seemed too risky. She just about tolerated Jack taking charge, but she would never submit to the rule of a butler.

'Or I could bring her with me,' he mused.

'No, Jack, don't do that. You know what she's like. There'll be an international incident. And if they refuse she'll be claiming that Prince Friedrich is a murderer because he did away with her cats. And, believe me, that's something to avoid.'

'But if nothing is done they will arrive one day on the doorstep to deport her, Gleb. Her nerves would never stand that.'

'I know, Jack, I know. But we're in a real bind here.' Gleb lay back and closed his eyes.

Jack noted the use of the royal plural. Gleb looked thin and exhausted.

'There is one way to avoid all of this,' he said finally and Jack knew from the way he said it that this had been his proposition from the start. 'Someone could marry her.'

Jack strolled home through an autumnal dusk. Newly fallen leaves lay in drifts on the sidewalks, overhead the glowing embers of a mackerel sky. He knew that what he was about to do was momentous. Gleb was entrusting to him a magnificent relic, a holy totem, *his* Anastasia. The notion quickened Jack. He would be a consort to a queen. He imagined with a frisson of delight inscribing his own name beside hers on the Romanov family tree. He would enter the royal domain. As Gleb had been connected by proximity, he would be related by kin. Kinship was important to Jack. It was why, he guessed, he had spent most of his adult life mapping the intricate patterns of family connections. To see a genealogical chart laid out in black and white was to witness the equations of living, the distillation of the untidy sprawl of generations into a magnificent but pleasingly minute order. Even the dead ends had their logic, the sad petering out of family lines of whom he was one. And Anastasia another. Ah yes, he muttered to himself as he thrashed through the crackling leaves, the great tree of life.

She had taken to Jack's proposal as calmly as if he had been offering a drive in the country.

'It is my dream to live in America,' she said. 'And my name, finally, will be recognised. No one can say that I am not Anastasia Manahan. *Niemand!*'

She would always have this capacity to surprise. She had suffered so many upheavals that major life changes had ceased to hold terror for her. Jack's own life had been so steady, so tied to one landscape, that he could only marvel at the movements and changes in Anastasia's. An imperial childhood in Russia, a series of clinics in Germany, a stint on Long Island, the war years in Hanover, two decades in an isolated Black Forest village ... her life seemed as volatile as the century itself. She was a chameleon, capable of taking on the hues of her surroundings without even breaking step, while a minor irritation – a power cut which plunged the house into darkness, the doorbell ringing too often – would send her into a frenzy. She was particularly sensitive to noise. A car backfired on the avenue one evening and she practically jumped out of her skin. Jack would never forget the look on her face. Terror and resignation.

'Hans, they have come for me,' she said simply.

There were times when her paranoia would infect Jack.

Once when the phone rang at three a.m., they met robed in the hallway and stood shivering as the phone shrilled. Anastasia was breathing rapidly, her eyes ablaze, her bony hand clutching the stuff of her dressing gown, another holding a handkerchief to her mouth (she didn't have her teeth in, he suspected). Jack became mesmerised by the incoherence of her unspoken fear. Who could it be at three in the morning? At best some European acquaintance who had mistaken the time difference. At worst, a drunk or a nuisance caller. And yet looking at Anastasia he believed firmly that he would find some voice from her past if he picked up the receiver. A voice from the dead. And so they both stood there until the phone exhausted itself and fell silent.

The scandal-mongers had, of course, ruled out the possibility that theirs might have been a love match. They would not have understood the nature of Jack's desire. It was not about lust, it was about veneration. He worshipped her. And it was she who had come to him the night after they were married, a small, slightly hunched figure, a cluster of dyed hair around a childish face.

'Hans,' she whispered. It was the first time she had used the nickname that would stick to him for the rest of their lives together. *'Kann nicht schlafen.* Can I share? When I was young, my sisters and I . . . Did I tell you? I am afraid of the dark.'

She crept into bed beside him, a shawl wrapped around her white cotton nightdress. He found himself trembling as she settled like a child into the crook of his arm and wound her arms around his waist. Here in his arms, the Grand Duchess Anastasia Nikolayevna. They lay clasped together. Through the blinds he could see a blurred moon. The trees dripped from an earlier shower. She pushed back the straps of her nightgown and there, there just as she had always said, was the trace of a bayonet wound, inflicted by the soldiers at the House of Special Purpose in Yekaterinburg. The sight of it almost made him weep. He traced his fingers over her ruined body. The blade's ruptured wounds around her chest and belly, the puncture marks on her thighs, even her sad feet. He felt himself in the presence of a martyr, as if by showing her wounds to him he would really believe. He was stung by an overwhelming pity for her. He pressed his lips reverentially on each of her scars. His tongue explored the whorls of her ears. He traced her whole sorry history on the geography of her skin. It was in this way he came to know her.

For Jack it has always been a question of faith. He believed. He did not need their proofs. For the court case, she had been poked and pulled at. They used measurements and gauges. Her handwriting, the bone structure of her face, the hidden crevices of her ears, her bunioned feet. All these they used against her. And her memory, of course. They wanted coherence, a narrative. And she had only her hotchpotch, patchy memory to offer.

He has trouble with the recent past, the days blurring into one another. He cannot justify the veracity of his own recall, particularly of his happy, documented childhood. The glorious contentment of infancy, the security of being a loved – and in his case – an only child, these do not comply with cataloguing. A family tree is one thing, but memory? It leaks and flows and shimmers, it fills the space provided. Anastasia is the only storm in Jack's life; while he is the placid port at the end of hers. He does not dwell on what he cannot imagine. He recognises that for Anastasia the violent rupture of Yekaterinburg, so monstrous and traumatic – her parents dying in a volley of bullets, her sisters skewered by bayonets, her beloved brother shot before her eyes – means that for her to recall the happiness is inevitably to relive the terror. Her memory, all memory, has been corrupted.

'Hans,' she says one evening as they sit out on the deck at Fairview Farm, Scottsville. It is a balmy summer's night, a clear sky overhead, moths fluttering at the open windows. She loves the farm – the chickens, in particular, whom she clucks at like a farm wife. She fetches eggs from the henhouse and produces them from her pockets mischievously as if she has magicked them up. Straw-flecked, they are treated with as much delight as if they were the work of Fabergé. Eggs and gold, this is Anastasia's story.

'Yes?' he asks.

In these soft, reflective moments, they are Mr and Mrs Jack Manahan, in their twilight years, sitting on the stoop. She is the long-suffering wife who grumbles mildly about 'this husband of mine'. *Mach ein Ende*, she mutters at him when he takes up her cause hotly, trying to justify her claims to strangers. Do other men treat their wives like this, she asks, when he leans crossly on the car horn, anxious to be on the road, while she fusses about the house. She has no concept of time; the clock in her room is always wrong. Departures trouble her; all of them seem sudden as ambushes, no matter how much Jack has flagged them.

'I want to live a long life,' she says dreamily.

'You already have, my dear,' he replies, covering her liver-spotted hand with his own.

'No,' she retorts as if he has contradicted her. She whips her hand away as if he has burned her. She is strange about being touched, some royal protocol, Jack thinks.

'I want to see 1986,' she declares.

The arc of eight years hence spans before them. It is an airy sensation, unlike the heavy torpor of the past that constantly weighs her down.

'Why 1986, sweetheart?'

'The comet,' she says crossly.

'Comet?'

'It comes back', she says, 'in 1986.'

Jack is perplexed. She talks in riddles, sometimes.

Another legacy of royalty, her cryptic language, the lack of necessity to explain.

'Halley's Comet,' she says. 'Papa showed it to me. He knew he would never see it again. Only Baby would live long enough to see it return, he said. So I must see it for him.'

Jack looks up at the vast heaven. A falling star flares and sinks.

'Baby,' she murmurs, 'poor Baby.'

Jack watches silently as she sheds her generous old woman's tears. If only the judges, the lawyers, a century of doubters could see her thus, he thinks. Then they, too, like him, would believe.

It seemed the world punished her because she had lived. Her presence, her hard-won survival was a thorn, a regal, off-putting rebuke. Jack remembered the TV interview she had given. He does not hold with television, it is too greedy for spectacle. It cannot suffer hesitation; Anastasia's silences were edited out. She looked small and mad on the screen, Jack thought, swamped in her pillar-box-red coat and matching hat – with a gold feather cocked jauntily in its band. The camera's avaricious gaze reduced her to a bent old lady staring myopically at the lens. A jutting chin, her moist and toothless pout, shielded by a Kleenex. She absolutely refused to smile.

'How shall I tell you who I am?' she demanded crossly, when asked to declare herself. 'In which way? Can you tell me that?' She buttonholed the reporter. 'Can you really prove to me who you are?'

Touché, Jack thought.

After all the years of facts and measurements, decades of interrogation, yards of testimony, the faulty lies of eyewitnesses, not to speak of those bloody Romanovs, as stubborn as she was – could they not recognise, at least, a

common family trait in that? – Anastasia had finally come
up with an existential argument, a question of her own.

Dalldorf Asylum, Berlin, January 1922

SHE HAS CONFESSED! The Unknown Woman has confessed. Clara Peuthert rushes from Ward B, her good hand a-flutter, her heart thumping with a queer excitement. It is not the breathy agitation that usually precedes one of her seizures, lightness in the head, a heaviness of breath as if a heavy black anvil is lodged on her chest. No, this is a strange, clammy lump in her throat which feels like fear, and a tripping murmur in her breast which feels like love. Doused in the rinsed, lemony light of early afternoon, she lurches down the corridor of House 4 towards the director's office. She has a palsied gait. Her right arm is frozen, the buckled hand turned outwards like the sly reach of a pickpocket, her leg drags lazily. Stripes of weak sunlight flood through the French windows, throwing a fretwork of light and shade at her feet. It is like walking through corn marigold. Usually, it is necessary to make an appointment to see the director, and in Clara's case it would be more normal for her to be frogmarched to the small windowless room at the end of the low block. But this is an exceptional circumstance and Clara is an old hand. She knows when the rules can be broken. After all, she is the only sane one here. She has a certificate to prove it – not mad, it declares, only pathological. Anyway, none of this is of any import in comparison to the startling news she is carrying.

Clara Peuthert is a tall woman, fifty-one years of age, large-boned but lean. Her unruly head of red hair clustering around her square jaw is one clue to the spitting rages which have brought her to the Dalldorf Asylum, not once but several times. That and her green goitred gaze and the taut cords of her neck. But in repose she has a glassy, seductive air; she has the capacity to mesmerise with the intensity of her flawed attention. Her interest in others feels to them like lavish flattery, as if she has bestowed grandeur on them. It is in this way she has gained the confidence of Fräulein Unbekannt, the unknown woman.

No one else had the patience. The doctors had long since given up. Her dogged muteness had defeated them. All their inquiries had come to naught. The questions had started two years before at the Elisabeth Hospital on Lützowstraße, where she was taken first after being dragged from the canal, wrapped in a rough blanket, her fingers numb, her teeth chattering. Who are you? What were you doing? Did you jump or were you pushed? Why did you do it? Where are your papers? Who are you? The nurses peeled off her seeping clothes. She resisted at first, flinching as they touched her, shutting her eyes tight. They realised why when she stepped into the white enamel tub. Her body was covered in scars, long, deep incisions and blistered weals on her stomach and torso.

'Who has done this to you?' one of the nurses asked urgently.

She was brisk and heavy-set with a cracked red face, a motherly woman. But the young woman, who had not uttered a single word, simply shut her eyes and shook her head. The nurse stood guard while she bathed.

'Can't trust you near water,' she said heartily, her laughter echoing in the white-tiled bathhouse.

Her merry voice was the only human sound, though the pipes gurgled and the bath tap dripped. The young woman made no move to stop it. She lay in the water like a corpse until the steaming water grew tepid. On the nurse's urging she stepped out onto the wooden pallet by the bath. The nurse noticed another wound on her instep. And another thing which made her smart with fellow feeling. *Hallux valgus.* The mysterious patient, like herself, had bunions. She allowed herself to be wrapped in a towel and dried gently, the nurse mindful of her wounds, though by the look of them they were several years old. She did not struggle when the nurse slipped a white chemise of bleached hessian over her head. She was as biddable as an overtired child at bedtime.

The nurse led her by the hand to a desk on the night ward. She made a list of her sodden clothes. Black skirt, black stockings, white linen blouse, underwear, laced boots, a brown shawl.

'No coat,' the nurse murmured in rebuke as she entered these details in a large ledger, 'in this weather!'

She sifted through the clothing, examining each item and shaking her head mournfully at the end of the process. There were no labels or laundry marks. They provided no clues to the wearer's identity. She bundled the clothes into a large linen basket and led the young woman to a bed near the desk so that she could keep an eye on her. In the morning, she was sure, when the shock had worn off, whatever had happened to the poor creature would become clear. A predicament of love, the nurse suspected, why else would a pretty young woman try to kill herself?

The nurse checked on her through the night. Scrubbed and clean and released from scrutiny, the young woman's sleeping features had eased into a pallid innocence. Some mother had crushed this face to her breast, a man might have gazed here with desire.

'But now, my dear,' the nurse ruminated aloud, 'you are

as much yourself as you will ever be.' The graveyard hours had made her pensive.

In the morning, before going off duty, she brought the young woman breakfast, a bowl of coffee, a slice of white bread. She ate wordlessly but with relish. Her face had lost its night's ease. In its place was a blank and haughty defiance.

It is this look that greets the doctor who approaches the bed during the morning rounds. He is alone. From the admission notes he has gleaned that groups of people agitate the patient. When she came to on the canal bank the night before stretched at the feet of a crowd of onlookers, all babble and alarm, she cowered and clapped her hands over her ears as if to shut out the noise. He has told the police officer who has arrived to question her to wait outside.

'Fräulein,' he says gingerly.

She does not raise her eyes from what seems intense contemplation of her hands. He draws up a chair, a rickety bentwood. The legs scrape along the speckled floor of the ward. She winces at the tiny scream.

'Fräulein,' he starts again, 'you must tell us who you are. Your family will be concerned. Surely?'

She looks up, but not at him. Her eyes follow the progress of a nurse bearing a jug and basin for a bed bath further down the ward.

'They will wonder where you are, if some harm has befallen you. Your mother ... Papa?'

The word seems to jar. She looks at him swiftly, an afflicted glance no more, then looks away again.

'Come, come, Fräulein.' He tries a hearty tone. 'You must let us help you. We need to know what brought you to such drastic action.'

She sits stony-faced, eyes down.

'It's a crime, you know,' he says sternly.

Certain words seem to unnerve her. Crime makes her draw the coverlet up in a grim bunch to her face.

'You can't expect to get away with it, Fräulein.'

She bunches the counterpane into a rosette at her mouth.

'Trying to kill yourself . . . well, the authorities may want to pursue it. You would do better to co-operate with us rather than trust to the tender mercies of the Berlin police department.'

Police. Another jagged word.

'Tell us, we can help you. Who are you?'

She shakes her head.

'Do you work, Fräulein?' he persists. He makes to take one of her hands. She withdraws it sharply as if his touch might burn.

'In a factory, perhaps?'

A tiny frown wrinkles her high brow. He is not sure if it is a furrow of concentration or distress.

'Would it be fair to describe you as a working woman?'

He is beginning to sound desperate, sitting there with his pen poised and a sheaf of papers on his knee, like a disconsolate fisherman hauling in empty nets. And then, slowly, she nods.

'Yes?'

Too keen. She turns away and buries her face in the pillow. The interview is over. He has been dismissed.

He came back every day for weeks. He was like a dog, eager and hopeless by turns. He would get exasperated by her silence, exploding into a kind of helpless anger, immediately followed by a respectful apology, afraid of exciting her ire. She seemed to watch his antics with an indulgent fondness. Sometimes he thought she was laughing at him, enjoying this cat and mouse game, toying with him. At other times he believed her baffled muteness was genuine. And it seemed that she grew used to, if not to like, his daily visits, his tenderly persistent interest in her. He

24

could not understand why it disturbed him that he didn't know who she was. It didn't disturb her. Other things did – the sight of the policeman who, in the early days, had sat in on a few sessions, a clumsy, incompetent oaf by the name of Krug. She clammed up completely then. He laughed at himself. Only he would recognise the difference between her general silence and the recalcitrance she reserved for Inspector Krug. In the end, though, she exhausted Dr Finsterl. (That was his name; in the absence of information about her he had talked about himself.) Willi Finsterl, aged twenty-nine, newly qualified intern at the Elisabeth Hospital. He had served at the Front. Wounded at Verdun, he said. Verdun. She did not want to hear about that, her hands went over her ears.

After six weeks of fruitless questioning, Dr Finsterl surrendered. One Monday morning he arrived at her bedside as usual, but instead of sitting down companionably he stood rather formally at the end of the bed.

'Fräulein,' he said, with an upward inflection so that it sounded like a query.

She plumped up the pillows behind her, a prelude to their halting routine of unanswered questions.

'Today you are going to be taken to another place. To Dalldorf.'

She cocked her head quizzically.

'It's an asylum.'

She cleared her throat. Dr Finsterl realised that this was the first sound he had heard her make. He felt ridiculously proud as if she were an infant uttering her first word. And then she rewarded him with a full sentence.

'I have done nothing.'

So used was he to her silence that he looked around, sure that somebody else had spoken. When he looked back at her, her features were set in determined repose.

'Who are you? Please, tell me,' he pleaded.

But after the brief sunburst he had lost her to the enveloping fog.

'We cannot keep you here any longer,' he said irritably. 'We have many sick people to care for. And you refuse to help yourself.'

He backed away and then he remembered.

'I have given you a name, by the way. I had to put something on the papers. I've called you Fräulein Unbekannt,' he declared, 'the unknown one.'

Fräulein Unbekannt. She liked the sound of it. She was grateful to Willi Finsterl; he had given her a little gift. Maybe now the questions would stop.

She is ordered to dress. She is given back the freshly laundered clothes they said she had come in with. Two orderlies take her by the arms and steer her along a polished avenue, vast and shimmering as if in a heat haze, then down two flights of stairs mottled with spots of peacock blue and fiery red from a vast stained-glass window several storeys high. They turn at the end of the steps and burrow through a maze of dim passageways. A burst of copper clamour from the kitchens. The hissing clouds of the laundry with its swaddled bins of soiled linen. And then out into a paved courtyard and into the yawning gape of an ambulance. She sniffs the air before they shut the doors. Rain on the way, an injured sky.

The ambulance rattles along noisily as she sits clutching the edge of the hard bench. It is a long journey. She begins to get panicky locked up in this metal box, this prison on wheels. Where are these men taking her? To a lonely field. They would blindfold her and then . . . At least she would know what she had done. Before they shot her they would have to read out the charges. There might even be a priest there who would hear her last confession. But what would she confess to? Not even to a name at the moment, except the one Dr Finsterl had given her. Guilt is her only constant. She has done wrong, hasn't she? All her thoughts end up like this. One question begging another.

The motor slows and comes to a halt. The driver and his companion get out with a thunderclap of doors. The metal box sways like a horse, glad to have shrugged off its mount. She hears their footsteps scrunching on gravel as they make their way to the back. The bolt slides open. She crouches in the furthest corner. It is too bright out there – leaf-shimmer, drenched sun-dazzle. The two orderlies, reduced to burly silhouette, clamber into the archway of light. She curls up on the floor. Their boots make a rackety advance. One of them reaches down and grips her arm. She beats at him with her fists.

'Steady on, darling, don't make this hard on yourself.'

She kicks out, catching him on the shins.

He howls and staggers back, but the other one takes hold of her hair. She bites at his wrist. It is hairy and smells of sea-salt.

'Agh,' he roars, 'the bitch has bitten me.'

He grabs her again by her hair, while his companion hoists her up.

'Finsterl was right,' one of them mutters as they tumble out into the daylight, 'this one really is crazy.'

'TRANSFER FROM ELISABETH Hospital!' one of the orderlies roars as they approach a long wooden counter in the entrance hall. There is nobody about. He raps a small bell on the counter top. A nurse, whom she will later find out is Nurse Walz, appears from a doorway behind the desk.

'Sign here and we'll be off,' the orderly says and pushes a set of papers at her.

'Ah yes,' Nurse Walz says, smiling, 'we've been expecting you, Fräulein.'

'Well, just you watch her, she's no lady and that's for sure,' the second orderly growls.

'It says here that she's depressed, melancholic,' Nurse Walz says, puzzled.

'Melancholy she may be, but she brawls like a fishwife. She's just taken a lump out of my arm.' He rolls up his sleeve and points to the teeth marks. 'That's all the gratitude they have, biting the hand that feeds.' He gives the patient a spiteful look.

'A few weeks in the cells might put manners on her,' his companion adds.

Is this a prison? Have they tried her in her absence?

'We are not jailers here, gentlemen,' Nurse Walz says sweetly.

She circles out from behind the desk and lays a hand tentatively on the patient's arm. The nurse is a young, slender woman, her dark hair pinned severely under her cap, her eyes a mossy brown.

'Come this way.'

She follows Nurse Walz through a pair of swing doors into a long yellow corridor. French doors give on to a veranda. The light is the colour of mown hay, though the gardens outside are coming into green leaf.

'In here, please.'

Nurse Walz opens a door with frosted-glass panes into a small, airless study. If the season outside is a mixture of spring and summer, this room is autumn. Dark panels of waist-high wood clad walls the colour of bonfire smoke. A huge desk straddles the far corner and behind it, bathed in the green glow of a lamp necessary in this dimness, an elderly man sits.

'This is the patient from the Elisabeth Hospital, Herr Direktor,' the nurse says, placing the papers on the desk and returning to her sentry position behind the patient.

'Thank you,' the director says without looking up.

He leafs through the documents. He is white-haired but balding. His moustache is matched by twin tufts of hair at his ears. His spectacles are like thin slivers of silver.

'Not much to go on here, Fräulein,' he says reproachfully. He sighs. 'I shall have to conduct an examination.'

He rises and steps out from behind the desk.

'Yes?' he says loudly, peering into the woman's face.

The patient is mute, not deaf, the nurse thinks, but she too stays silent.

'Please remove your clothes.'

The patient does not react. Perhaps she is deaf after all, Nurse Walz thinks.

'Fräulein,' the director commands. 'Your clothes, I must insist. We must carry out a physical examination.'

He points to a latticed muslin screen near the desk. The patient backs away slowly. She turns and tries to lunge at the door and as she does it opens and a young man in a white coat marches in, beaming broadly.

'Oh, apologies, bad time,' he says and makes to retreat.

'Ah, Hanisch, just the man!' the director says with loud relief. He snaps his fingers. 'Walz!'

For a minute the patient thinks a band is going to strike up and the doctor is going to dance. Then the nurse rushes at her and pinions her arms behind her back. She is bustled behind the screen.

'Be quiet,' Nurse Walz hisses at her, 'or do you want one of *them* to do it?'

Nurse Walz methodically unbuttons her blouse, unhooks her skirt, unties her boots, unrolls her stockings. They lie where they have fallen, washed up around her ankles. Nurse Walz pulls down her bloomers.

'Step out, Fräulein, would you?' the director's voice booms.

Nurse Walz pushes back the screen.

'My God,' Hanisch gasps, 'what has happened here?'

The scars again.

She stands naked and shaking as he runs his fingers along the rugged seams.

'How did you come by such wounds?' the director asks.

'Bayonets?' Dr Hanisch ventures, as if it were an endearing query of love.

The director shrugs.

The men move around her, picking up her hand, then letting it fall, examining her temples. They stare into the whites of her eyes; they peer down her throat. They beckon to her to stand on the weighing scales. They measure her height against a metal gauge on the wall. The examination ends with the dirctor giving her a sharp slap on the rump. She barely reacts; all the fight has gone out of her.

'Walz,' the director barks, 'cover her up.'

The nurse guides her behind the screen. She fishes for her discarded clothes and hurriedly puts them on, refusing the nurse's help. She gets the buttons wrong, her skirt is crooked, she does not bother to lace her boots. When she

30

emerges she has acquired the dishevelled look of the vaguely mad.

'Does she not speak?' Dr Hanisch asks.

'She may not speak,' Nurse Walz says, 'but she bites. She attacked one of the orderlies who brought her in.'

'Brutes,' Dr Hanisch says. 'I would bite them myself.'

A strange thing happens then. The patient smiles. Dr Hanisch looks gratified; he likes his humour to be appreciated, even by the insane.

'Put her in Ward B,' the director says, 'we'll try her out with the quiet ones.'

Ward B was a pit of noise. Fourteen patients crammed into a tall, narrow room. A row of internal windows looked out onto the yellow corridor, but they were placed so high even the sills were out of reach. The light, which had seemed fresh and golden outside, was wan and bleached by the time it had filtered through the unwashed glass. When Nurse Walz led her in, the din of argument within fell away. A motley collection of women turned and stared at her absently. For a few moments she held their dulled attention. Then they resumed their clamorous complaint. A nurse detached herself from the gaggle of patients gathered idly in the centre of the ward and came over.

'New one for you,' Nurse Walz said. 'Careful, she bites.'

Nurse Bucholz was tiny and round. She had to look up at the patient, but she compensated for her girth and lack of stature with the fierceness of her regard.

'Bed fifteen,' she commanded, 'by the door.'

There is a white bedstead and a tin locker. On the made-up bed is a grey shift, which Nurse Bucholz orders her to put on. Obligingly she pulls a screen around the bed and for the second time that day the patient undresses. Nurse Bucholz returns, whips away her day clothes and hands her a ragged robe to put on over her regulation grey, and a defeated pair of slippers. The patient watches sadly as the nurse removes the clothes. *Her* clothes, it seems. They were not fine clothes. Indeed most of them seemed home-made, but they fitted her and they bore a homely smell of woodsmoke not quite eclipsed by the Elisabeth Hospital's aggressive starching. They were the only things she owned and Nurse Bucholz was taking them away.

It was almost lunchtime. One woman with long ginger hair and a slack mouth approached her bed and stood staring at her, then pointed her finger and cackled noisily. The rest of them took up her laughter, though from their mouths it sounded more like ululation, a lament. A dry-skinned dwarf ran up and poked her about the ribs. She winced, her scars ajangle. A large, lumpen woman with thick spectacles dragged the dwarf away, smiling as she did and showing shyly the rotten stumps of her teeth. The patient put a hand to her own mouth, some reflex of old. She turned her back to the ward and climbed into bed, hoping that would shut out their crazed observation. She need not have worried. At that moment the kitchen trolley was rolled in. The kitchen maid lifted the lids off the basins sunk in the trolley and banged them together like cymbals. The slovenly occupants of Ward B all but stood to attention, filing to their places at the long refectory table set in the centre of the ward. At the second crash of the cymbals they sat down with military precision, clutching their wooden ladles. (They were not trusted with cutlery in case they did damage to themselves or others.) The kitchen maid dolloped a portion of mash and a piece of *wurst* onto each enamel plate. They ate noisily – slurps and belches – but with exquisite concentration. It was the only time that silence reigned in Ward B. They eyed each portion greedily while guarding their own with a shielding arm. That first day Nurse Bucholz brought a plate to her, leaving it on her locker. Turnip had been threaded through the mash; she could smell it. It made her heave. She turned her face to the wall. She would not eat their slop and she would never join them at their table, where they fed like pigs, snouts in the trough.

She could not sleep. It was too bright. Moonlight streamed through the uncovered windows. And there was the noise. The other patients roared out in the night. They had bad dreams. And even when they weren't having nightmares there was a constant undertow of protest – they muttered and spat and grumbled even in their deepest slumber. The woman in the next bed, the large one with the spectacles, salivated noisily and ground her teeth. The beds were close enough together that every bodily function was clearly audible – farts, the growl of stomachs. And they snored like furnaces. She lay sleepless and listened to the cacophony, loud and livid as a nocturnal forest. In their slumber they railed against their fate; perhaps because only in their sleep were they allowed to give vent to their pent-up frustration and rage uncensored. And it was the only time they left her alone. Only at night as she lay listening to their animal sounds, burrowing deep into the febrile muck of dreams, did she feel anything for them. It was a mournful kind of fellow feeling, tinged with her own disdain.

They were roused roughly in the dawn by the peel of a school bell wielded by Nurse Malinovsky. The morning call was the last task of her day. They were herded down the corridor in a long line, each according to her number. Oh yes, not only did she own a name now, she also had a number, 15B, the latest admission, the last into the showers. She watched, horrified, as the women ahead of her were pushed two to a tiled stall and a jet of cold water was applied mercilessly. Nurse Malinovsky checked for lice in their hair and soaped the underarms and crotches of the vacant imbeciles, who rocked and swayed placidly in the footbaths. The others squealed and shrieked and pawed one another as they tried to catch the leaping bars of carbolic soap, which turned into fish in their hands. 15B watched long enough to know that this she would never tolerate. She would not strip in front of these creatures. She fled back to the ward. Nurse Malinovsky followed her.

'What is it, Fräulein?'

She shook her head violently, shrinking from the nurse's outstretched hand.

'The showers are part of the treatment here, Fräulein. We find that immersion is often beneficial for the despondent, it invigorates the spirit. And it's vital for hygiene. I can tell you have standards in that area but for the others it's something that must be imposed. You understand?'

She warmed to the nurse's conciliatory tone. This woman was a lady.

'We won't insist for today, but it's important not to let yourself go, particularly in here.'

The din from the showers blossomed damply.

'I must go and tend to my water rats.'

Breakfast was not much better than lunch. Lumpy porridge, cold tea – they were not allowed anything hot in case they threw it over one another. And their distance from the kitchens meant that all food arrived tepid and looking as if it had already been partially digested. She ate at her locker again. She would not grub around with the rest of them. The nurses did not insist. She had learned her first lesson about Dalldorf. Resistance must always be quiet. Anything showy or noisy would land her in the company of the really mad in the lock-up wards. If she kept herself apart she might not be infected. She must not end up like these

34

poor demented creatures, whom she both despised and pitied.

After breakfast the women were supposed to make their beds, but except for a few even this task was beyond them and the nurses usually took over, turning in corners and thumping the limp pillows to make them seem fat. The patients were lined up again, this time for their daily exercise. They were paired off. She got the pigtailed dwarf, who insisted on holding her hand, swinging it gaily as they were led outside. The dwarf's palm was aged to the touch, but clammy as a frightened child's. Their destination was not, as she expected, the verdant stretch of green visible through the French windows, but an exercise yard at the back of the building, fenced in by a tall palisade. Nurse Bucholz led the charade, a risible attempt at leg-shaking and arm-swinging and leaping on the spot, followed by a trudge twice around the perimeter. Nurse Bucholz tried to keep them in step by blowing fiercely on a whistle to up their ragged tempo. The dwarf took four tripping steps to each one of hers; it was like being chained to a malevolent infant. When it was over, she rushed to wash her hands, scrubbing them almost raw to remove all trace of the evil little creature, a hag in a child's body. It was the first and last time Fräulein Unbekannt would participate in communal exercise.

They were put to work, each according to her malady. The delirious washed, the imbeciles hung out to dry, the melancholy ironed. She was determined that she would never join them. She would not drudge and slave. She was better than that. She must rise above the common throng; how else was she going to get out of here? Initially she was excused from work detail because there were further tests to be done. As she sat on the bed in the deserted ward she wondered what further humiliation they had planned for her. Within the hour Dr Hanisch and Nurse Walz appeared, sidling up to her slyly, and she feared the worst.

'Fräulein,' Dr Hanisch said tentatively, 'I'm afraid that it is necessary for us to conduct another physical examination . . .'

She wrapped her arms around herself.

'Of an intimate, female kind . . .'

She knew what he was saying. He would rape her. It was what all men wanted.

'It will be very quick,' Nurse Walz said, 'it won't hurt.'

What place was this, where women shepherded degradation with sweet words and lies?

'Lie down, Fräulein,' the nurse said, pushing against the rigid clasp of her body. She flailed wildly, catching Nurse Walz's nose. Blood streamed from her nostril. The nurse backed off, leaving a bloody trail on the bedclothes. Dr Hanisch snapped his fingers and two orderlies emerged, shouldering their way to the bedside. One grabbed the patient's arms and forced them over her head, the other clamped his hands around her ankles. Dr Hanisch forced her legs open. She felt him enter her. Cold, metallic, he was using his rifle barrel. She screamed. One of the orderlies clapped a hand over her mouth. He tasted of bacon rind. She waited for the rupture. She felt inside the cold face of some sharp instrument, a mirror perhaps. Were they trying to see right inside her? Dr Hanisch withdrew. The orderlies released their grip. No wonder all the women here were mad, she thought. He had done the same to them. Nurse Walz, still nursing her bloody nose, drew over a cloth screen – as if it made any difference now – and she and the doctor moved away. She could hear them whispering.

'Well,' Dr Hanisch said, 'it would appear our mystery woman is no saint. Not a virgin any more.'

'Perhaps there is a young man?' Nurse Walz said.

She drew the coverlet up over her pulsing innards as Dr Hanisch reappeared.

'Fräulein, perhaps we should send for your young man?'

What young man would want me now? she thought.

'Your fiancé?'

A vision of blood appeared before her eyes. Blood and death.

'Fräulein?'

She curled into a tight ball.

'None of that,' she shouted. 'No fiancé, do you hear? None of that!'

'She speaks,' Dr Hanisch said quietly.

'I will say no more,' she spat back.

SOME WEEKS PASSED and Fräulein Unbekannt was, for the most part, left alone. Every so often she would be subjected to another round of fruitless questions by Dr Hanisch, though he did not lay a finger on her again. But there was the hostility of Ward B to deal with. For both the doctors and the insane, silence was a provocation. The dwarf woman, in particular, would spend hours staring at her, trying to touch her and speaking in a childish babble, a language only she understood. Her face would become animated, her beady eyes would light up and she would wave her hands about. She smiled gleefully, her shoulders hunched up, her large domed forehead wrinkling as she wiggled her eyebrows. When she got no response she would shout and wail, squeezing out large childish tears, her tongue lolling on her fat lip.

'She doesn't want to play, Hanna,' Nurse Bucholz would say as the Fräulein recoiled from the touch of the dwarf's scaly claws. 'Come, let's go out into the garden. You can play there.'

When they weren't leading her into danger, as Nurse Walz had done, the nurses were kind to her. They treated her with a kind of wary respect; they allowed her to walk in the garden alone; they did not insist that she work. She felt she had been granted a special position, above the others, as if her present condition, nameless and without a history, marked her out as superior.

'Believe me,' Nurse Malinovsky confided in her one

night, 'it makes a change to have a patient who doesn't know who she is. In the lock-up wards alone, there are three Empress Sissies.'

The Fräulein blanched.

'No matter she's been dead for years. But we have to still treat them as royalty. Kiss their hands and the like.'

'Sissi, did you say?'

'Yes, you know, the Austrian princess, murdered in the street. Terrible business.' The nurse chattered on, not noticing the Fräulein's abstracted discomfort. Something had reverberated, a name, a notion.

She often sat with Nurse Malinovsky during the night. The nurse would take her to the kitchens, strictly out of bounds for patients, and make her cocoa. The two women would sit companionably amidst the dull sheen of stove and pot, and Thea – she had even trusted her with her first name – would natter about her life. She was engaged to be married to a doctor. She was doing night duty to save extra money for the wedding, a large affair to be held in Charlottenburg.

'My mother, bless her, is looking forward ever so much to the wedding. There are six of us girls and she's anxious to get us off her hands,' Thea said one evening. 'Is your mother still alive, Fräulein?'

Mother, mother. She racked her brain. Even the smallest question was a test. She repeated the word to herself. Mother. Even the word itself seemed strange. All words seemed strange.

'I dreamed of her last night,' she said suddenly.

Sometimes a shard of knowledge would cut through the mist she was in. The truth was she was troubled by dreams every night. In this one a woman – whose features she did not recognise and yet whom she knew to be her mother – appeared, dressed in a rich black coat with a fleecy collar. She was stepping into a carriage outside a large, imposing house. Inside the carriage a handsome young man was waiting. He had a silver smile, but instead of teeth he had a mouthful of pins.

'How strange,' Thea murmured. 'What could it mean?'

She did not tell Thea Malinovsky of her other dreams, the bad ones. Fire and water. From which she would awake with a scream buried in her throat but nothing emerging but a vast and hollow silence. It was this that terrified her most – the deep emptiness within. As if she were an echo chamber, a dark and aching void, filled with the sharp fragments of other people's dreams. She was afraid the patients of Ward B were infiltrating her darkness. They could not reach her during the day so they chose the night to send her their horrors and secrets, their ghosts and frights. It was another reason to stay vigilant. She willed herself to stay awake until dawn when the night terrors would creep back to their rightful owners – the mad occupants of Ward B.

She liked to walk in the garden in the mornings when the other patients were at work. She was allowed to ramble down the gravel driveway as far as the huge iron gates that separated the asylum from the outside world. Beneath the shade of the oak trees bluebells flourished and wild poppies waved in red delirium. The large house that contained the lock-up wards looked from this angle like a fine manor, while Ward B with its French windows thrown open could have been a summer pavilion. For a few moments she could imagine herself as the mistress of this grand establishment, the doctors and nurses as household staff. It allowed her to believe that she was in charge of rather than imprisoned by Dalldorf. It was a pleasant daydream until she remembered the dull-eyed occupants of Ward B; then the fantasy fell away. And she could never fully surrender to such fancies. The dangerous outside world, shimmering vividly outside these walls, had a habit of intruding.

She was returning from a stroll in the grounds one

morning in late May, and looking forward to a little nap in the ward before the patients returned from the laundry for lunch, when she was accosted on the driveway by Nurse Walz.

'Ah, Fräulein,' she said, relieved. 'I'm glad to find you. There are some men to see you.'

'Men?' She knew no men.

'Policemen,' Nurse Walz said.

The two women walked together towards the director's stuffy office. Since she had struck her, she noticed Nurse Walz was careful not to touch her. The director was standing at the door.

'That will be all, Walz,' he said, grasping the Fräulein by the elbow and guiding her inside. He closed the door emphatically. Two men in overcoats stood by the director's desk. They were blunt-looking men. One had a bristled pate, the other, a much younger man, had a lock of oiled hair which fell into his eyes. A camera stood on a tripod in the middle of the room. She felt a cold, creeping panic overtake her.

'Sit!' the director said, pointing to a chair standing a few yards in front of the camera.

When she hesitated he caught her roughly by the arm and forced her to sit down. She covered her face with her hands.

'Fräulein,' the younger man said. 'We only want to take a picture of you, that is all. My word of honour.'

'Let's get on with this,' his gruff companion said.

'This will help you, Fräulein. And help us to find out who you are. We will post these pictures all over Germany. Someone is bound to come forward,' the young man said, brushing his greased hair back from his forehead.

She did not believe him. Why did they persist in telling her lies? They were here to punish her. The young man stepped back behind the camera and ducked beneath a black hood. A hood! They were going to shoot her.

'Now, Fräulein,' his voice came out distant and muffled, 'why don't you give us a smile?'

41

It was a trick. It was bad luck to show your teeth to an ill-wisher. She tried to cover her mouth. The director, who had been standing behind her with a restraining hand on her shoulder, caught her wrist and bent her arm back behind the chair.

'We can tie her,' he said.

'I'm sure that won't be necessary,' the young man said, his flushed face reappearing from behind the hood. Then he disappeared again.

'Look this way, Fräulein,' he said from behind his cloak of darkness.

There was a blinding flash, a smart explosion, and everything turned brilliant white, then flared into splotchy darkness. She waited for the fire – first the explosion, then the fire, but none came.

'Lovely,' the photographer said, mistaking her rictus of terror for a smile. The director released his grip and she slumped in the chair.

'You may go now,' he said.

'There is just one more small matter,' the older police-man said. 'Over here, Fräulein.'

The director prodded her and she stepped towards the desk. The policeman grabbed her hand and dabbed her forefinger onto an inked pad. Then he pressed it firmly onto a little cell printed on a white card lying on the table, which at the top bore her new name, Fräulein Unbekannt. So she *was* a criminal. She looked at the blackened smudge of her fingerprint. As she bent over it, it looked like the tiny map of an unexplored country, the tracery of rivers, the whorl of mountains, the swirling vortex at the centre. It made her dizzy. She straightened and it reverted to a messy black mark, a child's legacy in mud. They were fools! How could *this* tell them anything about her?

She did not want to know anything more about herself than her face and afflicted body had already betrayed. That way her crime, whatever it was, would not be discovered. And without a crime there would be no punishment. The last thing she wanted was the arrival of some stranger, who would point a ghastly finger and declare – you're mine. When she wasn't being pestered by official interrogation, or subjected to Nurse Malinovsky's questions inserted slyly into their night-time conversations, she was left to drift, free to be anybody she wished, or nobody. She was surrounded, after all, by a bunch of crazy women who all knew who they were. Hilda Scharrel knew who she should be and it tormented her. She was the bespectacled woman in the next bed. I am Hilda Scharrel, she would declare on waking in the mornings to anybody who happened by, Frau Hilda Scharrel.

'Yes, Hilda, we know,' Nurse Bucholz would say resignedly. 'Now off with you to the laundry.'

'I am Hilda Scharrel,' she would remonstrate as if begging to be contradicted. Or she would amble off singing her name tunelessly to herself.

Hilda had been a strapping farm girl, though the light household duties at Dalldorf had turned her brawn to fat. Her fishy eyes peered myopically through bottle-thick lenses. She had a story; everyone had a story, everyone bar Fräulein Unbekannt. She had been promised to her childhood sweetheart, Jonah. Jonah Scharrel. When she spoke of him, her plain broad face would soften and she would smile her rueful, rotten smile. He had gone off to the war, but when he returned he no longer wanted his old life, a plot of land, the arranged future with Hilda. He had wept when the guns fell silent, he told her; while there was war there was hope. He spurned her fleshy comforts, her willing, aching loyalty and fled to Berlin. He wanted only the company of men, men who had seen action. She had followed him, dogging his every move, as he roamed from beer garden to brothel. She debased herself for him, Nurse Bucholz said. She had become a woman of the night, wandering the streets and offering herself to strangers,

43

sleeping in the gutter. Her sin, Nurse Bucholz said, had driven her demented. It was Jonah who had had her committed. She had happily complied, assured that his concern for her indicated a change of heart. That had been two years ago. Time had played tricks on Hilda. Adopting his name, she slipped into the future that she had been cheated of. Frau Hilda Scharrel, brimming with hope, waited daily for her husband to walk up the driveway and fetch her out.

'Once I am over my little weakness,' she would say.

A dentist came to Dalldorf once a month to do extractions. Hilda Scharrel was hauled off one Monday morning to have her rotting molars taken out. When she returned her plump cheeks had caved in, her fleshy top lip had become a thin line, her foul-breathed smile a gruesome gummy grin. She wept and raged for several days.

'What will Jonah say?' she howled, thickly beating her large fists against the pillow. 'My looks are ruined. First the specs, now this! He won't recognise me.'

She wept as copiously as she bled. For days afterwards she spewed out phlegmy cobwebs of blood from the raw cavities where her teeth had been and which were stuffed now with wads of sodden gauze.

For the first time since she had come to Dalldorf, Fräulein Unbekannt felt sympathy. It was a strange sensation, this reluctant leak of feeling. But she pitied Hilda's illusions, not her pain. She had trouble with her own teeth, the loose ones at the back ached constantly and her gums bled, but she had made no more than mild complaint about them. Once or twice Nurse Malinovsky had given her powders in the night to ease the pain.

'You really should get them seen to, Fräulein,' Nurse Malinovsky had advised, but she merely shook her head. She would be a fool to volunteer for any more torture than was necessary.

But watching Hilda Scharrel bemoan her changed appearance, she remembered the bad-luck smile she had been tricked into by the police photographer. There was no way she could take it back, but she could make sure that no one would ever see it again. She hurried along to Nurse Malinovsky.

'Would it be possible', she asked, 'to see the dentist?'

Nurse Malinovsky smiled. A return of vanity, a concern for the physical appearance, was always, in her opinion, a prelude to recovery. It suggested prospects, a future. The dentist, a weedy drunkard, happily obliged. He rarely got a willing patient; usually these wild women had to be held down. He removed eight teeth. He barely needed implements; they would have come away in his fingers.

'Not to worry, Fräulein,' he said, holding the teeth in his palm, 'the other teeth will grow into the space.'

'Take this one too,' she commanded, tapping her front tooth.

'But, Fräulein,' he protested, 'this one is healthy.'

'Take it anyway.'

'But it is perfectly good. No disease here, the roots are strong.'

'Just pull it out,' she said.

He was a biddable man and too afraid of losing his job. There was not much work for a dentist as fond of his spirits as Dr Winter was. In the world outside, patients distrusted a man with a tremor in his hand and the smell of drink on his breath. In here, though, most of them were more malodorous than he was.

'Do it,' she said. She recognised a weak man when she saw one.

He tugged and pulled and after twenty minutes of sweating, shaking effort he wrenched the tooth from its moorings. He felt weak and in need of a drink, but the patient hardly raised a whimper.

She was pleased with the result. It made her look gormless and mad. Nobody in their right mind would want to claim her, with a scarred body and now a ruined face. In some other life, the life after this, she promised herself as she nursed her throbbing mouth, I will have a false tooth made, a crown of purest ivory.

CLARA PEUTHERT IS admitted with the same commotion that accompanies all arrivals to Dalldorf – the bucking ambulance slewing to a halt on the gravel forecourt, the slamming of doors, scuffles and protests in the night air. The lights come on in Ward B and Fräulein Unbekannt sees for the umpteenth time a ragged, distressed woman bundled down the centre of the ward and deposited roughly on an unoccupied bed at the far end. The other patients come to with low groans and restive thrashings of blankets, screwing up their eyes at the violence of the light. This one is vociferous and flame-haired, trying to wriggle out of the iron grip of two orderlies who half steer, half drag her across the polished floor. Nurse Malinovsky takes up the rear, clicking her tongue.

'Now, Clara, hush up, or we'll put you in the lock-ups. That'll cool your ardour.'

Clara, distracted by the nurse's jocular rebuke, falls silent.

'That's more like it.'

She sits limply on the bed, where she has been deposited like a sack of potatoes. The orderlies tramp out. Clara meekly dons her grey shift and folds herself under the covers. Within five minutes the lights are dimmed and the ward returns to its rackety sleep. All but Fräulein Unbekannt, who lies awake, aware that at the other end of the room, Clara Peuthert is also lying motionless but alert, watching moon shadows on the ceiling. After a year and a half at Dalldorf the Fräulein knows the difference between careless slumber and vivid silence.

The newcomer is fêted in the morning.

'Clara!' Hilda Scharrel cries on waking, fetching her spectacles from the bedside locker and clipping them clumsily around her large ears. 'It's Clara Peuthert!'

A chorus of recognition ripples around the ward.

'You still here then?' Clara hollers. 'Hasn't your old man come to get you yet?'

Hilda, crushed, shakes her head. Then she regains herself.

'What are you in for?'

'Fucking neighbours,' Clara spits, limping down the ward, 'steal my money from right under my nose, then accuse me' – she pokes her breast violently – 'of being mad.'

'Your old trouble, then,' Minna Heck says.

Minna is the veteran of Ward B, a 67-year-old drinker and mournful depressive with yellow-greying hair and a hacking cough. Nothing punctures her gloomy resignation. She shuffles towards the showers; slow on her pins, she likes to get a head start on the morning line-up. She also has a stash of methylated spirits hidden in the shower block.

'I'm not a well woman, Minna,' Clara shouts after her, '*they* should make allowances.'

She completes the length of the ward, conducting a surly survey.

'Kick a dog when it's down,' she mutters, 'that's their motto.'

She reaches bed 15B.

'And who have we here?' she asks, narrowing her eyes.

Fräulein Unbekannt, still abed – exempt from therapeutic showers and lice checks – is turned towards the wall. She makes no move, though all her limbs are tense. She recognises challenge when she hears it.

'Oh, that's our Fräulein,' Hilda Scharrel whispers, 'somebody quite grand.'

The dwarf Hanna lets out a piercing shriek of laughter. 'And does her ladyship have a name?'

'Well, that's the thing,' Hilda confides, yards from the bed, 'she doesn't.'

'Don't be a clot, Hilda, everyone has a name.'

'No, really,' Hilda mouths, 'no one knows who she is. *She* doesn't know who she is.'

'All right, ladies,' Nurse Bucholz's voice interjects, 'way past the bell. On your way.'

Fräulein Unbekannt draws the covers up over her head. For some reason she is filled with dread.

She makes her way to the library, where she spends her mornings in the winter when it is too cold to venture out. She was six months in Dalldorf before she realised there was a library, housed in the main block. It was Thea Malinovsky who had first taken her there.

'Not a great supply of books, penny dreadfuls mostly,' she said bashfully, 'not your sort of thing. But there are newspapers, the *Nachtausgabe*, *Vorwärts*, the *Berliner Illustrierte*. We thought...' She hesitated.

They were strolling in the grass. It was a gusty morning of speckled autumn. Thea was coming off duty.

'That is, Dr Hanisch and I...'

'What has Hanisch got to do with this?'

'Nothing, really, nothing, it's just ... we thought the papers might help to jog your memory, fill in the gaps?'

Her face smarted with disappointment. She had begun to think of Thea as a companion, not a guardian.

'We only want the best for you, Fräulein,' Thea said, 'restore you to your life, or restore your life to you.'

An icy fury gripped her. She must never trust anyone in here. Ever!

It was in the library that she had her next encounter with Clara. She was sitting on the window seat in the bow window, idly leafing through a romance. She did not have the concentration to read. Plots confused her, the lines of print would swoon into one another. A word would detach itself from its companions – father, fire, water – demanding her special attention. Listen, it seemed to urge, listen to me! She would repeat it to herself, trying a different emphasis each time – light, heavy, nonchalant – in the hope that it would yield up its message, but it would remain contrarily neutral, or worse it would sound absurd, like the preposterous gurgling of an infant. She steadfastly avoided the newspapers, slung in an untidy pile on the oval mahogany table in the centre of the room. She had no intention of co-operating with Nurse Malinovsky's ruse.

More often than not she was entirely alone in the library, the other patients occupied at their morning work detail. In the afternoons, when they were given a few hours of freedom, Hilda or Minna might saunter in and thumb through the illustrated magazines. But they really came to gossip, not to read. The library was a place of assignation, neutral territory away from the prying eyes of the staff. Male patients from the other 'quiet' ward, situated near the kitchen block a good half mile away, congregated in the library after supper to smoke and study racing form in the papers. Half-hearted trysts were arranged, their illicit planning exciting more energy than their execution. Tekla Becker, the flighty teenage daughter of a wool merchant admitted to Dalldorf for nervous exhaustion (she had been caught *in flagrante* in a horse stall with a stable lad), spent weeks trying to set up a meeting with a shell-shock victim she had spied during male ward exercises in the yard. Notes were passed, smuggled by the kitchen maid, and elaborate alibis concocted, though the meeting in the library never actually took place. Tekla was discharged after only a few weeks, but it had kept her busy and had animated the entire ward in the process.

But in the mornings the library was a haven. The Fräulein enjoyed the solitude and the vacant sense of absence which she could indulge without fear of being roused with questions and promptings. When the door swung open that October morning and Clara Peuthert stood there, regally proprietorial, her heart sank.

Dalldorf had a soothing effect on Clara's temperament. It was not placid resignation, as it was with most other patients, but a surrender of her spiky bad temper. For Clara, the outside world was a seething sea of hostility, rising seasonally to a boiling spring tide which threatened to submerge her. At that point Clara's ship tipped, friends were transformed into scheming enemies, neighbours into opportunistic thieves, and her long-suffering brother, who arranged her committals, became the arch-villain of her interior calamity. Her physical complaints also eased at the asylum. The violent outbursts which preceded her admission were always matched by a worsening of her paralysis, but once she had spent her rage the palsy seemed to retreat, her hand ungnarled and hung loosely by her side, her limp became less pronounced. So much so that on the October morning when she marched into the library, Fräulein Unbekannt realised with a start that Clara, at peace, had a certain noble poise and a fiery, flawed beauty.

Clara trails her good hand along the glossy table top as she does a full circle of the room. Her fingertips brush against the scattered newspapers, but she doesn't bother to pick one up, though that is why she has come. The *Nachtausgabe* is her favourite; she likes the lurid stories, the loud headlines. But like Fräulein Unbekannt she expected to have the library to herself at this hour. She is unnerved by the peculiar girl from Ward B, the silent one, the oh so haughty one, sitting in the bay of the window framed by murky storm cloud, a novelette open on her lap, sitting there like she owns the place. But it is also the first time

Clara has got a clear view of her; in the ward she huddles in her corner bed, her back turned. She neither washes nor eats with the throng; instead of working she moons about the grounds. She is not required to take communal exercise, the nurses practically curtsy before her. All of which inflames Clara's democratic ire. So it is much against her will that she has developed a sneaking regard for Fräulein Unbekannt. Clara, known by all and sundry – hail fellow, well met on the corridor, cheery backslaps in the ward – has never managed to command such respect. While this pasty-looking invalid has them eating out of her hand. She has seen those little tête-à-têtes with Nurse Malinovsky, the cocoa drinks, the headache powders, and the way Dr Hanisch, usually so briskly non-committal, reserves for her a kind of deference. No doubt she has gone through the usual humiliations imposed on first-timers at Dalldorf, but she has garnered privileges it has taken years for Clara to earn. And she *is* just a girl. Clara sees how high and smooth her brow is, those grey, melancholy eyes, the cheeky nose and those lips, full and soft and – Clara searches for the word – blossomy.

Clara Peuthert, too, finds herself awestruck, not by the enigma of the Fräulein's silence, but by the clarity of her presence.

'Fräulein,' she says by way of greeting.

The young woman says nothing, as usual.

Inwardly, Clara's temper flares. Too grand to talk to the likes of me! But she quells it. She wants to be let in, after all. She wants the Fräulein to know she is a worthy person, that she has found an equal in this place full of crazed vulgarity.

'Excuse me, Fräulein,' she says softly, 'but may I say your face seems familiar to me.'

The Fräulein levels a cold stare at her.

'You do not come from ordinary circles, I can tell,' Clara persists.

Fräulein Unbekannt appears agitated. She puts a finger to her lips.

Clara feels a tremor of subversion. She has obviously been let into a secret.

Fräulein Unbekannt returns to her book, hoping that might shake off the attentions of Clara Peuthert. It's a library, after all. Hasn't she read the sign above the door? *Bitte Ruhe*.

Clara had found a mission. Excused like Fräulein Unbekannt from work, she took to spending every morning in the library. She knew she was not wanted, so she worked hard to ingratiate herself. For the first few weeks the two women shared a grudging silence, Clara thumbing through back copies of the *Berliner Illustrierte* while the Fräulein sat in her usual position by the window gazing off into the mid-distance. Her silence was a particular challenge to Clara. The yawning gaps of time made her twitchy. Her gift was for uproar and drama; stalling tension she couldn't bear. Sitting for days on end with Fräulein Unbekannt without a word passing between them was a punishing agony. At first it simply made her angry to be so coolly and indifferently shut out. She needed engagement; she was anxious for confidences and greedy for quarrel. But she persevered with her collaboration of tact and deference, so at odds with her own nature. In time she learned that Fräulein Unbekannt's silence was not dense and uniform. Sometimes it was leaden as fog, or grave and gloomy like the gathering of a winter storm. Or it might be buoyant and good-natured like the jaunty sweep of cloud flurry, or bleached and serene as a clear blue sky. Clara learned to distinguish the ebb and flow so at variance with her natural impatience. And, in the end, she was rewarded. With a smile. A strange lopsided smile, it had to be said. Dr Winter had obviously been at the girl's teeth. And after the smile, a greeting. She tiptoed extravagantly into the library on

28 October 1921 – Clara would remember the date like a lover's souvenir – and the Fräulein turned from the window and said bemusedly:

'Hello, Clara.'

Clara merely smiles and tips her head slightly at the Fräulein as she makes her way to her usual spot at the table. She plucks the *Berliner Illustrierte* from the top of the pile. They are running a serial in it that she is avidly following, 'The Girl with the Lion's Head', about a young woman with a mop of red hair. It is last week's copy – the asylum gets all the papers late so that the news has already been digested by the outside world and the papers have been rumpled and tossed by other hands before the patients get to see them. She begins to read. The only difference is that this time she reads aloud. She starts with the blocky headline, 'The Truth About the Murder of the Tsar'. Beneath is a portrait of the Grand Duchesses Olga, Tatiana, Maria and Anastasia. Clara traces her fingers around the glossy locks of their hair, the white lace cuffs of their dresses, their small clasped hands. She starts the story: 'Is One of the Tsar's Daughters Alive?'

'Mystery still surrounds the disappearance of the Russian royal family. The Bolsheviks would have us believe that the tsar and his family were executed in a basement room of the Ipatiev House in Yekaterinburg and buried in a mineshaft in the Koptyaki Forest. But we have reason to believe that one of the grand duchesses, Anastasia, the youngest, escaped from her captors and may at this moment be in hiding in fear of her life...'

The Fräulein listens dreamily. It is soothing just to sit while Clara reads. It demands nothing of her but that she receive. For a while she pays no heed to what Clara is reading. It is Clara's voice, snagged and husky, her slow rendering of the words – she is not accustomed to reading aloud – that holds the Fräulein's wayward attention. It is like the application of balm, the sweet stroke of a cool hand on burning skin, or the steady supplication of familiar prayer, the gentle cadence of a voice which, for once, asks no questions. But after several days of Clara's recitations, she starts to listen to the stories. Where, they speculate, is the lost Russian princess? One story has it that Anastasia was spirited away from the slaughter by White Army officers disguised as Bolshevik guards. Another that only the tsar was shot while the rest of the family was moved in a covered train, and Anastasia, dressed as a peasant girl, had escaped. No, no, she is in hiding in a convent in Zagorsk, or living under an assumed name in the Crimea . . . There are, the Fräulein thinks, as many questions about this poor girl as there are about me.

'Just imagine,' Clara murmurs wistfully, 'somewhere out there, a lost princess too terrified to speak.'

SHE WOULD NEVER understand why she had given in to Clara. Why her, when she had resisted the veiled threats and blandishments of everybody else? It was a surrender, she knew, after a battle of wills. Her own silence had managed to frighten or deflect. Hilda, Minna and the others had butted at it like enraged bulls, Nurse Malinovsky had toyed with it circumspectly, but Clara had matched it with a silence of her own – stifled, testy, combative. The truth was she was lonely. The monastic-like retreat she had shared with Clara had made her yearn for its obverse – the inconsequential gaiety of female companionship. As if that was something she had known and lost. And though it had been Clara who had pursued her, she felt as if her time at Dalldorf had been a kind of attenuated waiting, filled with a fearful certainty that someone would eventually appear and undo her. It had not occurred to her that it would be someone from within Dalldorf's walls and that her undoing, if that was what it was, would be so seductive.

If their friendship had been born in silence, it blossomed into a garrulous and sisterly hubbub. Gagged for weeks, Clara could not stop from talking. Out they poured, her stories of triumph and revenge, punctuated by rounds of laughter. She had a peculiar laugh, like a performance – she would throw her head back and shake her mane of hair as if she were about to sing, but the sound that emerged was not hearty but mirthless, as if she could only approximate gaiety.

Her life on Schumannstraße was a catalogue of comedy and grievance. She took in washing; it was the only thing she could do since the palsy had set in. Before, she pointed out lest anyone try to gainsay it, she'd been a supervisor in a laundry, with ten girls under her. It was a step down taking washing in at home, but at least she could work at her own pace. Before her latest bout in Dalldorf she had been saving for a trip – she had a sister in Heidelberg whom she had not seen since before the war. She had made the mistake of telling Helmut Schrader, her next-door neighbour, a no-good scoundrel, that she kept her cash in a biscuit tin beneath the floorboards. She did not trust the banks, she'd lost a fortune in enforced savings during the war. It was Helmut who had whipped the money, she was sure. He'd been in her apartment the night before the money disappeared. They sometimes had a drink or two of an evening, she and Helmut. They were old friends, she explained, if you know what I mean. Oh, they'd had some gay times. He had been a railway guard and sometimes – before the war – he had taken her on trips, smuggling her aboard the night trains and hiding her in the little caboose at the end of the carriage. Had they travelled! Danzig, the Baltic coast. He was out of work now and living on a supplement. He'd lost a leg – no, not in the war, though he liked to let people assume that – when he'd fallen in the depot in a drunken stupor and a decoupled carriage had rolled over him. He just stopped being fun then, Clara said mournfully, came over high and mighty, wanted to be faithful to that milksop of a wife of his. Anyway, she said, what a pair we would have made, him with a false leg, and me with this – she raised her dead arm. She screeched with laughter. When the money disappeared she had waited for him on the stairwell and let fly, screaming accusations so everyone could hear the type he was, and landing several well-aimed punches.

'I gave him a black eye,' Clara said proudly, as if it were a badge of love, 'a real shiner!'

The Fraülein listened to Clara's stories with a fond alarm. She liked the sense of being included, a witness to Clara's crowded and haphazard history, but she was aware of the imbalance. Soon Clara would turn to her for confidences and she would have nothing to say. It seemed a bitter twist that she had spent a year and a half being tormented to produce some proof of who she was, to explain away her wounds, to account for herself. Now that their questions had eased off, she was troubled by the consequences of their lack of interest. If they never found out who she was, would she spend the rest of her life here in Dalldorf, the unknown woman whom nobody had wanted? She had a title, nothing more. Fraülein Unbekannt. What she needed was a story. Something to offer Clara. But her mind, dulled by months of idleness, could summon up nothing. She could not even tell the time. Big hand for the minutes, little hand for the hours, she would repeat to herself, but faced with the implacability of a clock face the figures danced and threatened. Awakening from sleep, or roused from hours of withdrawn wakefulness on the ward, she could not tell if it was nine o'clock or a quarter to twelve. Was it nearly lunchtime, or was this the sunken twilight? Darkness seemed to stall, while mornings gobbled hours greedily. Her throat was thick with disuse, language like a wound, festering within. Yet Nurse Malinovsky had told her that she spoke out in her sleep, in tongues. Like Russian, Thea said. But in her waking hours she was a blank, a product of fire, which had left its mark upon her, and water, from which she had been saved. As if that had been the moment of her birth. Ordeal of water, baptism of fire.

Time quickened while she was with Clara. The deadening tedium of days on Ward B, the dangers and alarms of its nights, gave way to an exhilarating sensation of imminence. Each morning when she awoke she felt she was on the brink of a great discovery. Her sleep was less troubled, and if she woke in the small hours of the morning, she did not need to turn to Nurse Malinovsky. It was enough to know that Clara was there, even if she were snoring loudly at the other end of the ward. She had only known her two months and yet Clara's presence seemed as comforting as that of a cherished sister. Where others found Clara coarse and loud, she saw a woman wronged. She saw how Clara's appetite for life was mistaken for vulgarity, her passion dismissed as unseemly appetite. Could they not see, as she could, Clara's nobility, her sense of decorum? Why, for all the weeks they had known one another, Clara had never subjected her to the kind of crude questioning with which the doctors, nurses and inmates of Dalldorf had badgered her. Was that not proof of finer feeling, that she had never made a single demand? She felt both humbled and aggrandised by Clara's company. She had been chosen, singled out.

Clara was in the grip of a furious love. The Fräulein took up her every waking moment. Clara wished she had a name, other than that cold title she had inherited. Fräulein Unbekannt. She invented pet names for her – Princess, Sunny, Baby – but was too shy to employ them. No one had ever taken such heed of her. The Fräulein listened to Clara's yarns with a rigorous intensity. She seemed to concentrate on every word, her acuity never wavering. It was the kind of rapt attention Clara had always craved. As a girl she had been plain and gangly, the eldest lumbered with the disappointment of not being a son and eclipsed by the brothers who duly followed. Her education had been spotty, her brightness marred by her extravagant temper and, even as a child, her propensity for violence. She had broken a boy's arm in the schoolyard because he had looked at her oddly. Apart from this one youthful occasion, men did not fall at her feet. For affection, Clara

had always had to plot and scheme. Her dramatic looks –
the nest of hair, the startled eyes – did not fall within the
ambit of conventional beauty. Her mood swings were too
alarming. And then, in her mid-thirties, the seizures struck,
leaving in their wake a fluctuating deadness down the right
side of her body. The palsy had put paid to her ambitions
for love.

Now in middle age she found herself at last, and totally
unexpectedly, the object of intense interest and an almost
devotional vigilance. Oh, she rattled on, but only because
the Fräulein seemed to like it so. Clara made her laugh –
out loud. No one at Dalldorf could recall having heard the
Fräulein laugh. As time went on, she indulged in her own
mild speculation about the Fräulein; it was the only way
she could smuggle through the appalling tenderness that
afflicted her.

'Now you, dear Fräulein,' (Princess! Sunny! Baby!), 'you
are someone grand, I can tell!' she says one morning in the
ward.

The Fräulein is sitting on a chair and Clara is brushing
her hair. The poor diet in the asylum has left it dull and
lifeless. Clara, energetically brushing it with her good hand,
is determined to make it shine again. And it allows her the
illicit luxury of touch.

'How?' the Fräulein asks eagerly.

'Oh, by your manners, the way you sit, my dear, the
way you comport yourself,' Clara says. 'I may be only a
working woman but I know breeding when I see it.'

Clara glances at her covertly. The Fräulein is blushing;
Clara can see the quick flare of her thrilled embarrassment.

'I have worked for grand people in my time. I was a
governess once, in Moscow, before the revolution. When I
was a young woman,' she says.

'Really?'

'Oh yes,' Clara says sadly, 'I was a young woman once.'

'Oh Clara, I didn't mean . . .'

'They were quite the thing, I can tell you,' Clara says. 'They had royal blood in their veins. My family . . .'

Clara stops, lost momentarily in a trance of remembering. Idly she presses a shank of the Fräulein's hair to her lips. Then she resumes her brushing, the air crackling with static electricity.

'I call them my family because they were in a way,' she says. 'Madame was sickly, spent a lot of time in her room. Not robust, don't you know. I practically raised those children. I was nursemaid and mother both.'

Clara had seen the royal family once at a parade to celebrate the tsar's birthday.

'It was 18 May. Those poor girls passed me on the street. They were as close as you are to me. Why, I could have reached out and touched one of them. And Madame was at a ball in honour of the Grand Duchess Olga in Petersburg. Madame told me all about it. The dresses those girls had, you should have seen them! Once, I copied one for Madame. She had seen Tatiana wear it. She described it to me – organza it was, with netting and pearl details on the bodice and a full skirt that took yards of fabric. Of course, it did not look so well on Madame. She was not so young and after two children . . .' Clara sighs. 'Your body is never quite the same again.' She lays the brush aside and gathering up the soft bulk of the Fräulein's hair she begins to coil it into a loose bun at the nape of her neck.

'Oh look,' she cries delightedly, 'there's a little twig caught here. You must have picked it up in the garden. What have you been doing, my little princess, rolling in the hay?'

Something stirs. The thin ice over her heart splinters. A tiny eggshell sound. And she is suddenly in a new element where all is fluid and clear. A sensation, ancient and trembling, steals over her, like the caress of sun on a shorn meadow, or the blue certainty of a summer sky. The laying of hands on her crown, the sharp intake of love. A full, fat memory comes unbidden, lucid as a teardrop. She is a little girl in her Papa's arms. He has picked her up from where she has fallen. He envelops her in a blue and gold embrace . . .

'Fräulein?' Clara starts.

Mortified, she lets the Fräulein's hair fall into a fan across her shoulders. She does not know how the endearment sprang from her lips, but now it hangs between them like some petty, scented secret, revealed. She makes to apologise, but the Fräulein does not seem to register. When Clara leans over the girl she sees a stricken look on her face and a single tear glistening on her cheek. Clara cannot read her expression. Is it passion or grief?

It had been like a rift, that sudden opening up. A benediction from the past she could not summon up. She did not need to search any more, to pick through her water-logged and blood-soaked dreams for clues. She did not need to offer explanations or even seek them. In that flowering moment, it had been revealed to her. Whoever she was, she had been beloved.

ON A COLD January day the Fräulein walked alone to the shower block. It was mid-morning. Frost clung to the frozen earth, petrified icicles hung from the eaves. Clara had been called to the director's office on some business. She did not want to go to the library alone. She turned on the shower and stepped into its effusive rush. The brass shower head was like the tarnished face of a sunflower dispensing rain. She smiled up at it as the water gushed and hissed around her. The cold outside, the warmth within, made her light-hearted and she sang as she soaped herself – an aimless melody, the words of which she had long ago lost. For the first time in Dalldorf, she actually felt ... happy.

Clara, released from the director's office, had hurried first to the library, expecting to find the Fräulein sitting, as usual, in her glassy perch by the window. She stood nostalgically in the deserted room testing out the wan sensation of absence. She flicked through the old newspapers from which she had been reading aloud to the Fräulein and chose one. She folded it carefully and slipped it into her shift pocket. Then she made her way back to Ward B. There was no sign of the Fräulein there either, so she placed the copy of the *Berliner Illustrierte* underneath the Fräulein's pillow and then went in search of her. She found her in the showers. Or rather she heard her first, her small cracked voice echoing damply in the tiled fog of the shower stall. She stood by the doorway and listened. After a few minutes, the fractured singing came to a halt. The Fräulein stepped out, unwary, into the passageway and reached for a towel that hung just out of reach on the rail. Clara stood and watched as she stood, her back turned, blindly fishing for the towel. Her illicit nakedness thrilled Clara, the flawed, misshapen feet, the moulded calves, the fleshy, embarrassed-looking thighs, the dimpled bafflement of cheeks. And then the Fräulein turned around.

Clara had heard Hilda and the others talk about the Fräulein's scars but nothing could have prepared her for her first sight of them, a careless patchwork of puckered seams from breast to pubic hair. My poor baby, Clara thought, what is to become of you?

As if she had heard her unspoken plea, the Fräulein looked up. Her first instinct was to cover herself up, but something about Clara's piteous expression stopped her. She wanted Clara to see her as she was, a nobody, naked, ruined. Clara saw a princess with bayonet wounds.

'What is it, Clara?' she asked.

'I am to be released next week,' Clara said.

It was the news she had been dreading.

'We could run away,' she said as Clara wrapped a towel around her and rubbed her dry.

'Oh, darling,' Clara sighed, emboldened by the prospect of her departure.

'Don't leave me, Clara,' she begged. The steaming fog in the bathroom was retreating. She began to shiver.

'Come on,' Clara said briskly, to hide the tugging at her heart. Like every inmate in Dalldorf she wanted to get out. Who in their right minds would want to stay? 'Let's get your clothes on or you'll catch your death. We'll think of something. We'll get you out of here.'

That night Nurse Malinovsky tried to calm her. She had never seen the Fräulein so distressed. Spates of tears alternated with her old doom-laden silences. It had something to do with Clara, that was all Thea could divine. The nurse had watched the growing friendship between the Fräulein and Clara with alarm. Knowing Clara Peuthert of old, Nurse Malinovsky feared for her new-found companion. The pendulum swing of Clara's affection was the reason she was in Dalldorf in the first place; love turned to embittered violence in the blinking of an eye. At first she thought that such unlikely bedfellows would quickly fall out. Affection among the mad was rarely constant, she had noticed; their interior dramas were too insistent. Alliances were formed but they rarely withstood the competition of hysterics, tantrums, seizures, the true soul-mates of the insane. Anyway, fraternising could not be outlawed simply because she disapproved, and she had to admit that since Clara Peuthert had landed back in Ward B, the Fräulein seemed less suffering – yes, that would be the word that Nurse Malinovsky would use to describe her – suffering. She had even heard her laugh once or twice, as she and Clara walked in the garden or engaged in forensic perusal of the newspapers in the library.

That night, as the nurse turned back the covers and guided the still sobbing Fräulein into bed, she heard a rustle underneath the pillow. She slid her hand in and withdrew a crumpled edition of the *Berliner Illustrierte*, months old.

'And what have we here?' she mused.

The Fräulein looked at her blankly.

Clara Peuthert sidled over to the bed.

'I thought I told you, Peuthert, to go to bed,' Nurse Malinovsky said. 'Haven't you caused enough upset for one day?'

Clara ignored her.

'I brought it from the library. I thought you might like to have it,' she said to the Fräulein.

'Pilfering from the library now, Peuthert, is it?' the nurse said.

'I think you'll find it gives the Fräulein comfort,' Clara said smugly.

And, strangely, Clara was right. Propped up in bed, the Fräulein leafed through the pages of the newspaper, even after lights out when she had only the dim illumination from the corridor to read by. And Nurse Malinovsky noticed that, hours later, before she settled down to sleep, she carefully folded the paper and placed it under her pillow as if it were a solemn relic. Some time later, doing her four a.m. round, Thea Malinovsky halted, lamp in hand, by the Fräulein's bed, relieved to find her sleeping deeply.

'Sweet dreams, Fräulein,' she murmured softly.

I dream of sisters. The tangled limbs, the downy skin, the plaited ropes of hair, a shared bed. I hear their laughter floating in the thin blue air across sun-dappled grass. I am the youngest of them, impish and quick, the cleverest. A treasured child, princess darling of her Papa. And then Baby comes. A charmed child whom Papa has wished for so long, he wishes him into life. Papa has such power! We girls creep into the nursery; he lies in his crib, an angel in a white robe. Papa lifts him up and kisses him on the forehead. Our brother, our own little tsarevich. How blessed we are! We do not know how blessed. Those years of joy, the little pleasures. All shrunk and shrivelled like an apple left to ripen in the dark and forgotten. All pucker and decay. Our small world, perfect as a decorated egg, a shiny trinket, blue and gold, smashed into a hundred pieces.

For days she stays in bed. Clara tries to engage her in conversation, her old bright chatter, her raucous jokes, but the Fräulein cannot bear to enjoy what she is soon about to lose. She turns away and buries her head in the pillow. She pores over the grainy plate on the cover of the *Berliner Illustrierte*, which Clara has left for her like a love token. She is sure there is a message in it for her. Four girls turn their gaze on her. And there is a little boy in a sailor suit, his lips parted as if he is about to speak. She likes to say their names aloud, Olga, Tatiana, Maria, Anastasia and the baby, Alexei. Apple of their eye. Even in the photograph the girls cluster round him protectively, as if the sudden flash might alarm him.

The one who has escaped, the one they call Anastasia, is second from the left. She is the only one not smiling. Her hair falls down around her shoulders. Where the light catches it, high on her temple, it seems to turn to gold. The shadows of her sisters cast her face into half-shade, a pocket of it beneath her solemn eye, her left cheek and the dimpled point of her chin fall into darkness. A cuff of broderie anglaise rubs against a glimpse of arm.

The Fräulein runs her fingers round this face like a blind woman seeking knowledge through her hands. The candid childish gaze, fraught with premonition, is like an entry point, a way in. She examines it through a borrowed magnifying glass. The face enlarged and saucery as she tilts the glass. She trains the glass so close the features fall away into a speckled web and weave, as ink bleeds into paper. She is drawn into the blurry polka-dot engravure, the black pinholes of another world. As if she has turned inside out, the photograph a mirror and she is looking out, not in.

'Fräulein!'

She jumps. Nurse Walz bends over her.

'I know all these,' she says.

Nurse Walz looks at her, puzzled.

'One of them was rescued, they say,' Nurse Walz says, and, sliding the paper from the patient's hands, points to Tatiana. 'This one, I think.'

The Fräulein shakes her head.

'Which one, then?' Nurse Walz demands.

But she cannot shake off the odd feeling that has come over her. As if her very edges are melting, she cannot tell where she begins and ends. She is terrified and exhilarated all at once. Or else, after two years in the madhouse, she has finally lost her mind.

She toys with the girl's name. Anastasia. An-a-stas-iah. It ripples like a stream of over rocks. The first syllables twinned and echoed in the second. The name blossoms like a rose, petals crushed and enfolded. She shortens it – Ana – to make it fit the smallness of the princess who owns it. She compares it to her own. Unbekannt. The choppy indifference of it. A name for a logbook, a register. A name that allows no knowing, which lifts a bureaucratic hand and says – keep out, go back, dead end. She studies Anastasia, the little owner of the name – the dreamy tilt of head, the rounded jut of shoulder, the tiny pearls that nestle at her throat. Those eyes, the gravity of the rosebud mouth ripening for disappointment. Little girl, poor lost girl, lost princess. She returns to the photograph, but she finds the little girl is strangely absent. No longer imprisoned in the frenzied puzzle of dots, the grey and black patina of the photographer's flash. She has escaped!

Fräulein Unbekannt feels pregnant. Nauseous in the morning, sick with a delicious dread. Her belly flutters, the old wounds ache. A dream is growing there, a curled-up, day-old fledgling. Unfurling, hour by hour, the tiny thorns that will lengthen into fingers, the luminescent skull which will become a polished globe, the pink-raw flesh that will emerge as cherished skin, soft and feathery. A princess incubating. And no one notices that Fräulein Unbekannt is drowning, sinking fast beneath the waters of the Landwehr Canal. Not even Clara. Clara is too busy. There are papers to be initialled. Her brother who has signed her in must sign again to effect her release. Because Caspar Ruecker (Clara's maiden name; she does not like to dwell on her early unsuccessful marriage to Otto Peuthert, a fancy goods salesman, though she keeps his name) has been through the routine so often, he is lazy about details.

What matter if mad Clara has to stay an extra week in the loony bin? The journey out to Dalldorf is an imposition, and only possible on Monday afternoons when the ice rink, of which he is the manager, is closed. Ice-house, madhouse, he sometimes thinks, there's not much difference. Clara limps restlessly up and down the ward. She worries about Caspar not showing up. She frets about the apartment on Schumannstraße and the state it may be in. She remembers now the upturned table, the chairs flung aside, fruit of her struggle with the orderlies from Dalldorf amidst a snowstorm of featherdown. (She had ripped open the mattress with her bare hands in a frenzied search for her cash box.) But mostly she pines for the Fräulein, who has been sickly and totally withdrawn for days. Nurse Walz says she is as bad as when she was first admitted. She will not talk to Clara, or even meet her gaze. Clara is awed by the magnificence of the girl's bereavement. She does not know what to do. She fears that she has lost her Fräulein Unbekannt.

Nurse Malinovsky is sitting at her desk, drifting in the crystalline trance induced by the inky hours before dawn. The only one awake in a sleeping world, alert to the possibility of alarm, but soothed by the rise and fall of slumber all around her, she is thinking of her wedding dress, dreamily calculating how many yards of fabric she will need, when a shadow falls over her. Startled, she looks up. It is Fräulein Unbekannt, who has crept up soundlessly, pale and silent as a ghost.

'What have you there, Fräulein?' Nurse Malinovsky asks, still half-lost in nuptial reverie. 'A love letter?'

The Fräulein hands her the *Berliner Illustrierte*.

The paper, Thea notices, is cracked along the edges where it has been folded and refolded, then smoothed by careful hands. So this is what the girl has been mooning over, a photograph of the Russian royals. The picture has a pressed look, like a flower trapped between the pages of a missal.

'It's a sad story, isn't it?' the Fräulein says.

'Yes, Fräulein, it is.'

Nurse Malinovsky does not dwell on death, not when she is quickened by the future. A silence falls between them.

'Does anything strike you about the photograph?' the Fräulein asks.

Nurse Malinovsky studies the picture closely, her eye moving swiftly over the portrait.

'No,' she says slowly, doubtfully.

'Then you don't see any resemblance between the two of us?' The Fräulein points to the face of the youngest grand duchess.

Nurse Malinovsky looks again, then back at the insistent Fräulein Unbekannt.

'Well,' she says, gauging the Fräulein's pallid brow, the eager agitation of her grey eyes. 'It's true there is a similarity.'

The Fräulein smiles darkly, gap-toothed.

'What are you trying to say, Fräulein?' It is Nurse Malinovsky's turn to be agitated. 'What is it? Is it you, is that what you mean?'

Rising, she grasps the Fräulein by the shoulders and gently shakes her.

'Is it you, Fräulein, is it?'

Is it you? Is it you? Who are you? Where are you? Who did this to you? You, you. Who are you? The words swirled in her head, every question she had ever been asked, all rising together and rushing out of Nurse Malinovsky's mouth. It made her dizzy, as if the world had keeled over and everything had come adrift from its name. The room was spinning. She felt a kind of sea-sickness, as if she were on the brink of a vertiginous fall.

'Fräulein?'

The name, her name, brought her back from the edge.

'Fräulein, are you all right?'

The ward, the rows of iron cots, the mothy glow of Nurse Malinovsky's night light reassert themselves. In the moment when she closed her eyes, they had slid noiselessly back into their place. The nurse's face fills up her horizon as they stand, clasped together.

'Are you faint?'

Yes, oh yes, she was faint. So faint she could not be seen. The little princess had fled, unable to bear the cruel gaze of the world.

'Let's get you back to bed,' Nurse Malinovsky said, guiding her back to the ward. 'Try to get some sleep.'

Thea Malinovsky, shaken by the encounter, travels through the frosty early morning streets. The tram rings merrily as she alights from the back platform and hurries to the Café Luna to meet Dr Leon Chemnitz for breakfast. Their lives are like this, brief untimely encounters – she bug-eyed from night duty, he sticky still from sleep – meeting for just-baked rolls and steaming coffee before she falls into bed and he goes off to start his day at the Westend Hospital. He is in the café before her. He stands and waves to her. They kiss. Urgent day greets languid night.

Coffee comes. Leon gulps his down, one eye on the clock over the counter.

Thea barely touches hers.

'What is it, sweetheart?' he asks, nuzzling at her neck.

'The strangest thing has happened,' she says, easing away

from him and staring abstractly into a veiled distance. 'You know our Fräulein Unbekannt?'

Leon nods. He knows them all; the sad, the bad, the mad populate his early mornings.

'She tried to tell me something last night, something about her past.'

'So?'

'Leon, she as good as said she was Grand Duchess Anastasia, the daughter of the tsar.' She feels her eyes well up with tears.

'Oh, Thea, is that all?' Leon laughs indulgently.

Thea looks at him, offended.

'Well,' he says guardedly, trying to dispel the mood of recrimination, 'it *is* a lunatic asylum, Thea. What else would you expect?'

'But,' she protests.

'But what?' He is impatient with her air of preoccupation.

'The Fräulein is different. She's never made any claims for herself, that's what makes me wonder.'

'Wonder?'

'If she isn't telling the truth.'

'Come here,' he says, pulling her to him. This time she doesn't resist. Her hair tickles his chin.

'Even if she is, darling, what can you do about it?'

'That's just it,' Thea says. 'If I report this to Dr Hanisch, or the director, they will seize on it. It will convince them that their diagnosis is right, that she is crazy, and you know I have never believed that. But then if she really is, you know, who she says she is, then she shouldn't be with us. In Dalldorf, of all places!'

'Thea,' he says, 'Thea.' He loves her name; he loves just to say it. He kisses the auburn crown of her head.

'It's strange, isn't it?' she muses gently. 'It's as if the Fräulein has resorted to madness to save herself. As if delusion *is* her cure.'

IT WAS MONDAY morning. The inmates of Ward B returned from laundry duty. They usually came back in groups of four or five, with lone stragglers taking up the rear. Today they invaded together, a raggle-taggle army on the move. Fräulein Unbekannt could hear the tone of agitated alarm in their voices, even before they came in. It was not the usual mélange of individual complaint; some common grievance animated them. Hilda Scharrel led the bunch. She marched up to the Fräulein's bed. She was propped up on high pillows. Hilda noticed her pallor and that sour air of disengagement she gave off.

'Fräulein, Fräulein,' she said, 'have you heard? They're going to move us. Ship us off!'

An orchestra of grumbles and sighs tuned up from the knot of inmates gathered at her back.

'Nurse Bucholz told us at the laundry, let it slip more like, that Ward B is to be transferred, all of us, to another place, an asylum out in Brandenburg. In the middle of the country, God knows where. How will Jonah ever find me there?'

'Well, I'm not going,' Minna Heck declared. 'I'm too old for shifting. Only way I'll leave here is in a box.'

'What's this?' Clara demanded.

She pushed through the crowd. She was in her day clothes. She had been sitting on her bed beside her canvas bag of belongings all ready and prepared for Caspar, though he was not due until at least three p.m. All morning

73

she had been watching Fräulein Unbekannt at the other end of the ward. Twenty of her halting steps would cover the distance between them, but the silence emanating from the Fräulein had defied her. Clara knew its tenor – hurt, haughty and despising. But this commotion had given her an excuse.

'Nothing that need worry you, Clara,' Hilda said, 'you're getting out.'

'They're moving the entire ward?' Clara asked. 'What about the Fräulein here?' She cast an anxious glance at her. 'She's not well enough to be carted about the place.'

'Everyone,' Hilda said emphatically.

Her tone defeated them. The others retreated to their beds, for once their gloom matching Fräulein Unbekannt's.

'I'll come and visit,' Clara said to her, 'no matter where you are. I promise. I'll find you.'

But the Fräulein didn't answer. Didn't even seem to hear. She was miles away, in another world.

Anastasia remains sickly, too frightened to reveal herself. Chased away by Nurse Malinovsky. When the Fräulein looks at her beloved, tattered photograph it no longer has the piteous gaze of an icon. It has the glassy look of history. Dead history. Where has she gone? What dark corner has she crept into? What is she afraid of? The Fräulein feels a motherly concern for her, wandering aimlessly through the wards, searching in the garden, pressing her nose against the window of the library (after all, that is where she was born). She wants to call out – Anastasia – making shushing sounds as if to a cowering kitten. But words, she knows, are useless.

She watches Clara disconsolately as she paces up and down, clock-watches, checks her kitbag for the hundredth time as if there's something she's forgotten to put in. First Clara, and now the little princess, gone. Without Clara she would never have found Anastasia; now, she would have neither of them. Was it her fate always to be abandoned?

Clara is desperate. Caspar will be arriving any minute now – she checks the clock, it is, in fact, only ten past one. She's torn in two. She wants to go, she longs to stay. She hasn't had the stomach for lunch. She's been too busy racking her brains trying to think of some way to reach the Fräulein, who's lying there like death warmed up. So frail and weak, Clara fears that she will simply fade away. What will the poor girl do, without Clara's protection, lumped in with this lot? That Hilda, for example, likes to be top dog, Clara notes. She looks at them scraping their bowls, licking gruel from their ladles. The common mad, Clara thinks. Her Fräulein should not have to suffer them. She is too good, too fine, too noble to be locked away with them, with this. She surveys the crowded ward, the nonsense hum and idiotic babble of it. Her poor Fräulein with nothing, without even a name. A name, she thinks, a name.

Clara waits until the lunch trolley disappears. She waits until the inmates return to their beds. Some will read, others will fall into an afternoon drowse. She must act before that happens. She will need witnesses, even if they're all mad. A nurse would be even better, but Clara cannot depend on the presence of their ladyships Walz or Bucholz. Never around when they're needed. She roams in little circles, her bad hand is jumpy. She must be calm. Now she must be calm because later she will have to be mad. The clock shows two. It is time.

She hurtles down the ward, jabbing her finger in the air and shouting at the top of her lungs. The sleepy and the dull regard her jadedly. Another Peuthert drama. But it's spectacle if nothing else and so they watch – and witness.

'I know you,' Clara shrieks, 'I know you.'

The Fräulein looks aghast as Clara, hair adrift and spittle flying, lurches at her. She whisks the *Illustrierte* from underneath the pillow and waves it in the air.

'I know you, I know you,' she screams and stomps her foot.

Slack-jawed the ward looks on. That's curtains for her release, Hilda thinks; Clara will end up in the lock-ups for this.

'You are Grand Duchess Tatiana!'

The Fräulein's face opens into a smile. She draws herself up in bed, leaning on her elbows. Clara has found the princess. Not lifeless in a photograph this time, but here at last, at home, within. And Clara can see her! The only trouble is, Clara being Clara, impetuous, wild-hearted, has picked the wrong princess. The Fräulein stretches out her fingers and lays them on Clara's swinging arm. It seems to work magically. Clara halts in mid-shriek. The princess speaks.

'I am Anastasia,' she says carefully. 'Grand Duchess Anastasia Nikolayevna!'

The silence fairly thrums. Even the dwarf Hanna, sitting cross-legged on her bunk, and humming quietly to herself, stops.

'Hear that, you cretins?' Clara roars. 'Did you hear that?'

Dumbly they regard her. She turns and lunges out into the corridor, heading for the director's office. Weak winter sun glares in her eyes. Fräulein Unbekannt has confessed, she wants to shout out, but there is no need to act mad out here. She tries to compose herself before she reaches the director's office. Fräulein Unbekannt, the unknown one, has spoken, Clara practises, as she staggers and weaves. But she cannot contain herself. To me. To me!

My princess, Clara murmurs, my princess.

Nurse Walz, running in the opposite direction, sees Clara Peuthert's lurching progress from afar. She's been alerted, not by Clara's shrieks, but by the eerie silence she has left in her wake. Outbursts and rages are the norm, but silence means real trouble.

'What is it, Clara? What's happened?' she calls with yards of sun-striped floor still between them.

Clara's face is strangely illuminated, softened, positively beatific.

The two women draw level with one another.

'Clara?'

Clara staggers by, saying nothing. She seems not to even see Nurse Walz. She points silently towards Ward B. Nurse Walz hurries on. The patients in Ward B are where Clara has left them, a frozen tableau. Hilda stands sentry at the end of Fräulein Unbekannt's bed, Minna Heck is stranded in the middle of the floor, Hanna is crouched, cross-eyed, on her bed.

'What's going on here?' Nurse Walz demands.

Hilda thrusts a newspaper into her hand and points in dumb show at the Fräulein.

'It's her,' she whispers, 'don't you see the likeness?'

Nurse Walz has already seen the portrait. Thea Malinovsky showed it to her one evening and asked her cryptically if the young woman, second from the left in the picture, reminded her of anyone. Nurse Walz does not like riddles.

'No,' she had said impatiently.

'The Fräulein,' Thea had ventured, 'can't you see? Wouldn't it make sense?' Thea had gabbled. 'Her silence, her refusal to work, those scars?'

Thea had been too long on the night shift, she thought.

Nurse Walz takes the paper now from Hilda and pushes it into Fräulein Unbekannt's lap. Has the entire world lost its senses?

'Fräulein,' she barks, 'explain this!'

The Fräulein looks straight at her, straight through her.

'Not Fräulein,' she replies, 'Anastasia.'

It was as if I had fallen from the sky, a clear blue sky and

77

found myself suddenly among strangers. They hid me in their wagon. Have you ever seen a farm cart? No, I don't suppose you have. But I have. I know how these wretched people live. With their rough-hewn clothes, their poor black bread, and their pitiful belongings. I was lying in a nest of straw; it smelt of milk and rottenness. A man was driving the horses. Alexander, Alexander Tchaikovsky, the man who saved me. He drove the horses like a man possessed. His family huddled together in the well of the cart for warmth. His mother, his sister Veronica, his brother Sergei. I drew warmth from them too. It is a shameful thing to admit. I bedded down with subjects who once would not have dared look me in the eye. Alexander was a soldier, he had guarded us, though I did not remember him. They all looked the same to me, these people. He saw that I was alive and he would not bury a live body. He would have been damned for ever if he had. So he took me away, I don't know how. I can't remember. After the smoke and the blood, I was in darkness for a long time.

When I awoke I was wearing clothes, not my own, peasant clothes which smelled of woodsmoke, as if I had been smuggled into another life, a wretched, hunted existence. We journeyed, oh, for weeks and weeks like animals in the night. Bucharest, they said, Bucharest would be safe. It is all a blur, all dirt. Dark woods and fields. A cold starry sky overhead. The nights were bitter. The cart rattled dreadfully. Each bump on the rutted track was like a twist of the knife. My smashed head ached and sometimes there was only water to drink. Sometimes, no food at all. They tended to my wounds with cold compresses. That is all they had. But they shared what they had with me. I would not be here now if they had not been kind to me. A peasant, you see, is not the same as us, but if simple people are kind to me I do not remember at all that they are simple. Alexander was rough, yes, but he had come from nobility, way back. His grandmother had been a Polish countess, yes, he told me that. But he was like all men: he was hot. By the time we reached Bucharest I was with child. Frau Tchaikovsky, that should be my title now. Oh yes, I married him. Not for me, for the baby's sake. There was a ceremony in Bucharest in a large church, a Catholic church. It was the only time I came out of hiding. I never went out into the street. It was too dangerous, full of brigands and thieves. I stayed indoors, in one room that we all shared. High up. Alexander strung a rope from wall to wall and draped a blanket over it to afford us some privacy. Trees scraped up against the windows. I could hear the sounds of other people. It was a cauldron of noise, that place. Roars and shrieks in the night, the poor and their noisy, common rows. And when the baby was born, he was christened. We called him Alexei, after Baby. As soon as he was born I gave the child to Alexander's mother to look after. I wanted only that he would be taken away. Instantly. I was ashamed. I had betrayed my name with a bastard son. Dirt was all he was, more dirt.

They took the jewels they'd found in the seams of my corset and sold them. Sold them so that we could eat. There were diamonds, amber, I don't remember; we had sewn them in willy-nilly. The last to go was a long pearl necklace. They killed Alexander for it, stabbed him right through the heart and robbed him. Rumanians are quick with the knife. They had killed him for Romanov gold. I saw his body, what they had done to him. The blood, all blood. Because of me. I might as well have killed him with my own hand. I bring death to all who know me.

It was winter then. I had to get away. Berlin was the only place where I would be safe. I have family here, Aunt Irina, she would help. Alexander's mother did not want me to leave but I had to. They had been kind to me but I couldn't live as a peasant all my life. Sergei came with me. He was a sweet boy, sweeter than my Alexander. There was something sad and solitary about him, like a child in a great big lumbering body. We had to walk for many miles, through snow, hiding by night. Sometimes we would go on

*a train, but we had no papers. In any case, there would
have been questions. We had to be careful. As soon as we
reached Berlin, we found a small hotel. I was exhausted;
you cannot imagine how tired I was, how weak. I had been
so reduced. When I awoke I was alone. Sergei was gone. I
waited for days for him. I searched the streets, wandering
like some lost soul. First Alexander, now Sergei. He had
been like a brother to me, a faithful brother. Perhaps he
had been set upon as Alexander had. There are assassins
everywhere. Perhaps because of me, he too was dead. I
tortured myself with such thoughts. All alone in a strange
city, penniless and friendless, no one to turn to. I ended up
at the canal. A weakness overcame me, a terrible despair.
All belonging to me dead or gone. Mama, Papa, my sisters,
my beloved Baby. Gone. How can I explain? The waters of
the Landwehr Canal promised rest. It's true. I wanted only
to be dead. And I was saved. Again.*

SHE HAS BEEN given a new name – Fräulein Anni – and a new prison, this time on Nettelbeckstraße. Six months after Clara's departure from Dalldorf, Baron Arthur von Kleist had offered to take her in. Dalldorf, he declared, was no place for a grand duchess. The Baroness Maria had taken her on drives to Potsdam and Charlottenburg. They had viewed palaces and museums which the baroness had presented with a proprietorial flourish. This, she would say, pointing to a glacial lake of polished ballroom floor, or the marble sweep of a staircase, will remind you of home. They reminded her of Dalldorf, sugary, iced-cake versions of Dalldorf.

She had been given new dresses to wear. They even had monogrammed knickers made up for her with the initials AR, but she felt too foolish wearing them. Gerda, the baron's daughter, would spend the night on a settle bed in her room in case she should wake up and not know where she was. The hush in the apartment on Nettelbeckstraße unnerved her; there were no night-time noises here. Everything was soft and muffled – the beds, the sheets, the heavy drapes which plunged her room into a velvet darkness. And then, the questions started, all over again. Not the same ones – who are you? where are your papers? – but sly and unexpected questions as if she were being tested. When she complained of headaches, a doctor was called. She should have known better. What age was she? Had she suffered a blow to the head? What about those scars? There followed a procession of guests, sometimes as many as twenty at a time in the drawing room, a Captain Double-Barrel or a Countess Buxombosom, who would stand and gawp at her or sidle up to her with more queries. Would she speak Russian for them? As if she was some circus dog. At least in Dalldorf she had known who to be afraid of – the doctors wore white coats, the nurses, uniforms. Here a visitor in street clothes could turn in the blink of an eye into an inquisitor. She took to her bed, where sometimes it was possible to spend an hour or two alone, though the baroness hovered constantly. 'For fear of what you might do to yourself,' she said.

She wept at night. Lonely, solitary tears so that she would not excite the attention of Gerda, snoring decorously at her feet. She could not tell what she was weeping for. Perhaps it was the little princess whom she had housed within, a little girl in need of mothering. And the loss of Clara. She would wake up in the small hours of the morning – the silence woke her – and cosseted in her high bed she would long for Clara. Without Clara, none of this would have happened, and yet where was she? Her new-found status had turned Clara into an unsuitable companion, as the baroness had put it.

It was surprisingly easy to escape. Easier than she had thought. She simply said she was going for a stroll, to take the air. Gerda offered to come with her, but she declined. Gerda was getting on her nerves, in any case. She had found herself snapping at Gerda and, surprisingly, Gerda took it. Where such behaviour would have won swift retribution at Dalldorf, here it was tolerated, even admired. As if this was what the von Kleists expected of royalty – bad temper, disdain. But Gerda's watchfulness was a kind of weapon. Her eyes darted about suspiciously, registering everything with a greedy disapproval. She was particularly vigilant when her father was about. What a pair they made

– the baron, tall and stringy as a beanpole with leathery jowls, and his daughter, broad-faced, smooth-browed, small and plump. When the baron made the introductions he always used her title; with Gerda she was just plain Fräulein Anni.

Out in the streets of Berlin, the merry song of trams lifts her spirits. If they will not allow Clara Peuthert to call, then she will visit Clara. It is the only other place in Berlin she knows, though certain street corners in passing beg to be recognised. A glimpse of cobble, a tram-tracked square, the spire of a cathedral, all seen from the baroness's motor, have struck a chord with her, but the connection is so glancing that she has not remarked on it. These are echoes that belong to her, only her.

Clara's place on Schumannstraße is a far cry from the featherdown comforts of the von Kleists', but Fräulein Anni likes it there. Its chaos seems eerily familiar, the gloomy scullery, the small, dishevelled parlour where Clara sleeps on a divan, the strange clutter she gathers all about her. The rumpled tissue patterns from her dressmaking days, the tailor's dummy standing naked in a corner, a samovar that Helmut purloined from a first-class carriage at the Lehrter Bahnhof, an empty birdcage. Even the musty rankness of the baskets of soiled sheets Clara takes in with the intimate whiff of other people's secret lives coming off them, seems bracing. Today Clara's dirty linen seems preferable to the shrouded dust covers of the von Kleists.

Clara is peppering. The pendulum has swung. She feels the savage fury of the abandoned. Her princess has been taken away from her. She is shut out by those Russian emigrés who have filled her Fräulein up with notions of herself. They treat her, Clara Peuthert, as if she doesn't exist. Without Clara, the Fräulein would be a nameless little tramp in an asylum. But now, now she answers to *their* vulgar name for her. Fräulein Anni. Fräulein Anni. Like some music-hall coquette. The little peasant doesn't even know when she's being demeaned.

Clara hears the knock on the door, a loud, imperious rapping on wood. The landlord, Clara thinks, looking for arrears. She settles her dress and pushes back the tangle of hair which clouds her brow. She stumbles to the door and opens it an inch. Through the suspicious slit she sees the Fräulein.

'Clara,' she says, 'it's me.'

'What do you want?' Clara barks, wedging her good foot in the door.

'Let me in, Clara, please.'

For a moment, Clara softens. Perhaps it is the urgent appeal in the Fräulein's voice, or her tense air of anticipation. She looks paler and thinner than at Dalldorf, but her skin has a clear, well-tended look. Her face is shaded by a hat, a gorgeous white plush confection with a black satin brim rolled at the edge and trimmed with two raven's quills in front. Over her arm a camel-hair coat is draped. She is wearing a mauve satin dress – drop-shoulder, five-piece skirt, Clara notes – which sets off the colour of her eyes, which today seem emphatically blue. She looks the part, Clara thinks, her tenderness suddenly exhausted. They had made her look the part. Sour bile rises in her throat.

'Clara?'

She opens the door and the Fräulein makes to come in. But Clara grabs her by the shoulders and pushes her back out into the landing, prodding at her satin breast, pulling at the feathers in her hat and finding instead fistfuls of glossy hair.

'Stop it, Clara,' the Fräulein squeals.

Clara lifts her hand and swipes the girl across the cheek. Her blood is up; she has been betrayed. How dare she come around here in her fine bought clothes, her silly hat, her puny cries for help?

'You have betrayed me,' she roars and clouts the Fräulein again, a sharp cuff about the face. She falls, sprawling on a gloomy landing, dust on her dress, her hat flying. How ridiculous she looks, Clara thinks, lying there scrabbling on the stone floor.

'That's where you belong,' Clara cries, 'in the dirt!'

Clara staggers back and takes one last look at her princess, smeared and bruised and brought down, before she slams the door. Within, she leans against the wood and tries to reclaim her breath. And as her breathing steadies and her rage subsides, she feels cured. Cured of love.

Fräulein Anni staggered out into the street and started walking. Her cheekbone was stinging and already felt shiny to the touch. She carried her hat in her hand. The white pile was soiled and she had lost one of the feathers in the scuffle with Clara. She wandered aimlessly, patting her throbbing face, and wishing she was not dressed in such a fashion, her finery despoiled. A tram droned past and stopped and on an impulse she boarded it, not even bothering to check its destination on the front. She wanted to put as much distance as was possible between Clara and herself. She sat in a daze, nursing her flaming cheek and her hurt pride. She took no notice of where she was going. The only sensation she was aware of was a queasy humiliation. When the tram stopped at Invalidenstraße, she got off for no other reason than the motion of the tram was beginning to make her feel sick.

Invalidenstraße. It rings a bell; no, the tram rings a bell and leaves her standing there. It is her street, the street of invalids.

'Franziska?' a small voice says wonderingly. 'Is that you? Is that really you?'

A blonde young woman is standing on the kerb.

Obviously a shopgirl or somesuch, but despite that, she is smartly dressed. A hat of cornflower blue with yellow flowers, a dark blue suit with black lace and red braid and buffalo-horn buttons. She has begun to take notice of what people wear; it matters.

'Franziska?' the voice persists and for the first time she realises the woman is addressing her.

'It *is* you!'

Suddenly she is enveloped in a coiffed embrace. Sticky hair, cheap perfume. She clutches her hat and hopes the mistake can be sorted out quickly without a public scene on the street. The young woman steps backwards.

'My, how well you look! You've certainly come up in the world since we last saw you!'

She fingers the lapels of the camel coat.

'Are you staying in Berlin? Oh, come home, that's where I'm going now. You must meet Mother. She will be impressed. Just look at you!'

The young woman takes her gloved hand and, putting her face up close, says earnestly, 'It's Doris, you do remember, Doris, Doris Wingender.'

She nods. She wants to please the young woman, who is pretty and winning and obviously in need of a friend. She has a terrible urge to confide in her, though she does not know why. She wants to tell this complete stranger how she is being held against her will by people who think she is someone else. Perhaps it is this woman's easy familiarity, the presumption she has made of friendship, or the blows inflicted by Clara? Clara, Clara, what will she do without her? Clara, the only one who really knows her.

'Franziska?' the chatty young woman says again. There is something insistent and demanding in the way she says the name. A more urgent instinct than the need to confide takes over. Flight. She hears the approach of another tram, wheezing to a stop by the kerb. She pulls her hand away and clambers on as the tram is pulling off. The young woman stands on the kerb, shocked, rejected, baffled.

'Sissy,' she is calling. 'Sissy!'

It is Herr Franz Jaenicke, an acquaintance of the von Kleists, who rescues Fräulein Anni. Strolling through the Tiergarten he spots her, standing on an ornamental wooden bridge that spans a green lake. Weeping willows trail in the water, lily fronds carpet the still surface. He is one of several friends the frantic von Kleists have called upon to scour the city for the fugitive princess. So-called, Herr Jaenicke thinks. Baron von Kleist was out of his mind with worry. When Herr Jaenicke was summoned to the apartment on Nettelbeckstraße, the baron was pacing up and down the drawing room, smoothing the quicks on his worried fingers.

'I have been entrusted with the Grand Duchess Anastasia, and you,' he pointed a finger at his wife, Maria, and daughter, Gerda, 'you have managed to go one better than the Bolsheviks. You have managed to lose her.'

He paused and narrowed his eyes.

'If things should ever change in Russia, that girl could be our passport, do you hear?'

His wife, given to emotion, released a volley of sobs. Gerda bristled with resentment. It was not her job to be a minder.

'She has lost track of time,' Gerda said. 'She cannot even read the clock.'

'She knows the difference between night and day,' her father barked. 'It's been three days now.'

'Where shall I look?' Herr Jaenicke interjected, hoping to dispel the air of tense recrimination.

'*Ach, Mann*, who knows?' the baron snapped.

'Try that Peuthert woman again,' Gerda whispered to him on his way out. 'The two of them were thick as thieves.'

But Clara would not even open the door to him. She shouted through the keyhole instead.

'How should I know where the little tramp is? I know where she should be. In the madhouse. If you find her, bring her back there. That's where she belongs.'

Herr Jaenicke approaches Fräulein Anni carefully. He does not wish to alarm her, or to lose his prize by scaring her off. The timbers of the little bridge creak as he tiptoes up to her, but she does not even lift her head. She is deep in leafy concentration.

'Fräulein Anni,' he greets her, conversationally.

She looks up at him as he sidles up to her and smiles at him vaguely.

'Herr Jaenicke,' he says as if to explain himself. 'You look lost.'

'Oh no,' she says, 'I like the water. It's restful, don't you think?'

Herr Jaenicke remembers her dangerous predilection for water.

'Home to the unhappy dead,' she says.

'Quite,' Herr Jaenicke says. 'Now, Fräulein, don't you think it's time for you to come home?'

He lightly touches her forearm. She stiffens. He wants to grip her elbow and steer her away from here. Her unpredictable air of distraction fills him with unease.

'Fräulein, I beseech you, come with me now before there is any more trouble.'

'Trouble?' she all but screeches.

He darts his eye around to check that no one is watching. A passer-by could well mistake this scene for a lover's tiff, and him for a bullying suitor.

'What do you know of trouble, Herr Jaenicke?' she hisses.

This is getting out of hand, he thinks. Short of manhandling her, he cannot imagine how he will ever get her to budge. He tries one last desperate measure.

'Your Imperial Highness,' he ventures and offers her his hand.

Surprisingly, she takes it and smiling, not at him but to herself, allows him to lead her over the water and along a shaded path towards his waiting motor.

Berlin, 17 February 1920

THE WOMAN STANDS on the footbridge and stares down into the inky waters of the Landwehr Canal below. It is a metal bridge, half-mooned, with intricate cast-iron work. A gas lantern poised in the centre of it is held up by two curlicued struts which arc prayerfully overhead. Sleet sprinkles in its glow. Passers-by swaddled in scarves and hats hurry past, bent against unforgiving weather, intent on their destination. Their footsteps ring out metallic in the crisp air, their warm exhaled breath hangs in urgent, puffy clouds.

The woman pays no heed to the scurry of the toiling pedestrians. Despite her heavy black skirts, and her boots laced up to the knee, her feet and legs are numb. Beneath her linen sleeves goose-pimples sprout. She is not dressed for the weather; rather she looks as if she has just stepped outside on a quick errand. A young woman, she is small, thick-set, with dark hair pulled back from a high brow and knotted at the nape of her neck. Her lips are fleshy and could be described as sensuous but for their slight downturn which hints sourly at recurring humiliation. Her face, in repose, is mournful, dour even. From where we stand it is not possible to see her eyes, which are a pale slatey grey, though in sunnier moods they lighten to blue. She wears a tobacco-coloured shawl over her shoulders. It has a threadbare, lovelorn look. She is crying, silently, though she hardly notices her own tears. They are partly the product of the biting wind, partly the fruit of a despair which has gone beyond self-pity. She has no pity left for herself.

She is about to plunge into the water.

Her name is Franziska Schanzkowska. She is twenty-three years old. How small and sad the details of the suicidal. When she clambers onto the pedestal of the bridge and stands, gripping the high strut with her arm, she will look like the proud figurehead on a ship leaning out fearlessly over the waves. And then she will pause, arms aloft as if she is about to fly. It will be a fateful hesitation. For the man standing by the ruined fence at the water's edge, hands sunk deep into his pockets, stamping his feet on the trampled grass to keep warm, she will look like a creature of the night, a bat with extended wings glimpsed in silhouette. He will not have time to form a word of warning, just a strangulated cry like the one which jolts a dreamer awake from a nightmare, as she falls, her clothes flapping heavily like sailcloth. Down, down, she will rush. Headlong. Her intricate store of memories will drown as she enters the freezing water in an icy spray. It is what she wants. To escape memory. To become innocent. To enter history.

Yekaterinburg, Russia, July 1918

PAPA! EMPEROR AND *Autocrat of All the Russias, Tsar of Moscow, Kiev, Vladimir, Novgorod, Grand Prince of Smolensk, Prince of Estonia, Hereditary Lord and Suzerain of the Circassian Princes and Mountain Princes, Lord of Turkestan, Heir to the Throne of Norway ... Papa! They call him Nicholas the Bloody. Mother is 'that German bitch'.*

It is hot here; the rooms swelter. The windows have been painted shut, the glass has been whitewashed. It is like living in a blind blizzard. We cannot see the street outside because of the stockade they have built around the house. But when they do allow us out, to circle in the trodden yard, we can hear the sounds from Voznesensky Prospekt. The scuff of feet on the dusty street, the clop of horses' hooves, the breeze riffling through the leaves of linden trees. Yekaterinburg is a fine city. Ivanov, the barber who came to cut Papa's and Baby's hair, has told us of the sweeping Municipal Gardens skirting the city's lake, the gold and malachite in the hills. There are two grand hotels, the America and the Palais. I don't suppose that we shall ever visit them. We can see the golden dome of the cathedral. It faces our house, our prison, the Ipatiev House, but we cannot enter it. It is forbidden. So much is forbidden to us. Nuns from the monastery leave eggs and milk on the doorstep, *but the soldiers take them. We have to make do with leavings, black bread, rewarmed cutlets from the guards' room. Fifteen of us take turns to use the five forks they have allowed us. We must share cutlery with our jailers.*

The days are long; so little happens. We read – old newspapers, the same old battered books. We play bezique. Mama stays abed. She prays. God will save us, she says, God will save us. Papa says the White Army will come; they will save us. During the night we hear them. Well, we hear the lonely snap of gunfire. Baby's knee is stiff. He rode his sled down the stairs at the house in Tobolsk, where we were held before. I remember the terrible crash as he tumbled down one flight, then two. Everything falls. And then the bleeding started. Baby bruises easily and then he bleeds. Mama's little Sunbeam.

I should have been a boy. We all should. First Olga, then Tatiana and Maria. When I was born, Papa had to go for a long walk in the woods at Peterhof, so great was his disappointment. The curse of a fourth daughter instead of a longed-for heir, a first son. And then, Baby came. What joy! We would be nothing without him. We were nothing without him. It is not that we were not loved, but we were incomplete. All hope rested in him, the boy who would be tsar.

What will become of us? What will become of us that has not already, Olga says. We have come as low as it is possible. We live like captive dogs. No, dogs would be treated better. Our dogs, anyway. Once our guards were respectful. Even in the Winter Palace – we girls were all sick with the measles, all our hair shorn off, Mama was at her wits' end – they granted us our privacy. But now we are gone beyond such civility. Now they treat us as if we are guilty of something. What have we done? The worst of it is going to the lavatory; they will not let us close the door. They watch us as we ... they watch us. It is all dirt. Enough!

93

Once, when we were in Tobolsk, I saw Gleb. Baby's playmate, son of our dear doctor. He was standing on the street below. I was trying to loosen the window, just a fraction, to let in some air. Sometimes I think they mean to kill us by suffocation. I stood up on the sill to get more leverage and there he was, standing, looking up, shading his eyes with this hand against the glare of the afternoon sun. He waved to me, I am sure he did. I was so excited to see him. Dear, darling Gleb. He used to do funny drawings that made us laugh. I wanted to shout out at him, afraid he couldn't see me. He waved again and then a soldier came and pushed him away. I felt my heart sink. No, don't go! Gleb bowed to me before the ugly brute hustled him away. I was still standing on the sill when one of our guards came into the room and pointed a rifle at me.

'Citizen Romanova, get down at once,' he shouted. 'You have been warned to stay away from the windows.'

I crouched down, trying to get down from such height with some degree of decorum. By right he should have turned his back, or offered me his hand.

'The commissar will have to be informed of this,' he said.

I slid down and righted my dress, my hair. I could feel my face flush.

'No, no, please, don't do that.'

'You could be sending messages to the enemy.'

'I was just waving, that is all, to Gleb.'

How could Gleb be anyone's enemy?

'He is our friend.'

'I could be your friend,' he said.

He smirked. He put his lips around the barrel of his rifle.

We had to play the piano for them in the evenings in the drawing room. One of us would be sent for. Olga sometimes, or Tatiana. My playing wasn't good enough. I couldn't read their music. Their common, vulgar anthems.

'You Fell as Victim to the Struggle', 'Get Cheerfully in Step, Comrade', 'You Don't Need a Golden Idol'.

I died there, yes, I died. The girl I was. Skewered to the floor by a boy who had smiled at me in the corridor. There were freckles on the bridge of his nose. He would turn his back when I used the lavatory, while the others laughed and stared. Now he was staring at me as if I were nothing, a bag of meal. He knelt down and put his ear close to my mouth. He smelt of sweaty fear and spirits. I thought he was going to whisper something to me, a secret, a prayer. My lips were parched.

'Do not touch me,' I said to him, 'I am your sovereign.'

He started back, aghast. Then he lifted his rifle butt and smashed it down.

Their excitement, our terror, it was hard to tell the difference in the stench of blood and the high, piercing panic. It was a clammy summer's night. The heat had made them sweat. They sweated as we bled, it was an exchange. Their sweat, our blood. Stubble on their chins as they rummaged among us with their boots, mud caked on their toecaps. The sweet smell of warm, oozing blood. The air palpitating. The shudder of exhaled breath, a hoarse groan, the tiny twitching of limbs after death. They gathered at the doorway when it was all over. One of them struck a match, a searing sulphurous sizzle, and lit a cigarette. They passed it around among themselves, inhaling greedily. The smell of Papa. Papa! Save me!

He saved me once before. From the sea at Livadia. We were in the water, great waves of warm surf. Olga, Tatiana, Maria. And Papa. We rose to the crest of a wave, up, up, then down. Plunging beneath the boiling sea, all greeny, thrashing overhead. I see them bobbing, Maria's pale legs, Olga's striped bathing costume, Tatiana's hair in weeping ropes. My sisters, lost to me. Then Papa's hand catches me by the hair and drags me up, up out of the angry deep. I gasp, inhale great lungfuls of blue air. Baby claps his hands together on the beach. He thinks it all some great joke.

God saved me. No, Tatiana did, she fell on top of me, she shielded me. She is dead because of me. No, the jewels saved me. Mama had us sew them into the seams of our corsets.

I thought they were going to take a photograph. That is how we were arranged. Mama, Papa, Baby in front, the rest of us behind. They roused us in the middle of the night, Dr Botkin rapping at Papa's door at two a.m. on the orders of Yurovsky. We must be moved for our own safety. We washed and dressed. Papa carried Baby in his arms; his knee, you see, was still stiff, he couldn't walk. Tatiana held Jimmy, our darling spaniel. There was Anna Demidova, Mama's maid, Alexei Trupp, Papa's valet, the cook, Ivan Kharitonov and Yevgeny Sergeyevich, our dear doctor. How reduced we are! We trooped downstairs, through the empty first floor and down another staircase, out of a doorway and into the courtyard. Oh, the night, how still it was. Summer in full reign. Yurovsky led us to a doorway into the basement. We followed him through a series of hallways. This is where the guards must sleep. The air was foul; we were below ground. We were shown into a small room with a vaulted ceiling. It was entirely empty. It had one sunken barred window and wallpaper, striped wallpaper, I remember.

'Why is there no chair here?' Mama asked. 'Is it forbidden for us to sit?'

She was leaning on her cane; it pained her to stand.

Yurovsky ordered chairs. Mama sat on one. Papa with Baby on his lap on the other. They were going to take our photograph.

The soldiers filed into the room. Ten soldiers. I counted them. They stood all in a row behind Yurovsky. Too close to take a picture; they would never get all of us in. A strip of bare floor separated us, that is all. Yurovsky stepped forward. He had a piece of paper in his hand, a small piece, a little scrap. He began to read from it.

'In view of the fact that your relatives are continuing their attack on Soviet Russia, the Ural Executive Committee has decided to execute you.'

'What? What?' Papa says.

How sweet the silence was after all the frenzied clamour. They had howled as they shot us, barking and baying like hounds to drown out our cries and their deed. And now there was only an exhausted silence. It was so silent I feared they would hear the blinking of my eyelids.

I played dead. I closed my eyes and imagined myself away. It was a game I used to play in the long hours of our captivity. It was a kind of escape. I would pick a girl out on the street, a factory worker, a peasant girl, it didn't matter, and wonder – what if I were her? It was a treacherous thought; there is nothing accidental about birth. We were born to rule. But it pleased me to consider what my life would be like were I not Grand Duchess Anastasia, but someone other. A nobody, a girl of no importance.

Berlin, August 1914

BERLIN WAS A city at war, but when Franziska Schanz-kowksa alighted from the train she stepped into a sea of children, scabby, barefoot and raucous from the sun. Hundreds of the city's needy young had been sent on free expeditions to the Wannsee because of the great heat. For days on end the barometer had registered 86°F in the shade; there was not a puff of wind; the stagnant canals stank. After several hours standing in the stifling heat of the corridor Franziska had got a seat in a crowded brown compartment, crushed against the window. Once she had stowed her case on the overhead rack (it was the case her mother had brought from Poznan on her wedding night), Franziska had concentrated on looking outside the train at the fleeing countryside. The fleet-footed zebra stripe of silver birches, the brown frown of furrowed fields, the scattering of cattle freckling the tussocky meadows flew by as if they were as intent on change as Franziska was. At first she measured the journey by reciting the names of towns to herself as they passed – Slupsk, Karwice, Koszalin; these she knew from her father's lips. But after a while the little huddled towns and the weathered-looking stationhouses bore names she had never heard of. They all began to look the same, and not much different from what she had left. And there was something depressing about the eager faces of the shawlies who rushed up to the windows of the train at each station, offering up their battered baskets of bread rolls and hollering their prices as if they were pious imprecations. She turned her attention inward. Two men sitting opposite in army greatcoats had struck up a conversation. One was a dark man, heavy-set and florid with thinning hair and, as if in compensation, an elaborately curled handlebar moustache the kaiser would have been proud of. The other, a much younger man, was pale-eyed and slack-jawed with a protruding Adam's apple which looked as if it must hurt him to swallow. They were both in the reserves and were returning from exercises. At least that's what Franziska thought they said. The men's accents were heavy and strange. German in their mouths sounded nothing like the language she knew. Exercises. She could think only of the arm-swinging and leg-shaking that Miss Tupalska had ordered in the midwinter schoolroom to keep their circulation going. But that did not seem the sort of thing that would keep an empire's army in shape. For the first time she felt a pang of fear – what if she couldn't understand anyone? What if no one could understand her? She smiled nervously to stem her own panic and the young man opposite caught her eye.

'Fräulein!' he said and dipped his head slightly.

Franziska blushed.

'No German,' she mumbled, though it was not true, and looked away.

Her silence discouraged him. She turned back towards the window and, closing her eyes, she feigned sleep.

It was late in the evening when they entered the city. The fields and small stations had given way to tall chimney stacks belching out smoke against a ruby summer sunset. Streets bathed in the sun's bloody glow faded into waste ground or lost themselves in coal-dusted arches. At eye-level, a land-locked basin lapped rosily against a weed-choked embankment. Then they were climbing. High up, they cut through boulevards dotted with gaslight; the gables of apartment buildings rushing to meet at street corners like the proud hulls of ships, then veering away into long, vertiginous perspectives. The flinty gaze of wall-eyed warehouses flashed by, the open mouths of tenements gaped. The train wormed its way into the saw-toothed silhouette of the city, deep into its sooted tunnels, hooting self-importantly as it bridged latticed metalwork before elbowing its way with a weary belch into the station, leaving Franziska on Platform 2 stranded in a crowd of sunburned orphans.

The noise was deafening. The children's shrill cries, the bellow of porters, the bombast of trains bloomed in the cathedral vault of the station. The thick metal hand of a large clock suspended in the wafting smoke moved halt-ingly over Roman numerals, shivering slightly as if time here were heavy. The air was speckled with flakes of soot and rank with grime and sweat. Gripping her case, she pushed against the seething throng, battling her way out onto the street. She stopped for breath at the grand entrance, inhaling great mouthfuls of city air. She was here; she had finally made it. Berlin!

The sun had gone down, leaving the tall buildings steeped in an invalid's pallor. All around her the city was in a fever. Trams clattered and sang across a vast cobbled square. Overhead on an elevated bridgeway a train rumbled and roared. Knots of young men in uniform brushed by her, hands raised in mock salutes or holding tankards of beer aloft. A couple embraced hungrily at the kerb, his kitbag at his feet, her straw hat tipping, then falling from her shoulders, unnoticed, and swept away by the light ruffle of breeze which had sprung up. Franziska followed its path as it bounced and rolled on the cobbles at people's feet, its polka-dot ribbon fluttering gaily like a token of the frantic mood. From the brassy glow of a beer cellar across the square she could hear the brazen strains of music and triumphant voices raised in ragged harmony. A row of military trucks growled by, their tarpaulins flapping at the back to reveal a tableau of eager boys in field grey. One of them leaped down and rushed at Franziska, landing his fleshy lips on hers.

'Wish me luck,' he said, 'for the Fatherland!'

Before she could protest he had scurried after the lorry, clambering on board to the cheers of his companions as the truck slewed drunkenly away into the lilac twilight. Franziska wiped the taste of him off her lips. She felt a bleakness steal over her. This was what she had always wanted. Escape and anonymity. But she felt as lonely as the petrified house she had come from. *Her* fatherland.

There was nothing there for her. Only her mother and Felix. The house, once so vividly cared for, was crumbling into a wilful chaos. Franziska could not counter her mother's absent-minded determination to let her tidy kingdom slide into ruin. The kitchen descended into an encrusted mess of meals begun and not finished, broths and sauces left to boil over, loaves burnt to a crisp in the oven, as if suddenly in the midst of a task her mother would succumb to a lethargic amnesia. For years she had lost herself in the dead march of domestic chores; now she could not forget herself sufficiently to press on with the daily grind. The autumn hours, which she would have spent carefully pickling, were passed in a dreamy idling, as if doing nothing required all her concentration. She seemed not to notice the passing of the seasons. Beets and cabbages rotted in the ground. Marrows went to seed. Only her geraniums flourished, as if repaying all her years of prodigal pampering. They bloomed hectically, as if trying to catch her attention. She watched with the baffled air of a child when Franziska scrubbed around her, or cleared a space on the table to roll out dough or chop vegetables. Without her husband, Mrs Schanzkowska's avid skills of home-making were redundant. She had been trained to be a wife, but she did not know how to be a widow.

Franziska's father had died in the summer of 1913. His illness was unlike anything else about him; it grew quietly, stealthily. It was not like his nature, volatile and explosive. It bided its time. At first it was no more than extreme fatigue and such an aversion to alcohol that when he so much as whiffed a drop on another man's breath it would make him gag. He began to shrink. His skin, which had always been ruddy, turned sallow and pitted as a walnut, as if he was developing a hard carapace to protect himself. His fingernails fell out. They simply crumbled away like chalk dust. He ate feebly. He sat, jaundiced, liver-eyed, exuding a kind of insular gloom. For the first time in his life his thoughts turned inward, finding there some mesmeric focus. Franziska feared that his old outbursts of rage were bottled up inside him and would emerge in one all-consuming tide which would destroy them all. She it was who cajoled him into eating. When he toyed with his food she would pull the plate sideways and chop his meat or dumplings into bite-sized pieces, pointing to each morsel as she would to a child.

'Now,' she would say, 'try this one.'

Her mother shaved him with the cut-throat. He had always been careless about his appearance, but her mother's finesse with the blade rendered him frighteningly clean. Franziska could not bear to watch. If the blade were to slip . . . Felix took him for walks around the yard, guiding him tamely round and round in ever-decreasing circles, this cleaned and polished father, silent and acquiescent. They had finally made him weak, Franziska thought.

Felix was the man of the house now, taking his father's place in the fields.

'And the meek', her mother said, watching her slow, patient son, 'shall inherit the earth.'

Franziska tried not to remember her father's last days. A great hulk of a man all hollowed out by disease. He smelled dreadfully. Even if he hadn't, neither she nor her mother had much appetite for nursing him. It was not a lack of fastidiousness that prevented them from changing his sheets as often as they should have. It was indifference. His years of bullying and neglect had numbed them; their haphazard care of him was a kind of low-lying revenge. Franziska's surfeit of feeling for him had seeped away into a steely pity. She looked back on her fiery devotion for him as if it were a fevered illness that had run its course. But she could not summon it up again.

It was Felix who would sit with him when the open sores on his ulcerated legs meant he could no longer walk. And when he breathed his last Felix was by his side, while Franziska and her mother sat in the kitchen shelling peas. It was a noisy procedure with which the tinny report of greens in an enamel pot could not compete. He died cursing and swearing and bellowing for Felix, as if the very fact of his despised son was the meaning of his passing.

Franziska crossed the square scored by the sweeping curves of tram tracks like the skate marks on a frozen pond. She tried to dispel the eerie aimlessness she felt by striding purposefully along, but the wintry thoughts of home stayed with her. On her arm she carried Mother's Poznan coat, a bulky black broadcloth with an astrakhan collar, the most glamorous item of clothing her mother owned. She would hardly miss it, Franziska thought; indeed it would probably take her days to register that her daughter was gone. Franziska had run away, stealing away in the dead of night, with money purloined over months from Felix's trips to the market. Mother's eggs had paid for the fare. In her suitcase she had one change of clothes, a matryoska doll, and the pendulum from Grandmother Dulska's clock. The gentle swing of it trapped behind its door of glass had caught her eye as she was leaving. She drew up a chair and standing on it she opened the door and unhooked the pendulum, thus stilling the clock for ever. There it would stand at the time she had made her escape.

She hurried along, eyes cast down so as not to attract attention. She reached the far side of the square and turned onto a side street steeped in shadow. A balmy dusk was gathering. A mobile coffee stall stood at the corner, an iron contraption on wheels topped by two gleaming vats of grounds. A bearded man with an apron was dispensing the coffee from a metal tap on the side into slim glasses. The smell of chicory was pungent. She stopped to inhale the dark fumes.

'Fräulein?'

A fair-haired young woman of her own age, plumply good-looking and smartly dressed, was tugging at her sleeve. She proffered her steaming glass.

'Would you like to try?'

Was it so obvious, she wondered, that she had never tasted coffee? But she took the glass gratefully. It was piping hot. The initial taste was more bitter than she had expected, but there was a sweet legacy in her mouth from the sugar that the young woman had obviously laced it with.

'Thank you,' she said, handing the glass back.

'From the east?' the young woman queried. She had a fresh, curious face. 'You have come to Berlin to work?'

Franziska nodded.

'Do you have a place to stay? Some lodgings perhaps, or with some compatriots?'

'No,' Franziska said slowly. 'I must . . .' she started.

'Then you are in luck! My mother takes in lodgers. In fact,' she confided, 'she sent me to the station to meet the evening train. Our last lodger left hurriedly, and without paying, and my mother said, Doris, that's me, run down to the station and make approaches. There's bound to be some lost soul looking for a bed. But I was late. The streets are hopping, the war has brought the city alive. And then', she added ruefully, 'the smell of coffee. I couldn't resist.'

Doris handed Franziska her glass and she took another sweet, gritty mouthful.

'We could pretend that we met on the platform.' She took in Franziska's appearance in a swift, appraising glance, her creased, sober skirt, her rough-hewn tunic, the well-worn shawl. 'You look like a good sort, respectable...'

'I have very little money,' Franziska countered, 'and I have no work.'

'We'll get you work. Louise, that's my sister, and I are on the production line at the AEG plant. This war will make work for everyone.'

Franziska hesitated. Could she trust this friendly young woman? She could have an accomplice waiting round the next corner, ready to pounce. Then she thought of the meagre coins left over from her mother's egg money.

'Say you will,' Doris pleaded. 'It will save me from my mother. She will think I have done very well for her.'

Frau Wingender was a stout, raddled woman with a beery face, who stood crossly outside Beusselstraße 27 awaiting Doris's return.

'You took your time,' she barked by way of greeting. 'Dawdling, no doubt. And who's this?'

'This is Fräulein Schanzkowska. I met her at the station just as you said.' Doris nudged her.

'Yes, ma'am, I would not have known where to turn if Doris hadn't appeared.'

'A Pole,' Frau Wingender said, 'and with no visible

means of support, I'll be bound.' She turned on her heels and disappeared into the dingy mouth of the apartment building, hands on her hips. Franziska remembered the words of Miss Tupalska – you are a little Prussian girl living in the German Reich. Doris hurried after her, down the rank passageway that led into the bowels of the building.

'Louise and I can get her a job at the factory. They're crying out for workers there. And she can share our room. That means you can take in another lodger in Herr Wunder's old room.'

Frau Wingender paused. Franziska watched her broad, implacable back.

'Well,' Doris's mother said slowly, 'that's a thought.' She was relenting. Money was Rosa Wingender's primary creed.

'Very well,' she said, turning around to take another look at Franziska standing on the street, her feet aching and her stomach growling with hunger. 'But you, my girl, better get work quick smart. The rent is still five marks a week, job or no job. I'm not running a charity home here.'

Doris smiled winningly.

'Come on, I'll show you to the royal quarters.'

It was a long, narrow room on the second floor. A blanket hung on a string dividing it in half. Frau Wingender slept on one side on a divan pushed up against double doors, which gave onto the lodger's room. The girls slept on the other side, two beds crushed a thigh's distance apart and wedged beneath a tall window, which looked out onto the building's back courtyard. A pecked-looking tree, stunted by the lack of light, scraped against the pane. Mottled masonry bearing the geography of damp peered in from outside. Lines of becalmed laundry were strung across the blind windows opposite. The dust-mottled glass added to the room's stifled air. Cobwebs shivered in the corners of the high ceiling. Doris closed the shutters and pushed the two dishevelled beds together.

'There,' she said, throwing a dark green coverlet on top of the unmade beds. 'Plenty of room for all of us!'

She pulled open the bottom drawer of a large chest, which stood in the corner of the room, and deposited a nest of stockings and smalls on the bed. 'This can be yours and we'll find space in Mama's wardrobe for your dresses.'

Franziska opened her spartan suitcase.

'There's not much,' she said apologetically.

She fished out her second skirt, a creased linen blouse and her home-made bloomers and laid them on the bed beside the Poznan coat. Her fingers did not stray into the sateen pocket sewn into the inside spine of the case, where she had hidden the painted doll and the pendulum. These were things which she did not want Doris – or anyone else – to see. Here they seemed like guilty clues. Hurriedly she shoved the case under the bed.

'Wait till you get your wages,' Doris said brightly as she folded Franziska's scratchy underwear. 'We can go shopping at Jandorf's!'

Strange house. Unfamiliar noises – shouts rising up from the street, loud arguments from the courtyard below, the slamming of doors, a woman sobbing, the night terrors of an infant. Lying head to toe between the Wingender girls while their mother snored loudly beyond the makeshift curtain was almost like being at home, a child again between her own sisters, Gertie and Maria. And Walter. She would not think of Walter. When she did there was only water and death. She willed these old memories to lose their power. A new life was about to begin. A life of her own.

'RISE AND SHINE!'

Franziska opened her eyes to find Doris bending over her. She was already dressed and busily tucking a white madras blouse into the band of a whipcord skirt of powder blue. She straightened and turned back to the speckled mirror that stood on the chest of drawers.

Clamping a hairpin between her lips, she swept up the stray tendrils of her honey-coloured hair.

'I don't know why I bother,' she said as she slid a comb into the tidy bun at the nape of her neck.

Louise was sitting on the edge of the bed, braiding her hair into two plaits. The younger of the two, she had been given a more sober measure of her sister's noisy good looks. Her face was thin and long, where Doris's was fleshily round, her hair nut brown without the glossy kink of her sister's, her eyes frowningly dark. She knotted a bandanna round her forehead, and threw on a dark worsted tweed coat.

'But you have to make an effort. Where else would I get to wear these stockings? And I *do* love this skirt,' Doris said, smoothing her hand over the pale blue fabric. She perched her hat on top of her piled hair and twirled around in the blue-grey morning light. 'What do you think?'

'We're only going to the factory, Dor,' Louise said, 'not to a ball.'

'Hurry, hurry,' Doris said to Franziska, who was sitting up in bed with the coverlet drawn up around her shoulders.

She felt awkward and shy. She might have shared a bed with these girls, but dressing under Doris's scrutiny would be an ordeal. Nothing would have measured up. Her plain black skirt, her rough linen shirt, her threadbare shawl. Yesterday she had been glad of Doris's brassiness and her flirtatious friendliness. Now it seemed like a female challenge.

'We'll wait for you in the kitchen. Let you get dressed in peace,' Louise said, nudging Doris out.

Franziska splashed her face with water from a jug and basin on a stand by the bed and dressed hurriedly. She swept past the musty blanket which divided the room, passing the mound in the bed that was Frau Wingender. She was not an early riser. She liked to stay up into the small hours. The tell-tale beer bottles still on the table in the tiny scullery down the hall bore testimony to her predilection for solitary late nights. The girls were standing round the littered table, drinking tea. A sunken green light pervaded the room. A stove listed on the scarred floor-boards, a white ceramic sink hosted a pile of teetering saucepans, the doors of the wall cupboards all stood ajar as if a fruitless search had recently been conducted. Their shelves were crowded to overflowing – ill-matching cups and plates, the handle-less casualty of a jug shared quarters with flour bags, a jar of dripping, the tallow-spattered stump of candle, a pile of coupons, a blackened tea caddy, a dish of melting butter. It made Franziska think of home, but here it was not the hand of wilful neglect that was evident but a cherished, careless overuse. Looking at Doris standing there, neat as a bandbox, it was hard to believe that she had sprung from such wanton clutter.

'All set?' she asked cheerily.

She handed Franziska a lidded coffee pot of battered brown enamel.

'This will keep you going. We always make our own, cheaper and better than that muck they serve in the canteen.'

The three girls clattered down the stone steps of the hallway and into the dawn-blanched street. It had rained overnight and the cobbles were greasy underfoot. The streets were thick with people. They joined the silent throng, the wordless tramp of hundreds of workers, men and women, pale and glue-eyed with sleep, heads down, shrouded in the smoky, early-morning mist. The only sounds were the plangent leak of birdsong, the chafing of serge and gabardine and the steady clunk of boots on stone. They funnelled through the narrow streets, gathering more people as they marched. There was an odd comfort to be among so many strangers all bound for the same destination. They arrived at the factory yard at six-twenty. A great crowd had already gathered at the gates. A hooter from somewhere within brayed in short, sharp bursts like an animal bellowing to be fed. Doris pushed her way to the front of the crowd and spoke to a man in a cloth cap and mustard coat, who stood, clipboard in hand, at the entrance. They talked for several minutes while Doris gestured urgently towards Franziska.

'Don't worry,' Louise said, 'if anyone can get you in, Doris can.'

Doris skirted the patient crowd and rejoined them.

'When the gates open,' she said to Franziska, 'wait for your name to be called. You'll have to be examined.'

'Examined?'

'Oh, it's nothing, really. They just want to be sure you're fit.' She clapped Franziska playfully on the back. 'You've nothing to worry about. You're as healthy as a trout.'

At six-thirty sharp the gates opened and the crowd surged forward, leaving Franziska standing alone. It was only when the narrow entrance had devoured the throng that she noticed two policemen standing guard outside twin sentry boxes at either side of the gates. She felt a sharp stab of alarm. Their executioner's glare reached her across the

vast expanse of glistening cobble. She stood petrified, afraid
to move in case any movement would betray her. What had
Doris told them? Did they know her secret? Standing there
in the breaking dawn – the hanging hour – she felt as if she
had woken from a crowded, hectic dream to this her final,
bleak and solitary punishment. She inhaled, waiting for a
shot to ring out. Instead she was startled by a ripple of
laughter from behind her. When she turned around she
realised she was not alone. A couple of yards away a group
of headscarved women stood huddled together, arms
folded, faces smug with gossip. Several men also stood
leaning against a wall, heads bowed, chins sunk in gnarled
hands, caps pushed back resignedly. But unlike the merry
women, they stood apart from their neighbours, as if the
roll-call for work was something shameful.

'Müller, H.!' the man with the clipboard called and one
of them, a young man with a head of black hair and a
sailor's gait, marched towards the gate.

'Why aren't you serving your country?' one of the
women barked as he passed.

'Hush up, old woman!' he hissed. 'You don't know what
you're talking about.'

'Bergmann, S.!'

A pale weak sun was visible now behind the factory's
bulk. It gave a glassy look to the morning, as if everything
solid were thin as eggshell.

'Schanzkowska, F.!'

At first Franziska, lost in the humid glare, didn't
recognise her own name. Then she walked forward
gingerly, eyes down to avoid the gaze of the policemen
who paced back and forth on the apron of cracked
pavement outside the factory gates. They were both heavy-
set men. Wheezy with age, their double-breasted buttons
looked set to pop as they trod heavily, like patient
farmyard horses. She could outrun them, Franziska
thought as she passed. But there was no need. They were

not interested in her. The man with the clipboard looked her up and down.

'Report to the Shifting House. Herr Lindner.'

She stepped inside and found herself in a pitted yard. Blackened red-brick buildings bore in on her on all sides. A large shed on her left rose three storeys high, with elongated windows that stretched from floor to eaves; ahead a glass and metal walkway straddled between two further sheds. On her right a low block of offices led her eye through a square archway into a second yard beyond. She hesitated.

Behind her she heard the mournful clangour of the gates as the man with the clipboard pulled them to. She turned around and caught a glimpse through the bars of the few stragglers left outside. A woman with a child on her hip, an elderly man with a stooped back, a boy with a club foot.

'Not changing your mind, I take it,' the man with the clipboard hollered as he padlocked the gates.

Franziska shook her head.

'Then no more dawdling. Herr Lindner does not like to be kept waiting.'

She hurried across the littered yard. Underfoot were the rusty remains of shell bodies, and shavings of bright blue and copper shimmered in the small pools left by the overnight rain. She stepped over the rail tracks which criss-crossed the outer yard, winding their way from a dark entrance close to the gates round a corner into the inner yard, where the Danger Building was. This second yard was overshadowed by a tall chimney stack, but it was open-ended and over a far low wall she could see the metallic toss of the Spree. She paused at the entrance marked Shifting House and pulled open the heavy door. A muffled boom reached her from somewhere deep inside the building. She found herself in a large cloakroom, where dozens of barefoot girls were stripped to their underwear.

They were hanging their street clothes on pegs and stowing away their boots in metal cages on the floor. Not only their clothes but every piece of jewellery, every comb and hairpin had to be surrendered.

'All your metal bits and pieces, girls,' the Lady Superintendent called out, dropping hair clips and brooches into a large muslin bag. 'And that means stays, as well.'

'Oh, Auntie!' wailed a pretty, pert girl down to her corset and bloomers.

All the girls called the superintendent Auntie.

'You know the rules, 474,' the superintendent barked.

Auntie knew the girls by their numbers.

Once undressed, the girls donned gowns and aprons and soft cotton caps. They filed through a gap in a wooden partition at the end of the cloakroom. Franziska made to follow since it was from there that the dull rumble and boom she had heard earlier was coming. A bony hand on her shoulder yanked her back.

'Girl, girl, you can't go in there,' Auntie shrieked, 'you're not clean!'

'I *am* clean,' an offended Franziska bellowed back over the din.

'No, no, you don't understand, you can't go through there.'

She thumped the partition with the palm of her hand.

'No boots or street clothes beyond this point.'

Franziska looked down at her spattered skirt.

'I'm here to see Herr Lindner,' she explained.

'Ah, a beginner,' said the superintendent, 'don't they tell you anything? Out the door and up the stairway outside, if you please.'

Herr Lindner was a fastidious man, balding, with a sharp nose. He sniffed all the time as if he were catching a bad smell. Was it her? Franziska wondered. He peered through round spectacles as she knocked and entered his office. The far wall of the room was a trellis of glass and he was standing looking down at the factory floor far below.

'Schanzkowska, sir,' Franziska said, as he turned to see who it was.

He moved slowly to his desk and sat down with pointed deliberation.

'Schanzkowska,' he repeated doubtfully, shuffling papers in front of him.

'Doris Wingender in the Tailor's Shop recommended me and the man on the gate told me to . . .'

'Just so,' Herr Lindner interjected, silencing her.

He rose and with his hands behind his back came out from behind his desk and surveyed her. Up and down. Then he walked around her as she stood fidgeting and staring straight ahead. He paused at her back for several minutes and clicked his tongue.

'Not very tall, are you?'

He circled around her again, jutting his face close to hers.

'Look up,' he commanded. He stared intently at the whites of her eyes. Then he took her chin in his hand. Startled, she thought for a moment that he was going to kiss her.

'Teeth,' he said, letting his hand drop.

Her hand immediately replaced his, covering her lips.

Her father's words came back to her. Never let an ill-wisher see your teeth.

'Fräulein Schanzkowska, please open your mouth.'

She stood up, lips firmly pursed, her fingers knotted in a bunch.

'God grant me patience! In case you haven't noticed, Fräulein Schanzkowska, there is a war on. I have no time to dally. Please show me your teeth or I shall have to show you the door.'

She dropped her hand and opened her mouth slowly. He pushed up her upper lip and peered at her teeth. She closed her eyes tight, her cheeks smarting with humiliation.

'Hands,' he barked.

She held her hands out, palms down. He took them between his fingers and revolved them.

'Well, you're not afraid of hard work to judge from these.'

He dropped them.

'This is very fine work, Fräulein, it requires delicacy.' He enunciated his words carefully.

She burrowed her rough hands deeper into the folds of her skirts.

'Age?'

'Seventeen, sir. And three-quarters.'

'Married?'

'No, sir.'

'Are you willing to work in mercury?'

'Yes,' she said, remembering Doris's instruction to agree to anything she was asked.

'What about yellow powder?'

'What's that?'

'Trotyl, my dear.'

He sighed deeply and then with a military flourish he clicked his heels and walked measuredly back to his desk.

'Well, you're healthy and strong by the looks of you. We'll put you on trolley work to start with. That won't require much finesse.'

'Don't know why Lindner keeps on sending me women,' Franz Gering complained when Franziska appeared in the loading bay. He handed her a tunic and gaiters and a paint-spattered mackintosh coat.

'Not many men left around here,' a female voice called from the darkness of the loading shed. 'Real men, that is.'

This was followed by a large guffaw as several carriers emerged out of the shed to view the new recruit. They were a motley crew, some lanky teenage boys, a pair of beefy men, a couple of strong girls like herself.

'Well,' Gering conceded, 'at least you've got some meat

on you. Your job is to keep these bogeys moving. It may not look like much but you've got to keep the factory fed. You'll be on Team Four.'

The trolleys were deep flatbed trucks with high perambulator handles which ran on runners through the yards. They worked four to a trolley, hauling shells from the Finishing Shop to the Loading Yard, and carrying shell cases and cartridges from the Machine Room to the Danger Building. Day and night the machines ran, clanking and grinding, all polished limbs and burnished plates, a merciless cavalry of iron horses, rearing and neighing in the dry, fumy heat. They were tended to as if they were tethered animals not yet broken in. Franziska often overheard the machinists coaxing them tenderly into action, but once up and working they were driven relentlessly. Levers were yanked roughly, wheels cranked, the wide leather belts of the machines set spinning dryly, while the lathes whinnied and screeched. The din was tremendous. There was barely time to rest while the trolley was unloaded and filled up again with finished shells. Then it was back out into the yards again pushing with all their might, even though the tracks underfoot were regularly oiled. It was hot, sweaty work. Franziska was used to labour, but here she felt weak and puny, dwarfed by her surroundings and her own insignificance in this feverish cycle of masculine work with no visible harvest. One of hundreds – her assigned number was 670 – she was just one more body enslaved not to an end but to an effort, the war effort.

Franziska would never fully comprehend the geography of war, the great battle sites, the muddied victories of the Western Front, even later when she had good reason to. This was where she sited her war, in the tedious journeys through the yards and sheds of the munitions factory. She thought of the Tailor's Shop as the Home Front. Here caps and gowns were run up on treadle sewing machines. It was the only place in the factory where the loudest noise was human, full of girlish chatter and the comradely gaiety of a sewing bee. Elsewhere talking was either futile or forbidden. In the Machine Rooms it was too noisy to be heard – Franziska thought of the roar of battle – and in the Danger Building, it was a finable offence to speak. Here, Franziska imagined, was the mute imminence of the trenches. The workers sat in regimented rows, hooded and hidden, swathed in veils and fireproof overalls buttoned to the throat, weighing out trotyl on small hand scales or filling tiny bags from trays of powder. Their silent concentration on this minute work seemed to tick louder than any clanking machine. And their yellowing, discoloured skin marked them out already as weary survivors of some small, private calamity.

THAT FIRST DAY seemed endless. Outside the air was humid, the sky low and overcast, the sun glowered and glared but failed to smile. Inside, the dull light filtering through the mottled windows of the filling shops hung in dusty shafts along the alleyways between the machines. Franziska's brow seeped, rivulets of sweat poured down her cheeks unchecked. As the four carriers heaved and pushed their trolley – when it was full of finished shells it was so heavy their chins were at handle level trying to shift it – she felt like a horse tethered to a plough. When they lifted the shells off at the end of each run, two of them staggering beneath the molten, menacing weight, they cradled fifteen kilos between them. She was unbearably thirsty, but they were allowed only two comfort breaks per shift – one for the canteen, one for the lavatory. Any more and their pay would be docked. They were under the constant scrutiny of Herr Lindner, standing in his glassy cage high above the works floor. They must have looked like ants to him, milling around the clanking machines and trestle tables, Franziska thought. And at any moment he could move his foot and simply squash one of them for no better reason than they did not please him.

High on the gable of the works floor, under the arced legend which read 'Cleanliness, Gentleness and Punctuality', a placid clockface marked time. Franziska learned to concentrate on it. That way she could time each trip. Sometimes the minutes ticked by astonishingly slowly; at others, when Franziska dared to look up through the falling wisps of her hair, several hours had gone by. The lights in Herr Lindner's office went on at six p.m., like a magnified version of its occupant's glasses, adding to the air of vigilance as if his attention became more, not less, concentrated as the day wore on. In time, Franziska would not need to look at the clock or note the turning on of the lights to recognise the hour. She knew it by the twinges in her body – the dull ache in her lower back, the sharp tightening around her shoulder blades, the livid blooms of bruises on her calves and upper arms. But when the knocking-off hooter brayed at seven-fifteen p.m. that first day she fell to the floor of the machine shop and lay there exhausted amongst the metal shavings and sawdust. Way up above her through the skylighted roof she could see the sooted felt of a darkening sky and the sly grin of a half-moon. She felt protected lying there, the machines stuttering to a halt, the unaccustomed silence sprouting in her ears. She closed her eyes and was a child again, lying in freshly cut hay with a sea of blue overhead.

'*Sissy. Sissy,*' *a voice calls.*
Her mother calling her in.
'Franziska, are you all right?'
She opened her eyes to Doris.
'Yes, I'm just so tired.'
'You must be careful, Franziska.' Doris cast an anxious eye up at Lindner's perch at she helped Franziska to her feet. 'Lindner watches everything. If he thinks you're not up to it, it's the chop! War or no war.'

Released by the hooter's glare, the departing day shift was not the grim throng of the morning. The men, glistening from their toils, halted at streetside stalls for tankards of cider or walked three and four abreast their arms flung around one another, calling out bawdily to women standing in doorways, clusters of children at their feet.

The female workers chattered noisily at factory pitch, the echoes of the machines still bellowing in their ears. Doris and Louise, at either side of Franziska, gossiped across her, Doris, mostly, and though Franziska said nothing she felt included in their lazy, familiar conversation.

Frau Wingender was cooking when they got back to the apartment. A glorious smell of roasting wafted through the stairwells as they climbed to the second floor.

'I do hope that's coming from our kitchen,' Louise said.

Franziska heard the wistful tone. Frau Wingender's domestic chores were entirely dependent on the hour at which she started tippling. Two beers before dinner ensured a hearty welcome. Any more and they were likely to be greeted by the chaotic ruins of a burnt dinner, or the cold comfort of leftovers.

'Girls! Girls!' Frau Wingender beamed at the door.

Franziska found it hard to imagine that the slovenly heap they had left lying in the bed in the morning could be the smiling jovial *hausfrau* now before them, who bustled around the steam-filled kitchen, humming and stirring.

'Dear me,' she said, taking one look at Franziska. 'Look at this child. Dead on her feet.'

She sat Franziska down at the kitchen table and from one of her secret stashes produced a bottle of schnapps. She poured out a tumbler full.

'Here,' she said, thrusting the glass under Franziska's nose.

Franziska got a waft of father, that sweet, raw smell of spirits. As if he were standing beside her. She took the glass and swallowed the fiery brew in one go, as if to inhale her own memories, to have her father safely within again.

'Lindner put her on the trolleys,' Doris explained.

'It's not right,' Louise interjected hotly. 'It's too heavy work for a girl.'

'But I'm strong,' Franziska said, the alcohol coursing through her weary limbs giving her a peppery energy.

'Mmm,' said Frau Wingender, 'but for how long?'

She gazed at Franziska for several moments with a kind of bemused tenderness. Frau Wingender had two faces, Franziska was to learn, the cranky landlady of the night before and this ramshackle woman with her rapt spasms of motherly affection.

'Doris,' she commanded, 'fetch the tub. This child needs a soak or she'll seize up.'

The tin bath was fetched from its home – hanging outside by a hook below the kitchen sill – and Louise and Doris boiled two cauldrons of water. As Franziska undressed – less shyly than she had the night before – the Wingender sisters lathered some soap in the bath. When she stepped into the tub, she sank into a sea of foam. She had never been so grateful to be immersed, Frau Wingender's mutton stew bubbling on the stove and the tingling fire of schnapps within.

'I've had some good news, girls,' Frau Wingender said, as Louise rubbed Franziska down with a towel. 'We've got a new lodger for Herr Wunder's room. I met Frau Goldberg, you know, from Elberfeldstraβe, at the market, and she's sending me on one of hers, a nice Jewish boy, it seems. He's been with her for several months, she knows his mother. But she got the chance to take in a pair of army clerks and couldn't pass up the opportunity. Isn't that a stroke of luck?'

'A Jew?' Franziska said.

She thought of the peddler who pushed his cart through Borowy Las once a year, or the strange, secretive figures in long coats who populated the marketplace in Bytów. Never trust a Jew, her father used to warn them as children. But she had never met one not to trust.

'As far as I'm concerned, the only difference between them and us is that they don't go to church on Sundays,' Frau Wingender said. 'I only hope he won't be fussy about his food.'

The new lodger arrived the following week while the girls were out at work. As they ate their evening meal, they could hear his heavy footfall moving about in his room.

'So nice to have a man about the house again,' mused Frau Wingender, 'a respectable man.'

As opposed to Herr Wunder, who, it seemed, had led Frau Wingender up the garden path in more ways than one.

'He was a complete rogue,' Louise had told Franziska, 'anyone could see that. Anyone but Mama, that is.'

'She gets lonely,' Doris said apologetically, 'without Pappy.'

'Good riddance to him,' Louise muttered under her breath.

'He ran out on us when we were children,' Doris explained. 'Left Mama high and dry with nothing, no money, nothing. He has another wife and a couple of brats in Prenzlauer Berg.'

'It's why she has a weakness for a tipple,' Louise offered. 'And Max Wunder did nothing to discourage her.'

'We were just as pleased when he went, to tell you the truth,' Doris said. 'Imagine having Herr Wunder as a stepfather.'

'He was such a buffoon!' Louise confided, while Doris marched around the kitchen imitating him, sticking out her belly and blowing out her cheeks. 'And just imagine we would have been the Wunderkinder!'

The sisters exploded into laughter.

'And what's the big joke?' demanded Frau Wingender, puncturing their girlish jubilance.

The girls tried to smother their mirth.

'Nothing, Mama, just factory talk, that's all.'

'I hope you'll forgive these silly girls, Herr Fröhlich. I'll make sure they won't trouble you. Doris, Louise, I'd like to introduce Herr Fröhlich.'

From behind Frau Wingender's ample figure a neat young man emerged. He had close-cut, straw-coloured hair, a strand of which fell over his forehead, a long pale face, a small fleshy mouth. His eyes were a washed-out blue. Doris and Louise exchanged a sisterly glance. Franziska, who had not been included in the introduction, watched as Herr Fröhlich stepped into the kitchen, his hands behind his back.

'Herr Fröhlich has a job in the Tietz department store,' Frau Wingender announced grandly. 'In haberdashery.'

'And who is this lady?' Herr Fröhlich asked.

'That's Fräulein Schanzkowska, she lodges with us too,' said Frau Wingender. 'She shares with my girls.'

'Schanzkowska,' he said, 'one of our Polish cousins.'

He extended his hands. Franziska felt it would be too intimate to touch it. And she was ashamed to offer her rough-hewn fingers to this well-groomed stranger. She did a little curtsy instead. Doris and Louise exploded in a fresh peal of laughter.

'He's not the kaiser, Franziska,' Doris said.

'There's no harm in showing respect,' Frau Wingender said, 'you could do with a little bit more of it yourself, young lady.'

Franziska blushed and covered her mouth with her hand.

'My name is Hans,' Herr Fröhlich said. 'Hans Walter Fröhlich.'

Water clouded Franziska's vision. Was she crying or drowning? She could not remember what happened next; one minute she was standing avoiding Herr Fröhlich's gaze, the next she was stretched out on the floor cradled in Doris's arms while Frau Wingender fed her a thimbleful of schnapps.

'What happened?' she asked weakly.

'You fainted, my dear,' Frau Wingender said, patting her hand. 'They're working you too hard at that plant. You're not as strong as you think.'

'I think it was Herr Fröhlich,' Doris said wickedly. 'I wonder, does he have that effect on all the girls!'

For the first few weeks Berlin remained a series of interconnecting rooms for Franziska – the Wingenders' cramped quarters, the cacophonous apartment building, the winding route to work, the ordered uproar of the factory. She had to keep on remembering that she was in a big city. Apart from that first evening at the station she had not seen the sweeping boulevards, the great monuments, the glittering department stores that Doris so often talked about. It struck her as she rose each morning how similar her life here was to the one she had lived at home – the ceaseless labour, the huddled and impoverished intimacy of the Wingenders. Even the eggs – especially the eggs – were a disappointment. When Frau Wingender cracked open a shell at the table to make *stollen* bread, the yolk was pallid, the white more glaucous. The air around her seemed thinner, extenuated by too many people drawing on it. In those first weeks Franziska fell prey to a crushing homesickness; it was not just a yearning for fresh eggs or the ferny green freshness of the countryside. She had expected Berlin to enlarge *her*. Instead she felt diminished, as if her world would always be small and mean and limited, no matter where she went. It seemed her destiny to be confined.

Sometimes, though, there were glimpses. Sedan Day was one, celebrated on a balmy September afternoon. Although it had nothing to do with this war – Hans Fröhlich told the girls it was a celebration of the victory over the French more than forty years before – it felt like an endorsement of the kaiser's pledge that victory would be achieved before the leaves fell. Doris, Louise and Franziska took a tram into the city and walked the festive streets. In the large department stores, in place of mannequins, shop staff and customers filled the display windows to get a grandstand view of the parade as it passed. News-vendors hollered at street corners and every couple of yards there were advertising pillars loud with posters for circuses, music halls and athletic clubs. Cyclists frantically ringing their bells wove in between the crowds, dodging small children and street hawkers selling matches and single roses. The girls eventually found a spot at the edge of the pavement near the railway bridge at Friedrichstraße from which to view the proceedings. So great was the crush that Franziska could only see the high blue sky and the brave sunshine reflected in the vast glassy arch of the station and she linked arms with Doris and Louise, nervously terrified that she might get lost in the mêlée. She had never seen so many people together, a heaving excited crowd, men waving flags, women in high-built bonnets fluttered scented hankies, not to speak of the parade itself, a seemingly endless stream of soldiers in field grey. Their spiked helmets glinted as menacingly as their rifles, as if, Franziska thought, even their headgear was a weapon. The sun glanced on their polished, calf-length boots. Captured artillery pieces – from France, people said – were drawn by trucks, each one greeted with a deafening roar that almost drowned out the reedy pulse of brass and the shrill tremolo of penny whistles. The sheer spectacle of it, the noise and the crowds, the triumphant air, exhilarated Franziska; here, nameless in this raucous throng, she felt again the elusive whiff of anonymity. She was one more face in the crowd in a vast city in a huge empire. Here, at last, was the large world, she thought, the world she had imagined behind the thin horizon of home.

Afterwards they strolled in the city. The leafy beer gardens and coffee houses on the Kurfürstendamm were packed with parade revellers. The floury, just-baked smell of pastries, the spicy tang of cinnamon and hot chocolate wafted from open windows and pavement tables as they passed. But they couldn't have afforded to go into any of these places. When they scanned a menu posted in one of the restaurant windows, they discovered that dinner would knock them back seventy-six marks.

'That's more than we earn in a month,' Louise said ruefully.

Beside the menu, a notice from the war office urged – 'Do not eat two dishes if one is enough.' But even one would have been too much for the Wingender girls. An hour of aimless wandering and they were back on the tram to Moabit, to the crowded blocks and smoking chimney stacks that was their city.

It was a grey quarter, a grid of wide streets dotted with weekend landmarks. The public baths on Jonastraße, where she and the Wingender girls went to bathe every Saturday morning. Armed with bars of soap and towels they lolled in the steaming baths, shouting over the wooden partitions of the green tiled cubicles until the hot water ran out and their fingerpads went white and rugged from the cold. There was the church on Oldenburgstraße where Franziska went alone on Sundays (the Wingenders were not religious and Franziska only attended because she liked the familiar cadences of communal prayer and the dry touch of the wafer on her tongue). She no longer had access to the God of her childhood. Even if she had, He would surely be displeased with her. Instead she contemplated the pearly vastness of the church's interior and felt emboldened by the distance she had travelled from His wrath. On Turmstraße there were numerous beer cellars, many of them below ground, where she and Doris and Louise would venture on a Saturday night. They were infernos of noise, thanks to their low roofs and the crush of uniformed men, garrulous with war and ale, chanting and singing. Often it was too loud to talk or to be heard, though Doris invariably woke on a Sunday morning with a hoarse throat from trying. But Franziska was happy to sit in the smoky, raucous babble of a city desperately at play.

HANS FRÖHLICH TOOK his evening meal with Frau Wingender and the girls. Frau Wingender presided over these meals with a motherly familiarity, particularly aimed at Herr Fröhlich. He got the best cuts of meat and always a second helping of vegetables. He showed no sign of the finicky appetite she had feared.

'I always longed for a son,' she told him, 'but it was not to be. Now I have a gift of one, late in life!'

'Not so late, Frau Wingender!' Herr Fröhlich replied as she refilled his glass with beer.

'Oh, you flatter, Herr Fröhlich,' she replied, poking him merrily on the arm.

Doris and Louise raised their eyes to heaven in unison.

Franziska watched him covertly. His slender fingers, the untouched look of his skin. He had a boy's face, pale and smooth, the only sharpness in his features was the severe line of his nose. She had to be circumspect with him; after her fainting fit both the Wingender sisters had ragged her unmercifully. Who fancies Hans, who fancies Hans, they would sing.

'I do not fancy Herr Fröhlich,' she replied angrily.

'Herr Fröhlich,' Doris cooed, 'my, how formal we are.'

Any time he directed a question at her – even to ask her to pass the butter or the beans – they would nudge one another knowingly.

Under Frau Wingender's pointed questioning, Herr Fröhlich described his days at the department store. He spent his time among trays of bobbins and threads, lengths of ribbon, cards of binding and edging.

'So if you ladies would like anything in the line of trimmings, I may be of service.'

Frau Wingender beamed munificently.

He was lucky to be working for Tietz's, he went on. His father – who was in tailoring – had managed to swing an apprenticeship for him at the company's store in his native Düsseldorf. Then an opportunity for advancement had come up in Berlin; he might be in haberdashery now, but his plan was to become a buyer, and maybe eventually a manager.

'My dream', he said, 'is to go to America, the New World. Oh, the opportunities there! I'm taking English classes so that I'll be prepared.'

'English?' Doris all but shrieked. 'What with the war and all?'

'Commerce knows no boundaries, Fräulein Doris.'

'I like to see ambition in a young man,' Frau Wingender said approvingly.

'Tell us about where you come from, Fräulein,' Herr Fröhlich said to Franziska one evening as they sat over dinner. 'I've never been to the east, though if this war continues I dare say I will get the chance.'

'Where I come from?' Franziska repeated.

'Yes,' he prompted.

It was the first time since she had come to Berlin that anyone had asked her such a question. Frau Wingender, Doris and Louise had welcomed her into their world, but they had shown no interest in where she had come from. She sometimes thought that they considered Berlin the world and that she had simply emerged from some far-flung north-eastern suburb they had never heard of. But she was glad of their blithe acceptance, their total lack of curiosity.

'You won't have heard of it, it's just a one-horse town. Not grand like Berlin...'

'Grandness, Fräulein, is not everything.'

'Just so,' Frau Wingender said, eyeing Franziska reproachfully.

'And Berlin can be a lonely place, I have found, when you're far from home and not among your own.'

'Oh, come now, Herr Fröhlich, you must give our beautiful city a chance. I'm sure my girls could...'

'Mama!' Doris said crossly. 'Stop matchmaking.'

'No, I'm not,' she wheedled, 'but I have to say Herr Fröhlich would be far more suitable than the company you're presently keeping. She's seeing a very uncouth young man, Herr Fröhlich, not steady and respectable like your good self.'

'Mama, please,' Doris said and standing up she flounced away from the table.

Frau Wingender hurried after her with Louise in her wake.

'Doris, Doris,' Frau Wingender's wail echoed down the deep stone stairwell outside, accompanied by the angry clatter of her daughter's footsteps as she fled the building. Herr Fröhlich and Franziska were left facing each other across the strewn table.

'Oh dear,' he said, 'I seem to have set the cat among the pigeons.'

He smiled apologetically and leaned forward, joining his hands together on Frau Wingender's stained tablecloth.

'I was wondering, Fräulein Schanzkowska,' he started, 'if I might be so bold as to ask you something?'

Franziska dreaded what the next question would be.

'Perhaps you would agree to step out with me one evening?'

'Herr Fröhlich, Herr Fröhlich!' Frau Wingender propelled herself into the room as if a large gust of wind was at her back, hands aflutter and blushing furiously.

Herr Fröhlich retreated in his seat.

'You must excuse Doris, she flies off the handle so easily. Takes after her father in that respect, I'm afraid.'

She rummaged in a kitchen cupboard and produced a bottle of schnapps. She downed a large measure by the stove with her back to Herr Fröhlich.

'Whereas I, as you know, am placid by nature.'

She felt unworthy of him, Herr Hans Fröhlich. And she was ashamed of her own shame. Hadn't her great-grand-mother been a countess? She came from better stock than Herr Hans Fröhlich, a Jew, a tailor's son from Düsseldorf. Apart from his gymnasium education and his department store deference, the only difference between them was that he was on his way up from tailoring and she was a step down from it. Living in lodgings, pushing bogies in a munitions plant. And how long would that last? The war would be over by Christmas. Hadn't the kaiser himself said so? The soldiers would flood back from the Front. And who would need shells in peacetime? She pitched herself forward in time. She could be the wife of a store manager one day. She might end up in America, a bigger world than she had ever imagined. Whatever else might be said of Herr Fröhlich, he was going places. Desire did not come into it. Desire, she knew, could be murderous. Ambition, though, could harm no one.

She kept Herr Fröhlich's declaration of interest a secret from Doris and Louise. She was afraid that Doris would see through to her greed to better herself. And anyway she would only pester Franziska for every detail of the encounter. Perhaps it was the language, but Franziska had never managed to acquire the gossipy tone she had heard other girls use together in the factory when talking about young men. She could not even feign it. And there was no need to say anything just yet, anyway. She had not given

Herr Fröhlich an answer. Before she could she must find something new to wear. Nothing in her meagre wardrobe was good enough to step out in with Herr Fröhlich.

She persuaded Doris to come shopping with her, not that Doris needed much persuasion. When they stepped off the tram, the two young women stepped into a burnished day of autumn. The sky was a drama of matted cloud moving swiftly across a fitful sun. They stood at the corner of a little park, appliquéd with gravel paths and bound by a row of plane trees. Berlin was unexpectedly full of such green spots, a soothing antidote to the stern reproach of stone façades and flinty brick. The light frowned and smiled on them, one minute gilded and bright, the next stormy and cross. There was a stall nearby where a man was roasting chestnuts in a large flat pan. The charred fumes infused the air and for a moment Franziska was transported. This was the smoky, violent smell of home.

'Franziska?' Doris was tugging at her sleeve.

She started and swayed slightly, as if she had fallen into a pocket of trapped time.

'I know,' Doris said brightly, 'let's go to Tietz's and see your fancy man in action.'

'Doris, I've told you a million times . . .'

'I know, you don't fancy Herr Fröhlich. Well, then, what's to stop us paying him a professional visit? We're customers, after all, with money in our pockets, as good as any of his other ladies!'

The Hermann Tietz department store drew crowds across the Alexanderplatz like a honeypot. Under the awnings curious bystanders gathered to gaze at its window displays, while streams of customers milled in its arcaded entrance. A revolving door, all heavy mahogany and milky glass, ushered Franziska and Doris in with the flourish of a florid dancing partner. Within there was an impression of polish and crimson. The lobby gave onto aisles of deep red carpet. A wide staircase beckoned.

Franziska's eyes travelled up to the first-floor balcony, strung like a latticed necklace between the marbled necks of fluted columns. Her eyes soared in the cathedral height, up further still, two floors, then three and more, which receded up into a vaulted glassy distance. All around there was a sense of urgent bustle. White-gloved bellboys ornate in red and gold, guardians of the lifts, drew back their accordion grids to reveal what looked to Franziska like gilded birdcages. She and Doris paused for a moment as the crowds streamed round them, and the island they formed on the polished floor. Franziska could hear the shushing swish of skirts, the click of canes and soles on wood, vague snatches of small talk – *a silk cravat, no, no, my dear, that would not do at all, ten marks, well I never!, this way, I said, this way* – the railway station calls of the lift attendants, and somewhere in the midst of that the tinny music of an organ grinder floating in off the street. And yet, despite the crowd, a sort of hush pervaded, the quiet ooze of commerce, the mercantile discretion of the rich.

'Second floor,' a bellboy called in a voice barely broken, 'haberdashery.'

'That's us,' Doris cried.

The Ladies' Department was also on the second floor and Doris could not pass it by without a visit. She sidled up to mannequin displays, calling loudly to Franziska, 'Oh, look at this!'

She lingered by glass cases of gloves; she fondled a ballgown of French silk.

'You would need to save for months to buy any of these,' Franziska complained to Doris.

'I know, I know, but these will give you ideas. We'll buy the fabric at Jandorf's and go to a dressmaker. That's what Louise and I do, and can you tell the difference?' She twirled around the shopfloor, her pink cotton dress with the daisy sprig floating about her.

'Fräulein Hackerl upstairs takes a down payment. That way you can dress like a princess on half nothing.'

Haberdashery was a world in miniature. Everything was under glass, as if even the smallest pin was a treasure worth protecting.

'They're afraid girls like us will come in and rob the place,' Doris remarked under her breath as they trailed around the display cases, which housed pins and stays, spools of thread, spare bobbins in serried trays. Even the lengths of ribbon and the cards of lace were trapped beneath a pane of glass on the main counter, behind which an elderly and very idle shop assistant stood contemplating her fingernails.

'Ladies,' she said tightly as they approached. She was a blowsy woman with stiff, coiffed hair and a tight shelf for a bosom. 'May I be of assistance?'

'We're looking for Herr Fröhlich,' Doris said.

'Oh,' she said, looking Doris and Franziska up and down. 'I see. Well, I'm afraid Herr Fröhlich always takes his lunch at this hour. He leaves me in charge. Perhaps I can be of service? Unless', she added, 'your visit is of a social nature?'

'Please inform him that Fräulein Wingender and Fräulein Schanzkowska called,' Doris said sniffily.

'Snob,' she muttered under her breath as they turned to leave.

Franziska was relieved he was not there. She was happy just to wander around and see Herr Fröhlich's world, the trinkets behind glass, the rows of ribbons, the cards of stays and trims, the needle pouches, the silvery thimbles. So small, so neat, so ordered. She felt a rush of pity for him, remembering the largeness of his ambition and imagining him here in the midst of all these small shiny things. The city had diminished Herr Fröhlich even more than it had her.

'It's no job for a man, is it, really?' Doris mused. 'That's what Fritz says.'

Fritz was the bad company Doris was keeping and of whom Frau Wingender so disapproved. A lathe operator at the plant, he was large and noisy in his affections. He would sweep Doris up in his arms – when they met after the dayshift at the gates – and squeeze her so hard that it made Franziska breathless just to watch. But she did not trust Fritz. His brutish good looks, his size; his rough humour made her wary.

'Fritz says isn't it strange that Herr Fröhlich hasn't volunteered,' Doris said as they stepped out onto the Alexanderplatz.

In the first rush to the recruiting offices, Fritz had been rejected. A bad chest.

'Fritz says it's criminal to wait to be asked when your country is at war,' Doris continued.

'The war will be over soon, won't it?' Franziska asked.

'Fritz says the war would be over quicker if every fit man volunteered,' Doris offered slyly.

Fritz says a lot of things, Franziska thought.

'Fritz says he's a nancy boy,' she whispered, though they were in the middle of a crowded street, amidst the screech of tram brakes.

'What?'

'Just look how he earns a living, Fritz says, selling fripperies to women while real men are at the Front. And all he thinks about are his big plans. America indeed!'

Fritz says, Fritz says. Franziska knew what Fritz was. An angry man who couldn't hold his drink or his temper.

'Fritz has a brother, you know,' Doris said, slipping her arm through Franziska's, 'maybe when you have your dress made up we can all go out together?'

Franziska smiled and nodded, succumbing to Doris's conciliatory gaiety. She warmed to her friend's engaging directness so at odds with her own labyrinthine secrecy.

But *she* was not going to consort with a tool-fitter, not even to please Doris.

They bought Franziska's fabric in Jandorf's. It was not at all as impressive as Tietz's; here there were no bellboys or carpets, but crooked parquetry and unruly queues and a functional clatter in place of a gilded hush. But that did not deter Doris from ordering the assistant to fetch down bolts of cotton and cheviot, serge and poplin from the highest corners. She had a hunter's appetite for the task at hand. She fingered everything and compared endlessly, doing quick calculations in her head. In the end Franziska chose a blood-red velveteen which brooded and glinted depending on the light and felt to the touch like goosedown. And even though she had to hand over half her week's wages, she felt somehow armed against adversity walking out of Jandorf's swinging a brown paper package with the makings of a fine dress.

ELSBETHA HACKERL WAS a thin, pinched woman of indeterminate age – definitely too old to get married now, Doris asserted, as they knocked on the shabby door of Apartment 307. The Hackerls lived directly above the Wingenders, so when they were admitted it was like walking into a replica of the flat below, the same pattern of interconnecting rooms, a small scullery, one bedroom. Fräulein Hackerl used the equivalent of Herr Fröhlich's room to work in; the window gave onto the street and she had placed her treadle machine facing it so that she sat as she worked in a bath of dusty light. Her bedridden mother, installed like a gimlet-eyed raptor on a divan in the adjoining room with the doors flung open, ruled her life, though Elsbetha spent most of her day with her back turned to her.

'Red,' the old lady scoffed when Franziska and Doris unfurled the prized material. 'A whore's colour.'

'You must excuse my mother,' Elsbetha Hackerl said in a low, urgent voice. 'Being an invalid has made her irritable.'

But, according to Doris, even in full health, Frau Hackerl had been cranky and sour.

'Crimson is a very fashionable colour this season,' Elsbetha said loudly for her mother's benefit.

Frau Hackerl snorted and rapped her cane on the floor loudly. The stick was used when she needed to attract her harried daughter's attention, but the old lady also used it as a conversational tool. Elsbetha cleared a space on the window ledge for Doris to sit, sweeping up several unfinished pieces embroidered with large tacking stitches – the raglan sleeve of a brown linen jacket, a bias cut of a grey flannel skirt. Hanging from the shutters, around the mantel mirror, from picture frames and even from the gas-light bracket, other clothes skulked in various states of undress. A faint breeze through the window – opened a crack at the bottom – rustled through the room, fussing at the thin patterns lying on the table like crushed paper lanterns.

'Now,' Elsbetha said, stepping back to take Franziska in. 'What style were you thinking of?'

'Something with a Robespierre collar and French cuffs,' Doris commanded, 'and a five-piece skirt with a pleat each side. Franziska should make the most of her height, don't you think?'

Doris, a diminutive four foot eleven, considered the rest of the world tall.

'Indeed, Fräulein,' Elsbetha said gravely, 'you have quite a regal bearing.'

'Clearing length,' Doris went on, 'and we've bought Belgian lace for the chemisette.'

Fräulein Hackerl set to with the measuring tape.

'You have an hourglass figure, Fräulein Schanzkowska, what a trim waist!'

The seamstress swathed the velveteen around Franziska's face.

'Yes,' she said approvingly, 'this will be most becoming on you.'

She laid the velveteen down next to the spidery lace.

'Come back to me next week,' she said, 'it should be ready for a first fitting.'

'That's what she says to everybody,' Frau Hackerl shouted, striking the floorboards with her cane.

Elsbetha ignored her.

'I said, that's what she always says.'

'We heard you, Mother!' Fräulein Hackerl said loudly as she showed Franziska and Doris out.

'She's a little deaf,' she confided, as if that might explain away her mother's rudeness.

'A little mad, more like,' Doris muttered as Elsbetha Hackerl shut the door on them with a tight smile.

As they made their way downstairs they could hear the rap of Frau Hackerl's cane and her quavery voice calling for broth.

They collided with Herr Fröhlich at the Wingenders' door, which was, as usual, thrown open. Rosa Wingender liked to hear as much as possible of her neighbours' doings and she hated being alone. In the evenings, if her girls or her current lodger weren't at home, she would sit in the open doorway and engage in conversation with the passersby. She could recognise people by their footsteps, and at night by their pauses and lurchings on the returns.

Herr Fröhlich was out of breath, having taken the stairs two at a time. 'Ah, ladies,' he said, standing back to let them pass. 'Going out?'

Franziska was never sure of his tone. She wondered if she heard mockery in it, or was it merely the servile politeness that his work at Tietz's required.

'No, actually, coming in,' Doris replied pertly. 'We've been to the dressmaker's upstairs. Franziska is getting something made up.'

'For a special occasion?' he enquired.

'A lady, Herr Fröhlich, does not need a special occasion,' Doris said and swept by him.

Herr Fröhlich waited until Doris was out of sight, then he touched Franziska lightly on the forearm.

'Would the special occasion have anything to do with our conversation the other night?'

She had not given him an answer. She hadn't had a chance.

'Fräulein Hackerl says the dress will be ready next week,' Franziska said meaningfully.

He smiled broadly.

How easy it was to please him, she thought, with a pang of remorse. For her, it would never be that uncomplicated. 'Then I'll have to pray that the seamstress is as good as her word.'

It fitted perfectly, though it took closer to three weeks to be completed. Franziska stood in Elsbetha Hackerl's chaotic workroom staring into the pedestal mirror which Elsbetha had pushed into the centre of the strewn floor. She gazed at herself long and hard. Perhaps it was the crushed pile of the velveteen, or the succulent colour, or the moth-busy light of Fräulein Hackerl's room, but she felt transformed.

'With this dress you should wear your hair up, Fräulein,' Elsbetha said, holding Franziska's heavy hair in a soft nest at her nape. The seamstress's breast glistened; she used the front of her sober dress as a pincushion.

'It's so beautiful,' Franziska whispered. She twirled slowly in front of the mirror.

She wanted to embrace the dressmaker; she felt absurdly grateful to her. Elsbetha wrapped the dress in tissue paper and handed it to Franziska as carefully as if it were a baby. At the door she handed Elsbetha her first instalment. Fräulein Hackerl slipped the money into her apron pocket and put her fingers to her lips.

'Another one paying on the never, never,' her mother muttered from within.

Franziska donned the dress the following Saturday. Doris was splayed on the bed wearing her nightgown and robe and leafing through the *BZ am Mittag* desultorily. The headlines lamented the Battle of the Marne, but Doris was more interested in reading the advertisements aloud – tango clubs on Kantstraβe, Lunapark off the Ku'damm, which 'every Berliner must visit at least once' – or the sad, lurid accounts of the city's victims.

'Oh, listen to this one,' she was saying. 'Desperation drove Else Jupke, a 22-year-old woman from Wilhaus, to jump in the Spree River near the Schlütersteig. Boatmen came to her rescue and transported her to the hospital. She had recently arrived in Berlin to work as a buffet lady, but after only finding employment as a waitress and then losing her job, her apartment, and finally her money, grew tired of life.'

Doris sighed loudly, sated with a luxuriant pity for a despair she would never know.

I could be Else Jupke, Franziska almost said.

A battered suitcase filled with tiny treasures from home, buffeted on the street by the heedless crowd and the piercing wind. A small, down-at-heel creature, with mouse-brown hair which sticks out behind my ears. Giving off an untended air, the graceless neglect of the unloved. Serving behind the lunch counter in a uniform made for the girl who had the job before, a smaller, prettier girl. Hurrying home with the smell of wurst *and onion clinging to me, the faint whiff of the slaughterhouse. If I were a shopgirl or one of those new-fangled typing machine operators, I might get more respect, or a certain kind of notice. But Fischer's is a cheap place, where the customers are more interested in the size of the portions than the looks of the serving girls. They leave tips for a hearty meal, but not for a pleasing smile. And one day I arrive at work, late again since rising early is a problem. It is cold in the lodgings. In bed with my coat thrown over the thin blankets is often the only warmth and comfort there is. It is a long tram ride, the Number 6, which often sails by full to the gills and leaves me standing on the kerb. And when I arrive, Frau Fischer calls me over.*

'Else, you're late again.'

'But . . .'

'No buts, late once too often. You just don't have the right attitude. You're a lazy girl, there's something slovenly

about you. Something not quite right. I shall have to let you go.'

'Trying it on for size?' Doris asked, looking up from the crumpled newsprint.

Else turns towards the street and slowly fades . . .

'What?'

'The dress,' Doris prompted impatiently. Sometimes she thought Franziska too queer for words. She would fall into a strange, distracted mood as if she could hear voices that no one else could hear.

'No,' Franziska said boldly, 'I'm going out, actually.'

'Really?' Doris sat up abruptly, abandoning her previous languor. 'Why didn't you tell me?'

She peered up suspiciously as Franziska, head bowed, buttoned the dress at the neck and cuffs.

'Who is it? It's someone from the factory, isn't it?'

'Maybe.'

'Louise? Louise?' Doris yelled. 'Come in here quick.'

She felt in need of reinforcements. Louise was more adept at worming information out of Franziska. In rare moments of reflection – usually after a row with Fritz – Doris worried that she was too game, too direct. Louise ambled in from the kitchen. 'What is it, Dor?' she asked lazily. She had been steeped in a novelette, a penny dreadful, and resented being yanked away from it.

'Sissy here has been holding out on us.'

Sissy, Sissy.

'Go on, Sissy, tell us who it is!'

Something snapped within. That name, calling her back.

'Don't call me Sissy.'

'What?'

'Don't call me Sissy,' she repeated.

'Why ever not?'

'Just don't,' Franziska said evenly. 'It's a child's name. I won't answer to a child's name.'

Doris's teasing gaiety evaporated and she fell into a crestfallen silence. Even Louise backed away, startled by

Franziska's menacing tone. A look of puzzled shock passed between the sisters. Franziska saw it in the foxed mirror as she gathered her hair back just as Fräulein Hackerl had suggested. She had not meant to be so cold; sometimes she did not know what came over her. Doris had meant no harm, Doris was her friend. Without Doris she might still be walking the streets of Berlin. Without Doris she would never have met Herr Fröhlich. But the wave of cold, despising anger which had swept over her could annihilate all of that in one instant. An old memory stirred.

'You really want to know who I'm meeting tonight?' she asked, speaking to Doris's reflection in the mirror.

'Yes, yes, do tell!' Doris crawled on all fours to the edge of the bed. She was like a puppy, Franziska thought, a playful and forgetful puppy.

'It's Hans,' Franziska said slowly, savouring the moment. It was the first time she had uttered his name.

'Hans who?' Doris asked blankly.

'Our Hans, you know!'

'Hans Fröhlich?' Doris asked incredulously.

Franziska nodded.

'Well I never!' Doris looked agape.

'Aren't you the dark horse?' Louise added admiringly.

'How do I look?' Franziska asked, turning away from the mirror.

Doris answered by embracing her. Franziska clung to her, trying to garner some of her friend's sweetness and warmth, so as to dispel the icy chill which had gripped her only moments before. She knew the consequences of allowing that cold fury to take hold.

Frau Wingender could not hide her disapproval as Franziska waited in the kitchen for Herr Fröhlich, while Doris fussed with her hair. She had lent Franziska her black panne velvet hat and was busily setting a pin into

Franziska's hair to hold it in place. Frau Wingender sat glumly at the table nursing her first drink of the evening.

'It's highly irregular,' she said, eyeing Franziska crossly. 'I can't have my lodgers consorting with one another.'

'Mama,' Louise pleaded, planting a comforting arm around the dejected sag of her mother's shoulder. 'Just think, you've brought a young couple together.'

Frau Wingender smiled tightly.

'And there's a war on,' Doris added.

'As if we hadn't noticed,' Louise murmured.

'I mean, we must all find our happiness where we can,' Doris said, 'that's all.'

Herr Fröhlich appeared in the doorway, stepping diffidently into the tableau of women. He wore a dark suit, not his working one, Franziska noticed, and a crisp white shirt. The stiff collar chafed at his neck and he pulled at it uncomfortably. He fingered the brim of his hat.

'Frau Wingender,' he started.

The landlady shot him a look of quivering hurt.

'Be assured', he went on, 'that I will behave with the utmost propriety. You can depend on it.'

She relented a little, unable to resist this appeal to her sense of respectability.

'But of course, Herr Fröhlich, I wasn't suggesting . . .' She lapsed into a doleful silence. The last thing she wanted was to lose a steady payer like Herr Fröhlich.

'You be careful, do you hear,' she admonished Franziska as they turned to leave, with Doris still tinkering with her hat.

'Yes, ma'am,' she replied, though the words stuck in her throat.

How strange to be so close to him, her arm entwined around the rough stuff of his suit. Perhaps it was her new dress which seemed cooped up beneath the Poznan coat, but she found it hard to keep step with him. They seemed to move at a different pace. His proximity unnerved her; she had not been this close to a man since her father. Despite his slender frame, Hans felt substantial here beside her, solid and bulky. She stumbled once or twice on the uneven paving stones and felt the pressure of his hand on her elbow. This close she could see the crescent curl of his lashes. The sandy cliff of his brow was steeped in the saucer shadow of his hat. She could almost touch the corn-coloured speckle of his jaw. On his neck there was a red chafe mark from his collar. He had the hands of a musician, broad span, stunted fingers. His smell, like hers, was of Frau Wingender's coal-tar soap.

Night in Berlin with Hans was solemn and festive by turns. They strolled down the long placid sweep of Unter den Linden past the frantic clatter of restaurants and hotels, the autumn leaves swirling in cranky eddies at their feet. They halted by the Brandenburg Gate, dwarfed by its vast flinty span and height, gazing up at the winged chariot. Franziska could have sworn the columns were moving towards them, an army on the march like the inevitable progress of war. She shivered and Hans put his arm around her.

'Winter is on its way,' he said, 'look how clear everything is.'

The dark tent of the sky was littered with stars.

'My father knows all their names,' he said, gazing upwards.

Franziska looked at him, not the sky. His eager face turned towards the heavens, his breath forming plumes in the chilly air.

'Four years ago he brought us boys out on the roof to see Halley's Comet.' He laughed. 'I was terribly disappointed. I expected something bright and dramatic, and all it was was a shadowy blur. To me.'

To me, thought Franziska, a comet is a tin lamp.

'But my father told me not to worry. Being the

youngest, he said, I had the best chance of being alive to see it when it returns in 1986. Imagine 1986!'

Franziska looked up at the infinity of stars, as distant and impossible as the numbered future.

'I would be ninety-two years old!' He laughed again and squeezed his hand in hers. 'Funny, though, I feel it is a good wish for me from my father, that I would live a long life.'

'Is that why you have not signed up?'

He looked at her suddenly. An expression of puzzled hurt crossed his face.

'You too,' he said sadly. He let his arm fall.

'No, I just . . .'

'I have my dreams,' he said. 'And I'm afraid. I don't want to die. Is that so wrong?'

Yes, she thought, but only because he had voiced his fear. The naming of it could make it happen. She cast her eyes downwards, afraid suddenly for him. She could not bear to look at him, soft and tender as a boy. This was a secret he should not entrust to anyone.

'When the call comes,' he said finally, 'I won't hesitate.'

'Won't it all be over soon, anyway?' she asked. 'The war?'

Her voice sounded small in this vast garden of stone. But he had walked on and did not hear her.

They ambled in silence through the Tiergarten. The street lamps turned the trees into a cabaret of colour, all fiery tresses and brassy crowns, leaves tipped with a viperish gloss. In the distance the golden angel atop the Siegesäule glinted. A fireworks display suddenly lit up the sky, great sprays of pink and silver showering over them. The sudden flowering of the night raised their spirits.

'Come on,' Hans said, taking her hand, 'let's see if we can catch the rest.'

They took a tram to the Potsdamer Platz where the night-time crowd, usually on the move, a great procession of prostitutes and vendors, shopgirls and clerks and merrymaking soldiers, stood transfixed, gazing upwards at the crackling, illuminated sky. When the last of the fireworks trailed away, they went to the Café Astoria on Potsdamer Straβe. Hans chose a table near the window. Its interior was gorgeous as a cake. The iced glaze of the high ceilings was trimmed with painted cornices. The chequered floor underfoot lent a noisy, functional air to the bubbling warmth of the crowd. A carved counter gleamed with copper pumps and the bulbous glow of bottles. High mirrors behind it gave the impression of another café at the other side, a spacious second world inside the first. A strolling band played between the tables, gypsy musicians in red boleros. The three played together, but each seemed in thrall to his instrument. The violinist leaned into his fiddle as if the bow were whispering painful secrets to him, the stout accordionist, tethered to his burden, swayed nautically. The guitarist took up the rear in their procession, strumming floridly and holding the guitar high as if it were a fiery dancing partner. They played waltzes and polkas.

'Oh, this one I know!' Franziska said.

Hans clicked his fingers. The band gathered round their table.

'For the lady,' he said and slipped a coin into the violinist's hand.

At first Franziska felt embarrassed, but then she closed her eyes and sank into the music. In her mind's eye she was no longer in the Café Astoria but at home, dancing in the dark with her Papa, the dust of the yard at their feet as they twirl ... *and suddenly she's in the air, his hands an anchor on her wrists, her hair and the trees and the night sky an intoxicating blur ...*

The music faded. She opened her eyes. His hand was on hers.

'You were very far away,' he said.

He pressed his lips to her fingers.

'Tell me,' he said.

She looked away from his tender gaze for fear she might blurt it out. She damped down the urge to confess which his kindliness invited. There was so much he didn't know, couldn't know.

'Was it a better place than here?' he asked.

She smiled sweetly at him.

'How could it be?' It was a half-truth.

She stroked his graven chin. She brushed back the fallen strand of hair that clouded his view and admonished him to silence with a finger to his mouth. She looked at him and saw a child. A mop-topped boy, with an earnest gaze and a future as bright and optimistic as the new century. The river of life had brought Walter back to her.

WITH THE NEW year came the first rationing, then the war bread, fifty pfennigs for a black, sour-tasting loaf, then the metal shortage. Frau Wingender offered up her prized pair of brass candlesticks for the good of the cause. It was not all privation. In February millions of hogs were slaughtered to save on feed and Frau Wingender served pork every night for a month. They feasted on fat, even Hans, though Frau Wingender thought it was against his religion. The war dragged on, but Franziska refused to believe that it would ever impinge on Hans and her. If she saw returned soldiers on the street, hobbling on crutches, she would turn away. It was not her war; it couldn't touch her.

Their courtship was conducted mostly outside the apartment so as not to aggravate Frau Wingender's air of grievance. They went ice-skating at the Ice Palais, an open-air rink a tram ride away in Wedding. It was a tennis court in the summer, Hans explained, but with the onset of winter they had flooded it and let Mother Nature do the rest. Franziska ventured out gingerly onto the glacial floor, clutching onto Hans to stay upright. She had a poor sense of balance and the hired boots pinched her feet. She could not quite believe that there was no lake underfoot and that the thin, scraped surface would not crack if she leaned on it too heavily.

'There's no water under here,' Hans would say, laughing at her nervousness as skaters whipped and curved around them.

Hans was steady and graceful on the ice, and when she surrendered to his lead and the foggy band music blaring from the loudspeaker it was a strange sensation, like finding a new element that was neither air nor water. Afterwards, cheeks aglow and ravenously hungry, they had pea soup and sausages at Aschinger's.

On Doris's urging they went to Lunapark, a vast fairground at the end of the Kurfürstendamm. They went on the merry-go-round; riding side by side on painted horses, clutching the barley-twist poles as the carousel turned. They swung high on boats moored only by vast ropes and took a child-sized electric train, which ran on rails through a darkened tunnel where ghosts howled and paper skeletons swung from the rafters. Franziska had her palm read in a canvas booth. The gypsy who held her hand tenderly pronounced her both rare and lucky; she had double lifelines on both palms. The gypsy predicted fame and longevity.

'See!' said Hans. 'You and me both!'

All that spring they spent evenings in Hans's room – with the door left respectably ajar. From above they could hear the impatient rap of Frau Hackerl's cane. Franziska often thought of Elsbetha Hackerl overhead, peddling away fiercely, surrounded by her swathes of fabric, the sleeves and pockets and hemlines of strangers, and felt a stinging kind of pity for her closeted life. She, at least, had escaped that. Hans talked of his life at home. His father, lover of the night sky, a timid, hard-working man, nimble-fingered and deferential; his mother, large and blowsy and over-protective, given to easy tears. His four brothers, the two eldest already gone to the front, Ernst who helped his father in the business, Wolfie who worked as a clerk in a grain store. 'It must be wonderful to live in the countryside,' he said to her, 'to be so close to nature. I envy you.'

She did not have the heart to tell him that for her it was a dark, cruel world dominated by need and the stormy violence of her father's moods. A mean life eked out scrabbling in the dirt. So she dissembled. Papa became benign in the retelling, a bear of a man, earthy by nature but honest and sweet-tempered. Mother was a loyal, unharried homemaker, broken-hearted by Franziska's departure. Her sisters she left gathered around the family hearth, happily married and bearing children; Felix, the heir apparent, she sent down the mines, working for the good of the empire. Superstitiously she neglected to mention Walter; there was no need. He was dead. She could say that to herself now without flinching, but she could not say it to anyone else.

She thought of Hans's room as a cocoon, a safe place of shadows. Frau Wingender had saved her best pieces for the lodger's room. An armchair with a buxom rump and a short leg sat grandly in the window bay. A wardrobe, where his Sunday suit hung to attention, a tapestry screen over which he'd slung his greatcoat, an oriental rug, threadbare in places where Hans's boots were splayed. The small metal fireplace with its empty grate was the only reminder that there was a war on.

'They'll come for me soon,' he would say gloomily.

But she would not hear of such talk.

'No, darling,' she would answer him, soothing but defiant.

She practised these terms of endearment, so strange on her tongue. She would sit on the side of his dishevelled bed and he would lie with his head on her lap like a sleepy child. She would part the hairs on the crown of his head.

'No harm can come to you.'

When the war was over, they would reassure one another, they would go to America together, New York, Chicago, New Orleans. He taught her a few words of English. *Mann, Haus, Feuer.*

'See,' he said brightly, 'they sound the same as German.'

But to her they sounded as thin and flat as the promise of peace.

By autumn her world was peopled by women, war widows and wounded men. Even at the factory, the boys who had shared the trolley run with her had disappeared, replaced by a pair of beefy twins from near Poznan. She felt a proprietorial lurch when she heard the name. It was on the tip of her tongue to ask them if they had ever come across her sister, but she checked herself. If they answered her questions they would have questions for her. So she listened quietly as they grumbled about their lot. How marauding German troops had pilfered everything their family had, their meagre crop of potatoes and oats, their only horse. It was the first time Franziska had realised that this war had stretched its tentacles as far as home; as far even as Mother and Felix. A picture of her mother flashed before her, and how she might appear to a raw recruit standing at the door of their kitchen peering into the gloom. There they would find her, sitting vacant-eyed by the stove, wretched with loss, a poor spoil of war. The Poznan twins had been deported for forced labour – they gestured to the rain-soaked yard and the glistening perambulators of death they pushed all day long.

'And you?' they asked in unison.

Freckled girls with auburn hair and the same stout legs. Helena and Zofia.

'I have been in Berlin many years,' Franziska said haughtily. 'My fiancé is German.'

'Oh,' the girls mouthed together.

'An arrangement between our families,' she explained.

Well, it was almost true. They were as good as engaged.

The twins oohed again like a pair of frogs. How easy it was to deceive them with their eager eyes and their pudding-bowl hair. They pulled their weight on the trolleys, though. They were as strong as dray horses, hauling across the mud-spattered yard, sloshing through the murky puddles, rain dripping from their noses. Then Helena went missing. She had borrowed matches to light a candle at her lodgings and stuck a spare one in her kerchief for emergencies. The Lady Superintendent had discovered it when she went through her checks at the Shifting House and had marched her off to Herr Lindner's office. She had been suspended, twenty-eight days without pay.

'These Germans,' Zofia muttered. 'Feed off us, then treat us like common criminals.'

Franziska hushed her. She could no longer afford such mutinous feelings.

The year turned. One Saturday in late January she met Hans outside Tietz's. It was late afternoon, a pale and frigid sky labouring with snow-cloud. Franziska stood on the pavement lost in a kind of dream. An eerie sensation of absence would sometimes take hold of her when she was in the city. The largeness of the place, the sweeping expanse of Alexanderplatz, the shuffle and push of pedestrians, the shrill business of trams, the low drone of omnibuses were like some vast engine that did not require her. At first this sense of anonymity had exhilarated her, now it made her feel small and unnecessary.

Hans, pausing in the entrance amidst the eddy and whirl of the revolving doors, watched her and felt the tender bruise of love. Her small frame cowled in her mother's coat, the forlorn set of her shoulders, the strange lostness of her. And yet when he embraced her he sensed something in her that would not yield, some fiery reserve she was holding back. It perplexed him. Perhaps it was because she was a Catholic. He felt for an instant the quivering, wounded disappointment of his parents, but he banished it. He was German first, a Jew second. A citizen of the world. He strode towards Franziska and tapped her on the shoulder.

She jumped, startled, and turned around. Some awful fright registered fleetingly in her pale eyes before she recognised him. He kissed her full on the lips, his tongue insisting on entry. Deep in the ribbed fleshy cave of her mouth, he could dispel the guilty undertow of his feelings and drown the fear of falseness that afflicted him, as if this was some illicit love and he was an impostor.

She hung onto him, glad of the unexpected fierceness of his embrace.

'I have a surprise for you,' he said.

'What is it?'

'Oh, you'll have to wait and see.'

He took her arm and they hurried along the street, battling against a chill wind.

'Tell me,' she begged.

'No,' he insisted jokingly, 'it wouldn't be a surprise then.'

They took a tram, and then another, alighting on the Kurfürstendamm. She loved the way Hans knew his way around; she surrendered happily to his intricate knowledge of routes and timetables. It was as if she was being led blindfold through streets whose names she did not know deep into the knotted core of the city. They halted under a railway bridge as a train thundered overhead.

'Close your eyes,' he commanded. 'We're almost there.'

He guided her towards a door and pushed it open, then they ascended a flight of steps and halted while he knocked on another door.

'Now you can open them,' he said.

She found herself in an ill-lit hallway. On a plate below the door's brass knocker a sign read: Hermann Jünger, Theatrical Photographer.

'We're going to have our portraits done.'

Herr Jünger's studio was a large, dusty room with a raised platform shrouded in red velvet drapes. Around the podium a number of props had been carelessly set down – a sedate tapestry armchair, a small hexagonal cane table, a sagging chaise-longue. In one corner a crop of parasols was stacked, one against the other, their frilled trims like the layers of a child's petticoat, in another a large wicker basket stood agape, an unruly drooling of clothes issuing from its open jaws. A hatstand sported a rich confection of feathered millinery.

'Quick, quick,' Herr Jünger urged, 'or we shall miss the light.'

He pointed at the louring sky visible through the attic window, tinged with the pale fire of a winter sunset.

'Hans,' she said, grabbing his arm, 'if I'd known I could have worn something better than this.' She tugged despondently at her black work skirt.

'Oh, but we can dress up. That's the whole point. Herr Jünger will give us costumes. We can be anyone we like.'

'This is the theatre of life,' Herr Jünger said importantly. He was a raffish-looking gent, straggly dark hair, an unkempt moustache and an artistic gait. He set to rearranging the furniture, pushing the chaise-longue to one side and centring the armchair and the cane table. Franziska rummaged through the open chest, swathes of chiffon skirts and stoles and boleros encrusted with tiny mirrored eyeholes.

'That's our gypsy collection,' Herr Jünger hollered in mid-heave. 'The society stuff is behind the screens at the other end of the room.' He straightened, mopping his brow. 'And you, sir, will go for uniform, no doubt. Most of our gentlemen do.'

Franziska made for the far end of the room. Dipping behind the screens, she entered a bridal alcove. There, hanging from rows of pegs, was a sisterhood of dresses, ivory and cream, embossed satin, frothy lace, the filmy filigree of worked silk, the naked sheerness of netting. She fingered the hems and gingerly touched the sleeves and cuffs of the costumes, afraid at first to lift one down in case it might disintegrate in her hands. The drained and wintry half-light made them look like jostling ghosts. She savoured the sepulchral silence which seemed to sprout with presences, as if the owners of the clothes – for surely they had had owners once – had gathered in the gloom to watch and wait.

'Hurry, Franziska,' Hans called out to her.

She riffled through the dresses again, inhaling the secretive musty scent that seeped from their whispering folds. What lives must have been lived in these! Finally she chose one, a full-length silk with a half-moon neckline around which a layered bed of net had been sewn. The three-quarter-length sleeves tapered into a deep cuff of broderie anglaise. Below the waist it flared into a full skirt. It, too, was covered with a fine netting and here and there a tiny pearl-like bead had been sewn on, as if the dress were the exquisitely delicate haul of a miniature fisher god. She stepped out from behind the screen.

'Ah, the Tatiana,' Herr Jünger said, hand on hip. 'Modelled on a Romanov gown, made for one of the grand duchesses.'

'My God, Franziska,' Hans gasped, 'look at you! Transformed!'

He stood at the far end of the room, resplendent in a naval uniform, stiff collar and cravat, all sombre blue and gold, bright as a new coin. She saw the blood-red drape behind him and for a moment her vision of him faltered.

'Come, come, darling,' Herr Jünger said, steering her towards the podium where Hans was standing.

Herr Jünger settled her on the stiff chair while he tamped down the tufts of net which sprang up on her bosom and lap. Hans stood behind her, one hand on her shoulder, the other clasping a crested cap to his coined chest. Herr Jünger retreated a few steps to get a picture of them in his head, as he said, then he leaped nimbly off the platform and returned to the large hooded camera which stood on a tripod some distance away.

'Just lovely,' he cooed from behind the hood. 'Just hold that. And smile, if you will!'

He held up what appeared to be a smoking gun, which turned into a blue explosion.

Startled, Franziska moved.

'Oh no,' she groaned. Her face would be reduced to a blur in the finished product.

Herr Jünger rushed to reassure.

'No, no, darling, it will be just perfect. Framed, Herr Fröhlich?'

'Yes, why not! We can put it on our mantel and show our grandchildren.'

'Herr and Frau Fröhlich,' Herr Jünger declaimed, licking the lead of his pencil before jotting down their names in a notebook he had fished from his pocket. 'Come by next Saturday and all will be revealed.'

But it was an appointment they would never keep.

Franziska had thought soldiers would come to the door, that a general in a peaked cap would point a finger at Hans, as if he had done something wrong that he must be punished for and he would be dragged away. Instead his call came in the form of a letter, a letter from his mother. Dated 15 February 1916. His papers had arrived at home, to the rooms above the tailor's shop. For Ernst and Wolfgang too, she wrote. The ink was smudged where she'd paused to cry. He must present himself in Düsseldorf a week hence for training. Frau Wingender was distraught – where was she going to find another lodger if all the young men were being ordered to the Front? Doris bustled her away, leaving Franziska and Hans stranded in his room, his mother's letter passing back and forth between them, a page at a time.

'You're young and strong, you'll survive,' she said brightly. But she did not believe her own words. 'The war can't last for ever. It will be over soon.'

'We were saying that a year ago,' he said glumly. He stood like a frightened boy, already at a distance, lost in his own fear.

'Maybe there'll be an armistice,' she ventured.

'Oh Franziska, no false hope, please.' He turned away.

'You must live then, if not for yourself, for me,' she urged.

'All our plans, our dreams,' he said, 'going up in smoke.'

She nestled into his back, her head between the slender bony wings of his shoulder blades.

'Let's pretend then', she whispered, 'that you are going on a trip. A civilian on a journey. Home to see your mother. It's true, isn't it?'

He laughed grimly.

'There is no war here,' she said emphatically.

The evening light faded into a violent sunset, staining the dim room red. A flock of starlings wheeled outside the window, then fell like smuts of coal dust in the air. Darkness settled on them, standing clasped together, her arms wound around him, her hand on his heart. She thought if they didn't move they could hold this moment, stop the clock, halt the drumbeat of time. But finally he undid her hold and turning around he buried his head in the crook of her neck. His lips brushed the lobe of her ear, the downturn of her eyelids. She trained his fingers down the buttons of her blouse, then guided him along the intricate stays of her bodice until with a gasp his frightened skin met the cold globe of her breast. She offered it to him and felt a latching tug as his lips sucked the fleshy bullet of her nipple. They stumbled to the bed, the boy child at her breast, burrowing fiercely with his tongue and fingers as she parted her skirts and eased the rough cotton of her drawers down around her hips as she led him carefully in.

'There,' she breathed as he took stealthy occupation, releasing a joyous, baffled whimper. He had entered her, but she possessed him now; there was no way she could lose him.

She comforted him, soothing his half-delighted shudders. They lay for hours in the complicit night, as if they had coupled in the darkness of time's beginning.

'Franziska,' he asked hoarsely, as if her name was a question in itself.

'Yes,' she answered, as if it were another.

'Marry me?'

She moved into Hans's room. Frau Wingender was appeased. For her it meant that Hans's going was not a complete loss. For Franziska it meant getting away from the smothering intimacy of the Wingender sisters, Louise's doe-eyed empathy, Doris's pert unconcern. She hibernated there even though spring was budding in the trees outside. Hans had left his greatcoat in the wardrobe and she would sleep with it thrown over her so she could be enveloped with the smell of him – soap and candle tallow and semen. That was all she had left of her fiancé. No ring to wear, just the whispered endearment of a frightened boy which had to stretch across half a continent now, away to the west somewhere. She could not speak of it for fear she had imagined he had asked her to marry him and because of the niggling shame over how his promise had been made. Doris, for all her flighty gaiety, was proper with it. And if Frau Wingender discovered what had been done under her roof Franziska would find herself on the street.

Doris chided her for moping.

'Plenty of other fish in the sea,' she declared, linking arms with Franziska on the way home from the factory some weeks after Hans's departure.

'I don't want anyone else,' Franziska replied.

'Leave her be, Dor,' Louise interjected. 'Hans and Franziska were made for each other. He will come home safe and they'll get married. Isn't that right, Franziska?'

She was grateful to Louise for her stout defence, but she felt she had moved beyond the simple fellowship of the

Wingender sisters. Her life was no longer here with them, it was out there on the Western Front with her boy soldier. The newspaper headlines screamed – 'City of Verdun in Flames' – and suddenly it concerned her.

Frau Wingender was clattering pots in the kitchen and complaining loudly. She had spent the day doing battle at the market, which always left her short-tempered and cranky. Food was getting scarcer; yesterday for their evening meal there had been just potatoes with a scattering of salt. Famine fare, Frau Wingender called it. Today there was a cabbage broth and a knuckle bone of pork wheedled from the butcher's stall.

'Look,' she said to Franziska, 'it's nothing but gristle and the whiff of flesh.'

Franziska's stomach turned at the sight of the raw joint. She felt suddenly squeamish.

'Any letters?' she asked urgently.

'Oh yes, my dear,' Frau Wingender said vaguely as if post arrived every day at the household. 'Something did come for you.'

Franziska dashed into Hans's room – both she and the Wingenders still referred to it as Hans's room. There on the bed the letter lay like a small encapsulation of Hans, a white oblong sliver of him. She lay down and clutching the letter to her breast she sniffed the envelope, hoping she could catch something of him from it. But it had passed through too many hands. It was rain-spattered – was this the mud of Verdun, she wondered, here beneath her fingertips? – and the address had begun to weep. She tried to imagine the letter's journey from the muddied battle-field, nestling in a sack on a truck, rattling through the night on a train, and sorted by a careless hand before it found its way to her. How delicate and defenceless their connection was. She pressed her lips to the seal before tearing the letter open with impatient fingers.

My dearest Franziska,
Oh, how suddenly everything has changed. How I lived
and loved is now like a dream. A passing mood. Only one
thing is real now – the war! I should like to dream about
you, and to love you, but I have not time for you now. I am
entirely occupied with thoughts of war and suffering.
Around us hell has been unchained. The attack was terrible.
Our artillery kept up a barrage and after two hours the
position was sufficiently prepared for our infantry. It was
magnificent the way our men advanced. In the face of
appalling machine-gun fire they went on with a confidence
which nobody could ever attempt to equal. And so the hill
which had been stormed in vain three times was taken in an
hour. But now comes the worst part – to hold the hill. Bad
days are ahead. The French guns are shooting appallingly
and every night there are counter-attacks and bombing
raids. Where I am, we are only about a couple of metres
apart. We could be torn to bits at any moment by a shell in
the trench, covered in dirt, and so end – in the mud and the
filth. We are comrades here, but only in this, as candidates
for death. The stench of death is everywhere. There is never
silence. Even when the guns are not roaring there are
strange howls in the night. The wounded cry out, but there
is nothing to quell their pain. Even the healthy – several
lines were blacked out here, the censor's pen made them
indecipherable – *have nightmares in the midst of night-*
mare. They call out to their loved ones, their sweethearts as
I do to you, Franziska, my love.
Yours, as always,
Hans

SHE READ THE letter over and over again. It was as if it were from a stranger. Apart from the endearment at the end it might as well have been. She was angry with him, his letter like a report from some other world, as if he were already dead, passed into some cruel hell. Judged and damned. But what crime was Hans guilty of to merit such punishment? Had he murdered somebody? Even if he hadn't he would return a killer, a man who had taken life to save his own. The boy Hans was gone. She shook herself. Hans was not dead. Here was his handwriting. But where was his voice? She could not hear it, no matter how hard she read between the lines. Is this what war did to men? Made them disappear before they were dead? She hid the letter under the floorboards. She buried it in the hope that its nightmarish echoes might die away too. She hung Hans's coat in the wardrobe and shut the door on him. It no longer bore his smell; it too had turned malevolent. She could only get the whiff of blood and gunpowder from it now.

The punch clock in the Shifting House marked time for her, snapping her card between its metal lips, wheezing out the hours. She worked as if in a dream, numbed by a strange kind of bereavement as if she were already a war widow. Was this what had afflicted her mother, this glassy remoteness, an unshed grief? In her new decoupled state, she found her thoughts returning to home, but she could not quite conjure it up any more. The war kept on getting in the way. Home seemed as strange and dangerous to her now as Hans's muddied battlefield and sodden trenches.

Suddenly, the factory began to make her sick. The fumy smell of braziers, the heaving labour, the oily clangour of shells, the dry din of the machines, the fiery showers of sparks from the whingeing lathes. She could not eat in the mornings. The black bread made her retch; her stomach heaved at the smell of the coffee which Frau Wingender had managed to get despite the shortages.

'See!' she said, pouring for Franziska, 'see how I look after my girls.'

Franziska covered her mouth to stop the bile rising. She tried to hide her queasiness at work. Twice in one week her pay had been docked – once for taking an unscheduled lavatory break, another for leaving the trolley shed before the meal hooter.

'Plenty of young women out there who are hungry for work,' Herr Lindner had warned her.

If he knew she was ailing, he would have no mercy, she knew.

'I don't know what's wrong with me,' Franziska confided in Louise as they undressed in the Shifting House. 'Every morning I feel like this. Like death.' Louise gave her an odd look. 'The work is making me ill.'

'Are you sure that's all it is?' Louise asked.

'What else could it be?'

'Oh Franziska, you're not pregnant, are you?' Louise shook her arm vehemently. 'Are you late?'

Franziska said nothing.

'How late are you?'

Franziska didn't know. It could be a week, it could be three. She didn't keep track. She was bled; it was something done to her. If she didn't bleed, she didn't worry. In fact she was glad of it. Her life's blood every month, lost. Taken from her so she could never really be strong.

'Franziska, how late are you?'

She was not pregnant. She couldn't be. She had wished for the bleeding to stop and it had. Franziska knew the power of wishes. It was the men who were bleeding now. This is what happened during wars. The men bled and the women stopped.

'Hans is gone nearly two months, Franziska.'

'Hans has never touched me, do you hear?'

The room fell silent. Girls in their bloomers looked around curiously at the two of them, clutching one another angrily in the middle of the room. Tempers often flared in the locker rooms. The early hour, the long war, mothers leaving fractious children behind in the gunmetal dawn, husbands missing in action. A dropped hairclip, hanging a coat on the wrong hook could ignite the tinder box. Franziska lowered her voice.

'He's not that kind of boy. Maybe the kind you and your sister hang around with, but not my Hans. *Not* my Hans!'

The Lady Superintendent parted the two girls.

'Number 670, what's all this about? I'm putting you on warning!'

Louise sloped away, shaking her head.

'She's crazy, Auntie, really crazy,' she muttered under her breath.

'My, but you're getting plump,' Frau Wingender said to her that evening as she picked at her meagre dinner. Louise shot her a recriminatory glance across the table. They had not spoken since the morning's argument.

'Here's my girls going to skin and bone.'

She plucked at Doris's dimpled forearm.

'But you, Franziska, dear, are blooming.' Frau Wingender smiled sweetly, but appraisingly. 'I think it must be love.'

Had Louise told her something?

'Anyone would think you were pregnant,' Doris said chirpily.

'I am not pregnant, Doris Wingender, do you hear?' She rose from the table, her fist in the air. 'What have you been saying, Louise?'

'Nothing, Franziska, honestly, nothing!'

'Girls, girls, let's have no squabbling. Sit, Franziska, and finish your meal. I'm sure our Doris meant no harm. We all know what a gentleman Hans Fröhlich was, is,' she corrected herself. 'Didn't he give me his word!'

Franziska sat down, suddenly defeated. She was trapped; there was no way out.

Louise cornered her in the hallway.

'Listen, Franziska, if you're in trouble, there's always Fräulein Hackerl.'

Franziska laughed. What had the henpecked seamstress got to do with this? She had paid off her last instalment on the dress weeks ago.

'To make me new clothes?' she asked incredulously.

'Hush, Franziska, not so loud. Mama doesn't know.'

She steered her down the stairs to the next turn, where they whispered in the darkness.

'Doesn't know what?'

'Franziska, please, listen to me. Fräulein Hackerl is not just a seamstress; she can . . .' Louise sighed, then started again. 'Remember Mathilde Bender? From the cartridge factory?'

Franziska did remember her, a small, broad-beamed girl with a turned eye.

'She was going to have a baby and we, Doris and I, told her about Fräulein Hackerl. She had to pay, of course.'

Franziska looked at her blankly.

'Pay?'

'To have it, the baby . . . removed,' Louise said carefully.

'Removed?'

No, it couldn't be.

'It'll be too late if you don't do something about it soon, Franziska. You'll begin to show.'

'No,' Franziska cried and clapped her hands over her ears. 'No, it cannot be!'

I know you, Elsbetha Hackerl, secret killer of babies. Maker of dresses the colour of clotted blood. Impostor with your brown, earnest gaze and those slender capable hands, all kind words and reassurance. Silken-tongued. Passing yourself off in the suit of a seamstress. I know you. Pincushion for a breast. Wielder of scissors and knife. Do you use them when you ply your trade in the dark hours of the night, your secret trade? I know you, Elsbetha Hackerl. Midwife of death. Creeping up on the innocent, on the barely formed, yanking them from their safe, watery homes and throttling them until they drown in their own blood. I know you.

They will come back to haunt you. The unhappily dead. The cries of those you have extinguished will cry out in the night. They will have their passage into the world that you have denied them. They will insist on it. One day you will open a door and unwittingly let them in. There is nowhere to hide from the murder in your heart.

'Franziska?' Louise was shaking her as if she had fallen into a faint. 'You must do something, or your life will be ruined.'

The next morning Franziska volunteered for the Danger Building.

She worked on the monkey machine, which forced a mixture of amatol and TNT down into the waiting shell cases. It took four girls using all their might to haul on a rope which raised the beater, a massive stone weight. Then, at a signal from the monitor, they let it drop onto the powdered mixture until it was packed tight. It was tense work, but at least there was peace there. Gowned to the throat, with fireproof hats and masks, they couldn't talk to one another even if they had wanted to. They communicated by gestures, a dumbshow. Their task demanded the utmost concentration. The slightest error could cause a conflagration. Franziska was glad of the quiet after the clatter and roar of the trolley work and the idle chatter of the Poznan twins. There was something soothing about the deathly silence.

Another letter came from Hans. She did not open it. She hid it with the first one underneath the floorboards.

ON A BRIGHT May morning, billowy with cloud, Frau Wingender decided to spring-clean. She opened the window in Hans's room and threw the carpet over the sill to give it a good beating. Little flurries of powdery dust escaped into the blue buzzing air, making her sneeze. She was leaning out to retrieve the rug when she saw the figure of a woman halting at the entrance on the street below through a haze of flying fleck and spittle. From this angle all she could see was the woman's bare head and the rounded slope of her shoulders. She was carrying a shopping bag, too heavy for her, and it canted her over to one side as she parked her bicycle at the kerb below. Seeing Frau Wingender peering out, she shouted up.

'Frau Wingender?'

It was Frau Goldberg. Now what did she want, Frau Wingender thought irritably to herself, just when she was in the middle of housework. Frau Wingender waved and withdrew. Wiping her hands on her apron she made her way downstairs, leaving the room dancing with disturbed dust. She had no feeling of premonition. What everyone feared was the telegram boy. And by the time she had gained the courtyard she had convinced herself that Frau Goldberg was going to put more business her way.

'Frau Goldberg,' Frau Wingender said, smiling broadly. 'Come to send me another lodger! Another nice boy like Hans Fröhlich, I hope.'

Frau Goldberg's face suddenly crumpled. She dropped her provisions and buried her face in her hands.

'Frau Goldberg, what is it?'

'Oh, Frau Wingender,' she wailed, 'forgive me.'

'What is it?' Rosa Wingender felt the first pangs of alarm.

'It's Hans Fröhlich,' she said, 'I've had a letter from his mother. The poor boy is . . .'

'Dead?'

Frau Goldberg nodded miserably.

Trailing the feather duster behind her, she climbed the stairs and sat in the kitchen. Her manic energy for housekeeping had deserted her. She sat in a vague kind of stupor for almost an hour, at a loss as to what to do. She should really go to the factory. She could make it in time for the girls' lunch hour, get Franziska called to the gate, prepare her, somehow, for the bad news. The very fact of Frau Wingender turning up unannounced like that would be warning enough. Franziska would know immediately. But Rosa Wingender did not have the courage, despite opening a bottle of schnapps and downing two or three measures in quick succession. Better to leave the poor girl in ignorance; she would know soon enough. After several hours she went back into Hans's room; as if to convince herself he was really gone. She opened the wardrobe idly and found his overcoat. She felt tears well up at the thought of the young shoulders that would never fill it out again. Beside it was Franziska's dress, the one she'd had made by Fräulein Hackerl. The sight of their courting clothes made Rosa smart with recognition. Suddenly she knew. The girl was pregnant. That would explain the bickering with Doris and Louise, her strange, volatile moods. She lifted the dress out. It was only then she noticed that the dress had been ripped at the bodice and skirt, as if someone had taken a knife to it deliberately. For the second time in one day Frau Wingender was shocked.

'Is that you, Franziska?' she called out when she heard the footsteps of the girls on the stairs outside.

Franziska felt a sharp pang of dread. It was probably another letter. She could not bear another missive of despair which would have to be opened under the watchful gaze of the Wingenders. Louise, in particular, was weighing on her, pressing her unwanted tender counsel upon her, accompanied by an expression of doomed worry. She it was who had checked the casualty lists on Potsdamer Platz, seeking out Hans's name, until the authorities halted the practice; Franziska had superstitiously kept away. She did not want to see his name among the numbered thousands. The war did not own her or Hans; she would not let it. She ducked into her room.

'Franziska?' Frau Wingender's voice came from the kitchen. She was sitting at the table, tense with a day's waiting and the dread of being the bearer of such news.

Doris threw herself into a chair dejectedly. Louise, noting the bottle of schnapps on the table, put some water on to boil.

'She's got another letter, I suppose,' Doris complained. 'I should be so lucky. My Fritzie hasn't written once.'

Fritz Schnaller had at last won his place at the Front.

'Hush there, Doris,' Frau Wingender snapped, 'you have nothing to complain about. Think of poor Franziska.'

Her hand flew to her mouth and she hurriedly filled her glass again. Louise noticed the absence of the usual indulgent tone her mother employed with Doris.

'What do you mean, Mama?' Louise asked.

Rosa Wingender rose and left the kitchen. Louise made to follow her, but her mother shook her head and beckoned her to go back. The sisters, Louise frozen by the door, Doris sitting, suddenly alert, braced themselves. A few moments later they heard a sharp wail, like the strangled cry of a child. Louise rushed into Hans's room to find Franziska on her knees, her hand clutching the metal lip of the fireplace.

'Is it Hans?' she asked her mother, though she already knew.

'Drowned,' Franziska said.

'What?' Louise was convinced she had misheard. Doris brushed by her and hoisted the stricken Franziska up from the floor. She led her to the bed.

'Poor Hans,' Doris murmured over and over again. 'Poor, poor Hans.'

Franziska felt only a queer numbness and the oddest sensation in the pit of her stomach, dread giving way to relief. The awful tension of waiting was over. The Wingenders were only catching up with what she had known all along. Hans had been doomed. Not because of the war but because of her, Franziska Schanzkowksa; she had given him the kiss of death.

Frau Wingender hovered guiltily while her two girls ministered to Franziska, who sat pale and silent. Franziska read her distance as judgement.

'We were engaged, Frau Wingender,' she said defiantly.

Something in the girl's tone made Frau Wingender angry despite herself.

'Where's the ring then?'

Franziska did not reply.

'In your belly, that's where,' the landlady snapped. 'And the Fröhlichs won't want to hear from a girl like you.'

'Mama, please, not now,' Louise pleaded.

'Maybe, under the circumstances, they'd be glad to know they had a grandchild,' Doris offered.

'I doubt it very much,' Frau Wingender replied. 'A Polish brat?'

Franziska tried to imagine Hans's parents, but the picture of them which Hans had so lovingly painted was obliterated. They were Jews. She remembered what her father had said about Jews. 'Moneylenders, living off the back of us Poles, worse than the Germans. They stick to their own kind.' She could never have married Hans; it had all been a ruinous fantasy. There was no way now that she could escape from who she was. A stupid Polack, pregnant and alone.

She rose the next morning as usual. Her sleep, such as it was, had been tormented. Whenever she drifted into slumber the shadows seemed to come alive and she would wake with a start, imagining the wardrobe with its door ajar like an upstanding coffin. The empty grate seemed to roar silently. The carpet left draped over the sill was a dark wave about to inundate the room through the open window. Awake in the dewy dawn she heard faintly from above the rattle of Fräulein Hackerl's treadle machine and almost at the same time she could have sworn the child moved within her.

'Franziska, dear,' Frau Wingender said when she saw the girl, pale and hollow-eyed at the stove, 'you can't go to work, not today.'

Chastened by her drunken excess of the night before, she had reverted to extravagant mothering. 'Doris will explain to Herr Lindner, won't you, Dor?'

Doris edged round the table and placed a hand tentatively on Franziska's shoulder.

'I shall tell them that your fiancé . . .' She faltered. 'That you have lost your fiancé.' Overnight, Hans had gained a title, her fiancé.

'They always give compassionate leave in cases like this.'

Cases like this. She had been reduced to a case, a casualty of war.

'No, Frau Wingender, I must go to work. I want to go. What would I do here?'

'But, my dear, you've had a terrible shock,' Frau Wingender danced from foot to foot, wringing her hands in her soiled apron.

'I'm better off at work. It will take my mind off everything.'

'Are you sure, Franziska?' Louise circled round the other side of her. 'In your condition?'

A case with a condition.

She did not want their pawing sympathy. It made her feel wanly delicate like a shard of eggshell.

'Not a word,' she warned Louise as they entered the factory yard.

She did not want to hear whispers rippling behind her on the factory floor. Franziska has lost her fiancé. And is big with his child. Even her predicament was common.

'Late again, 670,' Herr Lindner barked as she hurried towards the Shifting House to the plangent mewl of the klaxon.

'Tell him,' Doris urged.

'You're on your last chance, do you hear?'

'But sir!' Doris objected.

'No buts, 459. We can't afford slackers here.'

Last chance. The words echoed in her head. The iron clangour of machinery took up the chorus like train wheels singing a distant, impossible destination. She undressed hurriedly and donned her gown and hat, gagging herself with her cloth mask as she passed through the partition to the clean side. She followed the snake of girls making their way down the corridor to the Danger Building.

'Hurry, hurry, girls,' she could hear the Lady Superintendent urge other latecomers, 'there's a war on, in case you hadn't noticed.'

The silence of the Danger Building was like a balm; here all was quiet, under control, the trestle tables with their trays of trotyl, the girls masked to hide their liverish-coloured skin, the roots of their hair gone ginger from the suffocating powder. Bea Bratzl was already at work at the head of the table, weighing out the powder on a pair of scales, while either side the girls were filling bags. Franziska made her way to the monkey machine, joining the girls hauling on the rope to bring down the beater. They took it in turns – once on the beater, once holding the shell case in place so the powder would be firmly packed, once as the monitor giving the signal for the beater to drop. All morning they worked, the numbing thud of the beater rising and falling. The only noise was the distant rumble of the machines, their fiery spit and whine, as they pounded and packed. Just before lunch, Herr Lindner appeared with his clipboard and prowled around the tables. He was checking up on her, Franziska was sure. He stood behind her, so close she could hear his habitual dispproving sniffle.

'Dawdling again, 670,' he said.

She turned hurriedly to Bea Bratzl and surreptitiously gave the signal for the beater to be lowered in the hope that she could escape further admonishment. But as she did something caught his eye – she would never know what – and as she stepped back and the beater was coming down, he leaned forward and she was blinded by the fiery dazzle of his spectacles. She saw his flinty face change, melting into terror, the fright of death, the awful banality of his flailing hands and the pink insides of his mouth and then the whole building shook, a ghastly fire-red roar and a ball of flame engulfed him. Something soft and bloody spattered her, a piece of his flesh, and then the blessed darkness came. Oblivion.

It was only a few moments of darkness but it changed everything. Franziska would often wonder what had happened in that lost trapdoor of time like a gaping hole in her eggshell universe. It was as if she had been born again in a fury of blood and fire. When she came to, it was to a choking spectral devastation as if colour had been drained from the world, the building reduced to a floury rubble, a charred smell in her nostrils, her lungs clogged with a gritty dust. In her ears the frantic breathy yelp of an alarm. She was on the ground, prone, her cheek crushed against a hand, not her own, the magnificently intact hand of a man, the only recognisable part of a bloodied, scorched mound beside her. When she tried to speak her lips burned. The faces of women peered over her, large and overblown, mouthing at her, but she could not make out what they were saying. Apart from the panicky shrill of the hooter everything else was silent.

One face swims into view, a young woman's, brown eyes, long hair in plaits swinging at her shoulders.

'Franziska, Franziska,' she is saying, 'are you all right? Can you hear me?'

She wants to drift away from this insistent voice speaking in code, calling this name, adrift and meaningless in the choking dust and charred flesh.

'It's Louise, can you hear me?' the girl keeps on saying, lightly tapping her on the cheek every time she closes her eyes to ease her burning lids. Her eyeballs are aflame.

'Sissy,' the voice says and the sky turns blue, a rectangle of cornflower blue, a bed of gold beneath her.

'Sissy,' the voice calls again. 'Sissy!'

A hand grasps hers. It feels cold on her searing skin. Then there is another rupture. She is lifted and swung like a turkey carcass onto a canvas hammock. A bumpy journey. Her nerve ends scream. She feels the rough brush of women's skirts against her cheeks. Mother! But when she looks up all she can see are the menacing gallows of blackened machines. A rush of cool air hits her crackled face. They are outside now, footsteps cracking on bulbous cobbles. Then she is hoisted into a dim metal capsule, an engine coughs and revs, and a terrible juddering starts as if they have placed her on an assembly line, a pale green egg in a sea of field-grey grenades. Then with the flick of a switch the movement stops, the engine throb subsides with a throaty growl. A cymbal clap, a pair of metal doors swing open and she hears the swift tattoo of footsteps again. The lazy clop of horse's hooves. Papa! They are travelling down a long corridor, light like the sick colour of parchment, an air of hushed urgency. They pass white ghosts with shoes that make no sound. On they run. She can hear the heavy breaths of her bearers, messengers with bad news, dodging the explosions, the angry spat of gunfire. And then, suddenly, the flurry ceases. She has reached the benediction of a white room. She returns to the easeful dark.

FOR WEEKS SHE drifted, pain her only clock. It ticked slowly, biding its time before rising to a booming crescendo on the hour. She would come to, the light a jagged mosaic. She was swaddled in white, a corset of pain at her waist and temples, her left foot strapped tightly, her hands paws of gauze. She tried to shield her eyes from the piercing sun-dazzle, but her arms were too heavy. Protest reared up in her throat. At first no sound would come, then only a breathy rasp. The first time she howled it startled her; she did not know where the sound had come from. She lay silent and tense in case the noise, her noise, would bring the building crashing down around her. Everything was imminent with danger. Edges hurt. The corner of the locker beside the bed was sharp as a bayonet blade; the fat bulb of a white enamel jug seemed to pulse. The curved end of the iron bedstead pressed against her imprisoned feet. White screens billowed around her. Mooned faces emerged from their folds with a whisper of starch and a tinny crash of metal. Disembodied hands tended her, pushing her gently back into the deep.

'You're a very lucky girl, Fräulein Schanzkowska.' Dr Spitzer stood with his arms folded, beaming broadly. 'Saved from the jaws of death.'

She closed her eyes. Conversation wearied her; she could feel the irresistible pull back into her white world of sleep.

'Now, now, Franziska,' a female voice admonished, accompanied by a light smack on her cheek. 'You must listen to Herr Doktor.'

Franziska opened her eyes to a nurse's fat lips almost brushing her cheek.

'But', the doctor went on from his lofty height, 'we could not save the baby.'

Baby? She played with the word. Baby.

'The explosion, you remember?'

The man was clearly mad, Franziska thought. She knew where her baby was. In the river, under the water. Where all lost babies were.

'Walter,' she whispered.

'Yes,' the nurse agreed sweetly. 'Walter.'

'It will all come back to you,' the doctor said, 'in time.'

He was right. Bit by bit she remembered and when she didn't the Wingenders were only too happy to furnish her with details. She had been taken to the Charity Hospital, along with four women from the Danger Building, all of whom had since been discharged. Herr Lindner had taken the full force of the blast. Franziska remembered his hand, his perfect, unbloodied hand. He had literally been blown to pieces. As bad as anything they had seen at the Front, Doris Wingender informed her cheerfully. She remembered the look on his face, as if he had seen right through to the murder in her heart. Another one killed by her careless hand.

'You must put all this behind you,' Louise said when she came to visit. 'Pick up the pieces.'

That was all that was left of her. Pieces. And scars. Wounds on her belly, a dozen or more. A shaved rectangle of hair around her ear where a piece of metal had lodged. A heady sensation of weakness – her legs could barely carry her – and the frightening delicacy of a new-born. I am lucky, she would tell herself, I have survived, mouthing the brisk comfort brandished by Frau Wingender.

'A miracle,' she declared, 'nothing less. I'm not religious, mind you, don't go to church, chapel or meeting, don't hold with it. But this,' she said, gazing beatifically at Franziska's wrapped and scarred body in the bed, 'this could almost convert me.' Franziska tried to imagine Frau Wingender throwing herself upon the mercy of a god. Perhaps her god would be different. Franziska's was a god of vengeance, who ruled in fire and blood.

Frau Wingender rattled on, her conversation peppered with gossip and hearsay. Fräulein Hackerl was on the breadline, she said, thread could not be got for love nor money. She was doing piecework for the army – gunlock covers and rusk satchels. As for coffee, she said, they'd laugh at you in the Kolonial Stores if you went looking for coffee. Frau Wingender wrinkled her nose. They were using potato filler in the bread. The Engeles downstairs had lost a son. Like Hans, she said, at Verdun. Those Englischer, she said, they chop off the heads of babies, did you know? Brutes, savages. Enough, Franziska thought. Enough. She longed for the timeless drift of the early days in the hospital, those hours of dreamless drowse, barely knowing who she was. How free she had felt. Knowing nobody. Owning no name. Like a pure spirit, all flight and air, swift as a cloud on a blue day.

June blossomed outside. Her first journey on her feet – a stiff-limbed shuffle leaning on a cane – brought her to the casement. She pushed open the window and looked down. She could smell jasmine and mock orange; the perfume seemed delicately pungent, a feminine assault on the furry, etherised smell of the ward. She peered out of the window gingerly and down below there was a garden, or rather a patch of green with a stone arcade ranged around it and a large apple tree in blossom in the centre. Patients from the male wing were pushed into the sun-trap in the afternoons or, if they were ambulant, they hobbled out to take the sun and to smoke. They were mostly soldiers, young men in half-hearted uniform – a civilian shirt with field-grey pants, sometimes only their hats remained like a cocky reminder. They hunched and lurched on their crutches like thwarted greyhounds, still in twos and foursomes as if they couldn't lose the habit of drilling. Amputated at knee or thigh, their trouser legs were pinned discreetly in a gruesome show of etiquette. Franziska wondered idly why – as if what wasn't there must be emphasised. There were shell-shock victims too, with their crazed gaits – some like slippery ice-skaters, others tilted as if battling against an unseen wind. She watched them from above inhaling the petal-laden air. But she did not want to be close to these young men with their hair curling around bandages, and the blunt violence of their lopped-off limbs. They might flirt with the nurses, but they would want to trade stories with her, a fellow casualty of the war. With the windows thrown open their conversation drifted upwards. Even from this distance she could smell defeat amidst the perfume. So she waited until the shadow of the male wing opposite had crept across the quadrangle, plunging it into a grainy shade, before she ventured down to walk alone in the cool cloister.

The gravity of her illness still hung about her. Because she had lain for weeks shrouded by screens the other patients kept their distance. The crone in the next bed with her pallid complexion and gnarled hands was suffering from tuberculosis, the nurses told her, but she drew up the sheet and turned away if Franziska came near, as if she might be infected with the germ of death. The hours lay heavy on her. Sick time moved more slowly, marked less by the passing of days than by her own unswaddling. Each week a new area was exposed. First her hands, emerging pale and shrivelled and covered in tiny gashes. Then the cummerbund of cotton round her waist, one layer at a time as if she were shedding an outer skin. Her belly and torso were riven with deep gashes, some of which had been stitched, others of which had joined of their own accord.

'You'll always bear the scars,' the surgeon told her. 'But you're lucky, you heal well.'

He pressed on the raw tram-track wounds. She winced.

'See how the skin has made a perfect seam,' he said admiringly of his own handiwork.'

Nobody mentioned the baby. And Franziska, staring at her ruined stomach, could not believe there had ever been one. Obliterated like the phantom limbs of soldiers, blown clean away. The bandage around her head was the last to go. She felt unblinkered without it, as if only now her mind was free to roam. Images of the blast assailed her unbidden, the deafening roar, the crushing weight of masonry, followed by the sickening silence. Herr Lindner reared up, face agape, the tiny splintering of his spectacles as he fell. She did not want to think of him. He had left a wife and three children, Doris had told her. She covered her mouth with her hand, remembering how he had insisted on examining her teeth. She tried to steer her thoughts towards the future. Where would she go? What would she do?

The Wingenders came to the rescue.

'You'll convalesce with us,' Frau Wingender announced grandly. She was desperate to make up to Franziska, but Franziska knew that she could not afford an extra mouth to feed. The factory would not take her back, and anyway she would not want to return to the scene of her crime. 'Once we have you home, you'll be right as rain in no time!'

Frau Wingender beamed at Dr Spitzer, and pushed Doris forward.

'This is my daughter, by the way!'

Whereas the hospital had been light and airy, the apartment was sunk into a deeper gloom than when she had left. The war had taken hold of it and laid it bare. Frau Wingender had taken the mirror over the mantel in the girls' room to the pawnbroker's on Rosenthaler Straße and the foxed landscape in the lodger's room (tactfully the Wingenders stopped calling it Hans's room) had been removed from its frame so the wood could be fed into the kitchen stove. The tapestry screen had disappeared and there were bare boards where the carpet had been. There seemed hardly a trace of the life she had so recently lived here. Certainly no trace of Hans could be found. When she looked in the wardrobe, his overcoat had gone: Frau Wingender, in her last act of patriotism, had handed it in in one of the cloth collection drives. But she had left Franziska's dress, as mutilated as she was herself, a red velvet folly belonging to some dreamed-up life that had barely existed.

Franziska settled into the mournful remains of her old room. She handed over her invalid's welfare to Frau Wingender in its entirety. It was barely enough to cover the rent, let alone food, but Frau Wingender was glad of any income. In Franziska's absence rationing had taken hold. There was no more talk about victory; now all conversation revolved around the daily battle with coupons, the new currency. Eggs were down to two a month, a pound of potatoes daily, a half-pound of meat a week. Sugar was as rare as gold. Even their light was rationed. Curfew at eleven; the gas cut off at nine.

Franziska would go shopping with Frau Wingender. It gave her something to do in the long days when Doris and Louise were at work. It was as good as a full-time occupation. Queuing at the butcher's stall could take as long as three hours. Franziska shuffled upwards in the line praying that the 'Sold Out' sign would not go up before it was her turn. Standing pained her; the wound in her foot ached, her head throbbed, but though she longed to sit down she could not afford to lose her place in the line. Then it was on to the bakery to haggle for loaves. Even the food they did manage to get was not what it appeared to be. Strange impostor ingredients found their way into everything. Coffee was now roast barley with not even a whisper of cocoa powder; there was sawdust in the bread. An egg substitute appeared made of dyed potato starch. Buying clothes was out of the question without a purchase permit. Women were allowed only three dresses, two for work and one for Sundays. Franziska spent a whole day at the cobbler's with a pair of Doris's shoes worn right through. The shoemaker attached a pair of wooden soles to them; they crippled her, Doris said, but at least they didn't leak. No one talked any more about the war being over; they worried instead about the next cut in rations.

Winter came early that year and the Wingenders huddled in the apartment like cave-dwellers in a primitive dark, wearing their outdoor clothes and their leaky shoes, their stomachs acidy with hunger. They had entered War Time.

WAR TIME WAS hungrier than hospital time; it devoured weeks of tedious occupation, the daily diet of bleak queue and bare larder. It induced a numbed torpor, standing in the shuffling crowd on the pavement outside the bakery on Ottostraße, while snow fell in downy flakes. She could forget herself as the line inched slowly along the dreary, ill-lit street towards the mouth of the bakery. She could forget everything. The other women in the queue jostled and pushed as they neared the wicker baskets piled high with flat, black loaves. At first she would get infected by their urgency, but she was afraid since the accident that sharp elbows and the heaving of crowds might reopen her wounds. When a big push came, usually induced by a panicky rumour at the back that supplies were running out, she would stand aside, often losing her place. A kind of dull-witted indifference overtook her. What did it matter if she got her bread two minutes before the next woman in line? The only reason she stuck with it was that she could not go back to the Wingenders empty-handed.

It did not escape Frau Wingender's notice that when Franziska queued for bread it took her twice as long as when she sent one of her girls, or went herself.

'You must fight your corner,' she admonished Franziska, 'it's our bread, we're entitled.'

Frau Wingender was beginning to regret having taken Franziska back. The girl had not been right since that explosion. She would come across her in the kitchen, in the

183

middle of washing up, elbows sunk in the greasy cold water, staring off into the distance in a kind of vacant trance, as if she had forgotten where she was. She would not hear Frau Wingender approach and yet the smallest noise – the scrape of a teaspoon in a cup, the clank of a pail in the courtyard below – produced a kind of startled panic as if in her ears it had been magnified to a terrifyng boom. She complained of headaches, cradling her skull in her hands, her fingertips vainly trying to quell the noises within.

Doris and Louise found her strangely withdrawn. Even Louise conceded that whereas before she had been secretive and odd, now she was acting as if she was not all there.

'As if', Louise said, 'she was lost in time.'

She was. Everything seemed veiled and distant to her, as if the explosion had impaired her hearing and encased her behind glass. It was an underwater sensation, everything muffled, and then suddenly a crash of plates or the far-off wail of a siren would explode furiously. Her body was busily betraying her. It gave off the pretence of healing. New skin was growing on her hands, forming a spidery skein over the red raw parts of her, but it was less robust than her birth skin. It felt as fine as bone china. The tattoo of fish-bone scars, the shrapnel wound behind her ear, the star-shaped mark on her foot had all closed over, just as Dr Spitzer had predicted, but she felt they had enclosed a poison within, a festering, vaguely menacing lethargy, while her head boomed and echoed. She found it harder and harder to drag herself out to the market. And when she did, she found she couldn't get her mind around the trade of coupons and papers. Once she presented her ration card for soap – one bar of fat-free per household – at the butter store and the Wingenders went without lard for a week.

'You imbecile!' Frau Wingender shrieked when she returned home.

'I was the cleverest of all the Schanzkowskis,' she roared back, but it was a hollow claim. Now memorising a simple list of provisions was too much for her.

She had shouted to hear herself above the din inside her head. But Frau Wingender, taken aback by the violence of her outburst, took to keeping a strict eye on her. She noticed other strange habits. How the girl's face would become animated and she would move her lips as if engaged in some heightened internal conversation; sometimes she would raise a finger as if lecturing to a small child, but no sound came out. She hid her mouth constantly behind her hand – a shy habit Doris and Louise used to tease her about – but which now, in the light of her other strangenesses, took on a furtive air. Frau Wingender stopped asking Franziska to do errands; she couldn't afford any more short-changing on the potato allowance. Shortly it was not to matter anyway. By February 1917, there were no more potatoes.

The potato harvest failed and the Swedish turnip, originally introduced to fill out the potato ration, became their staple diet. Not only did it replace potatoes but it found its way into the bread, even marmalade, so they said, though it was a long time since a pot of preserves had found its way onto the Wingender table. At least, Frau Wingender reasoned, the turnips were genuine and not some cobbled-up vegetable made from starch and dye. She baked and boiled them, she made soup out of them, which she served the girls for breakfast instead of coffee, she concocted a casserole, a glutinous mix of beef bouillon cubes, potato scraps and – turnips. At a certain level of deprivation Frau Wingender came into her own. The lack of beer helped. The breweries in Berlin had closed down and even on the black market she could not have afforded a bottle of spirits. Sobriety made her capable but, unfortunately for Franziska, less tolerant.

*

Afterwards, Frau Wingender blamed the turnips for Franziska's first bout in the asylum in Neuruppin. She came home from the market one afternoon in April. A watery sky hung over the city and Frau Wingender felt washed out, as much by the sullen weather as by the news she had heard at the market.

'Guess what,' she hollered as she set down a loaf on the table. Franziska was in her room, moping as usual, and Frau Wingender often conducted conversations with her between rooms in the apartment.

There was no reply.

'Franziska?' she called again, doubtfully.

She tiptoed out into the hall and pushed the half-open door with her hand. The girl was standing by the mantel, dressed in her wounded red dress, scored by knife marks. She looked almost gay in a ghoulish sort of way with her pale face and her ruined hands.

'America has entered the war,' Frau Wingender said redundantly.

Franziska started to smile, then hurriedly covered her mouth with her hand.

'Don't I look nice?' she asked. 'Fräulein Hackerl made it for me.' She twirled around and the crushed fabric briefly flared at her heels.

'Oh yes, my dear, you're a real princess,' Frau Wingender replied mockingly. 'Now, any chance you would lend me a hand with the dinner?'

'What are we having?' Franziska asked in an imperious tone, as if she were the woman of the house and Frau Wingender a domestic. The cheek of her, Frau Wingender thought. Then she softened. The girl obviously had no idea how preposterous she looked, dressed up like Lady Muck in the middle of the day, in a dress as maimed-looking as herself.

'Turnips,' she said brightly, hoping to puncture the air of caged madness coming off Franziska. 'For a change!'

She followed Frau Wingender into the scullery. She donned an apron and turned the turnips out onto the chopping board. Then she fetched the carving knife from the sink. Standing there in her rich, torn velveteen, knife in hand, her hair falling in distressed trails around her face, she looked vaguely menacing. Frau Wingender was suddenly afraid. Hesitantly she turned her back and busied herself at the stove.

Franziska started to slice through the stringy white turnips. There were still traces of clay on their whiskery skins. She attacked them viciously, stabbing at their hard hearts, cursing them under her breath. For her they were not just meagre war rations, they were the clogged earth of home, sodden and stale and poor. She had gone right back to the beginning. She halted in mid-slice, swept the pieces into the hollow of her apron and going to the window she threw them out, turnips and peelings; even the knife leaped in a silvery tizzy. Below it rained turnips; by the time Frau Wingender had rushed downstairs and into the yard there were already three or four ragged-looking children scrabbling for the pieces. She was lucky to retrieve the knife. She decided it was time to send word to the asylum.

Neuruppin Asylum had none of the white order of the Charity Hospital. It was as loud as the factory, except here the noises were human, not industrial, outside and not inside her head. High, piercing shrieks, the low moans of the mad. Franziska was wearing the red dress when she was frogmarched into the hospital between two orderlies in white coats, who had collected her from the Wingenders. She had not protested; she was glad of the movement, a trip in a motor. Doris and Louise waved from the windows above as she was taken away, as if she were going on a jaunt to the Wannsee. Frau Wingender planted a moist kiss on her cheek.

'It's for your own good, my dear,' she whispered.

Franziska looked forward to the destination. Sea air, the flap of bunting, the lap of water. When she found herself alone in a soft, silent cell, wearing a striped uniform of rough ticking and her hands strangely straddled behind her back, she was not alarmed. Through the high, barred window she could see a scudding blue sky, a budding branch. A nurse brought her meals on a tray and fed them to her as if she were a delicate baby. Spoon by spoon. And it was real food. Some potato, even a little meat, one morning a beheaded boiled egg. She had not had an egg in months; the gelid yolk, the slippery white tasted like nectar. Indeed, Frau Wingender was right; it was doing her good. She felt a great calm descend, the hours passing in blameless idleness, sitting trussed in her bandaged room. Everything inside her was dead and laid to rest. She did not speak since there was no one to speak to. No one addressed her by her name. She found it soothing, this mute kingdom in which she ruled. Memories started to sink; she had difficulty sometimes remembering that there had been a life before – the apartment, the factory, even Hans seemed like some fevered manifestation of her own lonely yearning. Weeks went by. Asylum time was deceptively elongated, it did not gag and halt as ordinary time did, it was steady and pensive, sacred as an empty church. One morning – at least she thought it was morning judging by the brave light flooding the cell – two stout nurses entered her lair and cornered her. Gingerly they approached, making hushing sounds as if she were an unbroken horse in a narrow stall. They removed the strange harness they had put her in and backed away fearfully when she was liberated, as if she might bray and whinny at them. Some days later a doctor came. She saw him spy through the barred porthole in the door before entering. As he stepped inside, a flood of noise accompanied him, the metallic clangour of other doors locking shut, the rowdy babble of the wards. He stood at a distance, a foxy-haired man with a grey-flecked beard, which he stroked pensively with his eyes downcast. He began to pace up and down as if he too were confined, while she sat on the low, hard cot and counted his footsteps. He was a burly man, but graceful with it, and his stride was generous so he covered the distance from wall to wall in four steps, whereas it took her seven. That was how she had kept time. Finally he cleared his throat.

'Fräulein Wingender,' he started.

For a minute, baffled, she looked around wondering if somehow Doris or Louise had slipped into the room behind him, but there was no sign of either of the Wingender girls. Had time suddenly speeded up? Was she already released from her feathered nest and back again in the apartment on Beulestraße? She made to speak, but he raised his hand like a policeman.

'Since your mother committed you, we feel you have made much progress. We believe, further, that you are no longer a danger to yourself, or others, as you were when you came to us.'

He paused and she tried to voice her protest again, to tell him who she really was, but he raised his monitor's hand. She wondered how the confusion had started and why this man thought Frau Wingender was her mother.

'We find', he said, sighing grandly, 'that the rest cure is the best thing for war strain.'

'I am not Fräulein Wingender,' Franziska said loudly before he could proceed. 'There's been some mistake . . .'

'Now, Fräulein, let's not ruin our chances of recuperation by any silly talk,' the doctor countered swiftly. 'We have enough people in here who have notions about who they are. Besides, your mother is to come tomorrow to sign your release papers. We don't want to have to send her away disappointed, now do we?'

Franziska shook her head silently. What did it matter who she was, or who he thought she was. And Frau Wingender was as close to a mother as she had now, she who had once had two. So she buttoned her lip and smiled sweetly.

'That's more like it,' the doctor said, offering his own oily beam. 'Silence pays in here.'

She was to return to Neuruppin twice that year, and once in early 1918 to the asylum at Schöneberg. Each time Frau Wingender signed her in as her daughter – it was the only way she could have her committed. They were short stays and always followed the same pattern. The drumming ache in her head would become a dull roar. The tinselly shiver of tissue paper or the distant barking of a shut-up dog would set up a throbbing in the wound behind her ear. In her feet she could feel the painful thrum of the trams rumbling in the darkened streets down below. Her limbs were like a barometer, predicting the stealthy change in her interior climate. Then the nightmares would start. Fire and water. A river where the bodies of the dead might rise up to the surface at any moment. She would stare into the water and find not her own reflection but a child's staring up at her. Damp curls and baby teeth. Or she would be lying in a trench where soldiers scrambled trying to get a foothold as the mud walls slithered and seeped with blood. Then a blinding flash and always fire . . .

Returning to the Wingenders was like going back to the Front.

'Imagine, the tsar of Russia has fallen!' Doris informed her triumphantly after her first time in Neuruppin. 'His captors have him chopping wood.'

Fritz was home, invalided out, which helped Doris's good humour.

'I feel sorry for the tsar,' Louise said, 'bad enough that we have to go without. We're used to it. But royalty are different.'

'It's good news for Germany, Fritz says,' Doris said. 'At least we're not fighting on two Fronts.'

The second time she was admitted there was the great workers' strike. Doris and Louise had joined thousands of workers who had dropped tools and marched on the Alexanderplatz.

'Oh Franziska, you should have seen it,' Louise said, eyes shining. 'So many people all together. Until the police moved in. I nearly got struck by a baton myself.'

The third time Franziska was released, she came home to defeat.

THE CITY AWOKE, alive suddenly with dislocated wraiths – soldiers, stragglers, beggars, the unemployed. They emerged as if out of the dark underground, stumbling dazed onto the streets, idle and hungry. There had been a revolution, the kaiser driven out, but apart from bands of soldiers wearing red armbands who roamed raggedly about bragging triumphantly and the daily snowstorm of flyers falling from the roaring wings of planes overhead, Franziska saw little sign of it. For her and the Wingenders there was only defeat. It hung over the city like a smothering cloud. It even had a taste, sour and metallic like blood in the teeth. The streets were full with crowds venting their anger with old war cries, as if the thirst for blood had entered their veins. Protest was their only work. Doris and Louise had been laid off. The smoke-stacks and warehouses around Moabit lay idle, the stores opened but with as little to sell as before – rotten cabbage, handfuls of pocked potatoes, stringy bread.

In the spring Franziska found a job in the fields, sowing turnips. It was an hour's walk from where the train set her down to get there, followed by a day of back-breaking labour. All that year she slaved, bent over double in the ragged fields, despising the work, though she was glad of the couple of marks it yielded. She would pick bunches of wild chives or radishes and chew on them as she worked, their sour taste as pungent as the defeat all around her. They left green stains on her teeth, which rattled loosely in her head. She was permanently hungry, something which her illness had up to this protected her from. This sudden return of appetite tormented her. She fantasised about meat, memorising the succulent pork of her childhood, the pulpy texture of it, soft and yielding, and particularly the crescent of translucent fat on each cut, oozing with bloody juices. She ate again the sweet cherry windfalls from the orchards of home. She dreamed of eggs or the pith of oranges. She looked a sight, her teeth rotting, her hair wild. She no longer recognised herself when she looked in the mirror. At the end of May the putrid body of Rosa Luxemburg was fished out of the Landwehr Canal, her skull smashed. Franziska heard talk of it in the charity kitchen where she ate in the evenings. This really was the end of the revolution, they said. Franziska wondered what they meant. How could the corpse of a dead woman make any difference to history, which marched on regardless?

She toiled through the long, hot summer, seeing nothing beyond the end of the drill she was working on, the end of the day, the stain of sunset in the sky. Her strength returned, she had grown a new skin, but she felt she had sunk as low as she could get.

The year turned. It was mid-February. A dusting of light snow settled on her shoulders as she trudged home. It was bitterly cold. She wrapped the worn remains of the Poznan coat around her as she made her way to the small country station. Ahead of her, hooded figures hurried along the rutted track towards the distant lights of the city. She hurried after them, if only to keep warm. They travelled in a cold carriage. The lights in the train worked only intermittently and when they did they cast a blue sickly light on the pale faces and frostbitten hands of the passengers. As they reached the outskirts of the city,

Franziska remembered her arrival in Berlin five years previously. She longed to be back there, caught in that moment of anticipation, instead of here stranded in an exhausted aftermath.

She wished she was going home to the Wingenders, where at least there would have been warmth and food, but she had left her lodgings on Beulestraße in the summer of 1919. She had told Frau Wingender she was going home. She had a home to go to after all. Now there was a republic of Poland, not just the dreamy empire of her father's drunken sentiment. The Wingenders were happy for her. Doris helped her pack, what little there was – two suits of clothes, the matryoska doll, the tarnished Dulski pendulum – into her battered suitcase, which had survived the war in a nest of cobwebs under the Wingender sisters' bed.

'What a shame you're leaving,' Doris said sadly, 'just when things are improving.'

Things were improving for Doris. Fritz had secured a job in a printer's shop in the days following the Armistice. It was an unskilled job, feeding the furnace and dragging bales of paper around, but the shop had the job of printing travellers' coupon cards and when one batch was ordered to be destroyed Fritz simply pocketed them and made a killing selling them off at exorbitant prices. The Wingenders shared in his ill-gotten gains. And Franziska too – she gladly devoured the extra bread rations, the eggs, even a chicken or two. But when she looked at the Wingenders she saw a family unscathed. They had lost nobody, whereas she had been robbed of everything. It was easy for them simply to put their lives back together again. Franziska had no old life to put back together. For the first time in years, she thought of Borowy Las and her heart softened at the thought of it.

Frau Wingender packed her a lunch for the journey – a bread roll, some *wurst*, a hardboiled egg. She embraced Franziska on the threshold. Franziska inhaled her beery smell for the last time.

'There will always be a home for you here,' she said tearfully.

But as she watched Franziska make her way down the stairs and out into the street, she hoped fervently that this was the last time she would see the girl. She had brought madness into the Wingender home. She was a too concrete reminder of the war and Frau Wingender, with the help of Fritz's black-market trade in forged coupons, was determinedly on her way back up.

Louise had accompanied her to the station. They said goodbye at the entrance on Franziska's insistence.

'You're going to a better place,' Louise said bravely, 'you should be with your family, your real family.'

Franziska nodded dumbly.

'Write, won't you?' Louise pleaded.

She turned away and entered the dark cavern of the station. She wandered among the echoing halls and the belching smoke, mingling with her own kind – refugees with dishevelled luggage, Russians and Poles. A babble of languages streamed past her. She walked as far as the platform serving trains to Stettin and the east. And then she turned around abruptly. She could not go back. That would be one defeat too many. She made her way towards the station's back entrance and slipped out onto a dark, dim side street. She loitered there for several minutes with the pretence of a woman anxiously awaiting her sweetheart. Then she made her way back through the throng towards the main entrance, making sure that there was no sign of Louise before she stepped out into the rain-soaked square. Time slipped away. She was in a late summer's evening in 1914. She was arriving in Berlin for the first time. There would be no one to meet her. Nobody knew her name. She was free at last.

This time she found lodgings in a hostel on Füsilierstraße, above a bakery. The dormitories were full so she was given a tiny cupboard of a room on the turn of the stairs, which had been used as a store for flour when there had been plentiful supplies. A coating of white dust lay everywhere. There was a hard bed and a chair; the door opened out because there wouldn't have been enough room for it to open in. It had no window, just a rusted skylight. During the night, the yeasty heat from the bakery oven rose upwards making it toasty and warm, but by day it was like an icebox. Days would go by when Franziska would not speak to a living soul. She rose at dawn and made her way to the train station, rattled to her destination in the country, walked to the farm, where she fed pigs and milked cows, then returned to her caged box. In the evenings she would go to the charity kitchen on Linienstraße. There was a certain bleak freedom about it, this absolute reduction of her circumstances.

She alighted at the Anhalter Bahnhof and drawing her coat about her she hurried out of the station. Usually she walked to Friedrichstraße and took a tram. She liked to peer out at the vulgar nightlife of the street, the red glow of restaurants and neon-lit clubs, the Wintergarten and the Metropol theatres, and feel the dangerous pulse of the U-Bahn underfoot. But on an impulse she turned left, away from Friedrichstraße, and towards the canal. Cold as it was, she could not face the stifling confinement of her little room. It was dark and another half-hearted snow shower was flailing about her. She felt drawn to the water, its unflurried depths indifferent as time itself. She paused on the bank and watched the silvery surface, speckled with florets of snow. She was about to move on when she became aware of someone standing close to her. She looked up and saw a young man. A pair of hollow eyes regarding her intently, his shadowy face buried in the upturned collar of an army greatcoat and the shade of a forage cap. He was stooped slightly, his hands thrust into his pockets, and beneath his coat she could see a ragbag of civilian clothes, a grubby collarless shirt, the worn and patched serge of trousers, a scuffed and thirsting pair of boots. He smiled at her unexpectedly. People did not smile at one another much these days; it cost too much – a demand of some kind, or the offer of some trinket or illicit food which could not be afforded. She turned away and began walking. He started to follow her. She quickened her step but she could still hear his slow, dogged pursuit. She stopped suddenly and wheeled around. He halted too.

'What do you want?' she demanded.

'What do you think?' he said.

'Why are you following me?'

'It's a free country, isn't it?' He laughed grimly. 'Or so they tell us.' He moved closer to her. He smelt of rotting leaves, the ferment of autumn, some stale dark place. She took a step backwards.

'Don't come near, do you hear?' she said. 'Or I'll scream.'

'I have money,' he said quietly and fished from his pocket a wad of notes. 'Look! I can pay.'

'I don't want your money,' she said. 'What do you take me for?'

He moved closer again, but this time she stood rooted to the spot, mesmerised by the cash and horrified by her own fascination. She had never seen so much money.

She wanted to reach out and touch the notes.

'How much would you pay me?'

He threw several notes on the ground. She scurried to pick them up before they blew away. She was on all fours on the pavement like a dog sniffing for scraps. He bent down and helped her up, as she clutched the money in her hand.

'Your place then,' he breathed.

'No, no,' she said, panicking.

He bore her across the street, away from the water, her arm bruising beneath his wiry grasp. They walked grimly together for several minutes before he steered her down a side street. It sloped downwards gently. The branches of the bare trees arched overhead, bearing smudged petals of snow. The street was lined with apartment buildings, their wide entrances, sheltered from the snow shower, littered with the crackling leaf-fall of autumn, scurrying to and fro.

'Here then,' he said, thrusting her into one of their dark doorways.

He grappled with her coat, pushing it roughly off her shoulders. It fell heavily around their ankles. His unshaven face crushed against hers as he sunk his cold hand beneath her skirt, scrabbling for the feel of flesh. Up close his mulchy smell intoxicated her as she clung to him. Some primal memory of desire stirred. She shut her eyes, trying to hold onto it and to shut out the vision of his devouring stranger's face. His mouth tasted of sweet tobacco. As he entered her she thought of the money crushed in her hand. She clenched her teeth as he came, bellowing, his head thrown back as if he had been grievously wounded. Then he slumped against her, his head on her shoulder, as heavy as a corpse.

'What is your name, Fräulein?' he whispered in her ear.

'Sissy,' she said.

'Mine is Alexander. Alexander Tchaikovsky.'

Alexander Tchaikovsky told her the story of his life. There in a doorway in Berlin, leaf-crackle and spilt semen at their feet, crushed up against her, so close that afterwards she would not have been able to say what he looked like. He spoke hoarsely in her ear like a man possessed. He and his family had fled Russia after the revolution – his mother, his sister Veronica, his brother Sergei, and his wife.

'Wife?' she repeated, but he took no notice and went on with his urgent story. They had reached Rumania, hiding by day, travelling by night. They had hoped for refuge in Bucharest, but it was chaotic there and work was almost impossible to find. Then there was a further calamity. Sergei had been killed in a street fight.

'Rumanians', he said, 'are quick with the knife.'

His wife gave birth in the winter of 1918. A son, Alexis.

'A little tsarevich of our own,' he murmured.

His story tumbled out, more frantic than their copulation had been, as if this was what he had paid her for. He had left his wife and baby behind and travelled to Berlin in the hope that if he got work he could send for them. But he was like all penniless refugees. Nowhere to live, no skills but soldiering, no country to go back to. And no papers.

'I had one thing of value, though,' he said bitterly, pulling away from her. It was the first time he had met her gaze. 'A pearl and diamond necklace belonging to the Grand Duchess Anastasia. Some old emigré paid me a fortune for it.'

'And how did you come by that?' Franziska asked.

'Never you mind!' he said roughly.

He hitched up his trousers, buttoned his coat, and stumbled away into the white-flecked night. She settled her clothes, pulling her shawl around her, and felt in her pocket for the money he had given her. It was safe. How easy it had been. Then, with a sharp pang, she thought of Hans, and a hot wave of shame washed over her. Her fine young man, her dead boy soldier. She hurried out onto the street and made her way back to the canal, hoping that the sound of her boots on the cobbles and the searing cold would drive all thought of Hans away. On reaching the bank, she made for the bridge, intent on getting back to Füsilierstraße as quickly as possible. She was shivering and realised that she had left the Poznan coat where it had fallen. But she couldn't go back. She checked again on the money stashed in her pocket. She paused at the apex of the bridge and withdrew the crumpled notes. One by one she threw them into the water, watching them sink like the watery drifts of snow. She stared down at the dark waters. In the summer children swam here. Skinny urchins yelling to one another as they plunged in, calling out names ... *Walter, Walter!*

She started. Who was calling? But it was herself, her own voice howling into the wind. She felt his presence close to her. She peered again into the canal and there, there he was, the bright curls, the chubby face, the baby's smile. She climbed up on the parapet to get a better view. No, no, there was no mistake. He was there.

'Walter,' she called. 'Wait!'

Here he was, after all these years, not gone at all, but here, waiting to save her.

'Baby,' she sobbed.

It was then that she jumped.

Letting go is like breathy flight, an astonishment of air. In her mind's eye she is a hollow painted doll, tossed carelessly by an unseen hand, undone with each revolution, her outer shell unravelling to reveal a small, then smaller, version of herself until she is no more than a tiny wooden egg. Then the stormy mastery of gravity takes over, the greedy suck of earth. She falls; an overwhelming descent, turbulent and graceless. She cannot draw breath, it flies fleet-footed past her as she tumbles, buffeted and smacked by the stuff of her skirts, which flail around her, smothering her vision. They turn to sodden stone as she breaks the surface of the water. The shocking chill of it makes her gag. Her heart feels as if it will burst through its cage of bone. It is a white moment, flecked by sleet and icy spray and the clenched pain of her entry. White turns to a cloudy green. She is plunged into a murky underworld, billowing sails that were her clothes, her hands like dead white fish. Sprigs of bubbles whisper at her cheek. Down she sinks, her lungs filled to bursting, her limbs straining to ascend as her skirts puff and wave and her hair streams around her like trails of wayward seaweed. Down, down ... water gurgles in her ears. She can hear a heartbeat, loud and booming; she is

nothing now but water and air. It is over ... she has
entered history.

Borowy Las, 1900

'SISSY?'

Her mother's voice, harried and querulous, arches across
the golden stubble. She peers through the loft opening of
the barn and sees her mother far below. Dour-skirted,
hands wringing hessian, stray hair weeping from the
kerchief bound around her head, she stands in the rutted
yard outside the house huddled under its sagging thatch.
Sissy dips down, sinking into the springy bed of fresh-
mown hay. The stalks tickle her cheeks; she inhales their
dry, grassy fumes and gazes at the airy doorway of
porcelain blue. She drinks in the vast and cloudless sky,
intoxicated by its blue sheerness.

'Sissy,' Mother calls again half-heartedly, before turning
back towards the cowering house.

In her blue and gold shell Sissy sings absent-mindedly to
herself – Valerian, Gertruda, Maria Juliana and Felix. Her
brothers and sisters. Valerian is the eldest and almost a man
already, then come Gertie, Maria and Felix. Her own name
is Franziska, diluted by her brother Felix, whose lisping
first attempts at speech produced this double sibilance of
sound. Sissy. Strung together their names form an incanta-
tion which lulls and mesmerises her. She repeats them
because they are magical. They will keep evil away. She
is three years old. It is the first full, fat year of the

new century. A translucent teardrop of time. It is the life before Walter.

Gazing through her portal of blue, she is in the inside world. There are two worlds – the inside and the outside – but so far she only knows the first. The world of house and yard and stable. The leering pigs and screeching chickens, the silly heedless geese. Deep mystery of orchard, white lilac and bird-cherry, knee-high florets of cow-parsley and wizened trunks like Grandfather's bunions. The sanctuary of bowl and wood that is the kitchen, warm and dark and hidden like her own heart. Rough comfort of a pillow, her head between the forked limbs of sisters. The outside world is field and river, town and market, far-flung, wide open.

Her father stands swaying by the stove. He has been out in the village drinking. The work, bent double in the dusty, dry meadows, gives him a thirst which must be slaked. The warm stench of labour and drink rises off him as he blunders around the dim kitchen. Her mother steers him to the table. The lamp's glow leaves a halo on the pine. Sissy watches him in the oily light, his rough hands crouched by the tin plate. His head is bowed, his chin resting on his broad chest. He laughs quietly to himself, a ruminative chuckle.

'Papa,' she whispers.

He looks up and smiles, a leathery face cracked open by the breadth of his beam.

'Princess!'

'Sissy!' Her mother appears from the scullery and without looking up barks, 'Bed!'

She bears a bowl of broth and a loaf of black bread to the table.

'Princess,' he says and blows her a kiss. He waves a hand perfunctorily, then runs it through his dark hair. Steam rises from the bowl. He tears a piece of bread from the loaf and eats hungrily. Her mother circles around the table, eclipsing Sissy's view. Her hands are sunk into the small of her back.

Papa chomps mutely, then noisily slurps his broth. He wipes the wet ends of his moustache with his sleeve.

'Princess, indeed,' her mother says. 'Don't fill the child up with notions.'

There is a crash as Papa drops the ladle and thumps the table with his fist.

'Notions? If she has airs and graces it's not from me she gets them,' he shouts. 'I will call her what I like and I won't have you gainsaying me!'

Mother retreats to the scullery.

'Isn't that right, Princess?' he whispers to her.

Papa! Later as he dozes by the stove she perches gingerly on the arm of his chair. She loves to be this close to him without him even knowing. Secretly she traces the crevices of his weather-beaten face with her fingers. She knows the sharp gristle of his eyebrows and the vertical line that divides them so deeply that she can fit her little finger in the cleft. She knows the flare of his nostrils and the nest of hair which emanates from their dark caves. She touches the speckled bush of his moustache and the sickle marks of his rare smile. His ears are large and cavernous. Here there is more hair. So much that Sissy thinks that inside her father there is only undergrowth, a mottled tangle that sprouts from his ears and nose and creeps up his chest. There are even tufts of it on his lower knuckles. She follows his hair line down to the promontory of his widow's peak. The skin there is softer, shiny as a polished egg. Time has ploughed across his brow, leaving furrows deep as potato drills. She travels down the sharp line of his nose, leaping from its tip to his wet open lips. She taps lightly on his teeth, then fingers the bristled sureness of his chin. Next his craggy neck, lined like a tree trunk. She thinks she can

guess his age by counting the rings. Now she is journeying
blindly in the stretched tendons of his jaw until she strikes
the knotted hardness of his Adam's apple. She presses
softly on it and it moves like the stone of a plum in a pickle
jar. His eyes snap open, a bleary, flecked-brown gaze. His
arm flails and sends her flying.

'Get this child off me!' he roars.

He looms over her as she picks herself up, rubbing a
bruised elbow.

'Princess,' he breathes. He cups a large hand around her
head. 'Look at you, straw in your hair. What have you
been doing? Rolling in the hay?'

He parts her hair with his hands and picks through the
strands, plucking pale papery stalks from her dark, night-
damp curls. Papa loves her hair, though Mother, washing it
bad-temperedly, says it is a curse. It is Papa who takes the
comb to it, patiently undoing all the tangled clots and the
matted pockets of resistance until he has completely tamed
it.

When she is five, Papa takes her to the market. It is half a
day's journey by cart. It is the first time Sissy has been
beyond Borowy Las. She and Maria sit in the back,
swinging their legs over the edge. Felix sits up front with
Papa. It has rained. The wheels of the cart groan as they
rumble into pooled craters in the road, spattering her
boots. She squeals and Papa gives her a dark look. Maria
puts a finger to her lips. She is six years older than Sissy.
The first time she made this journey with Papa she had
squabbled with Felix, and Papa had warned her he would
set her down at the next gate. When the bickering
continued, he halted the horse and lifted her down off the
cart and left her at the side of the road.

'Why not Felix?' she had wailed.

'Because I need Felix.'

Maria waited all day for him to return. Papa found her sleeping in the ditch at midnight.

Dawn streaks the frowning low sky. Sissy's stomach rumbles with hunger. There has only been time to gulp down a beaker of warm milk which Gertie prepared before they left. Gertie has stayed behind to look after Mother, although she isn't sick as far as Sissy knows. The cart smells of damp wood and stale milk. They travel through the grizzled countryside past muddy fields Sissy has never seen before. Cows bellow beneath the dripping trees. She looks down each small lane winding away secretively or burrowing into the furred rumps of fields. She peers over unhinged gates, sadly ajar, leading to churned-up farmyards. Even the houses with their gables close to the road seem forlorn. They are stuck here on the bend of a road or at the puddled end of a lane, while she is moving towards the bright thin line of the horizon.

Beyond which is the sea, Valerian has told her. He is gone now. One morning early he disappeared. He had had an argument with Papa. Sissy heard them shouting in the yard. It was as if their cramped house was not large enough to hold Papa's feelings.

'Son,' he roars at Mother when he comes back in. 'I have no son.'

Valerian has gone to Gdansk. For days Sissy walked as far as the shrine at the crossroads and waited. The small statue of Our Lady the Traveller set in a portal of stone marked the boundary with the outside world. From there she would be the first to see Valerian return with his swaggering gait and his bright smile. He went off before when farm work was scarce, but he came back in time for the harvest. But this time, Mother says, is different.

'Your father has driven him away.'

Gdansk! She likes its name. Like the cranking clangour

of cranes, the whiplash crack of breaking ice, the salty spittle of sea. She has never seen the sea, only the big lake near Borowy Las. Gertie took them picnicking there once in the summer. She and Maria and Felix had paddled in the green and soupy shallows while the lake sulked, flat and warm. It stretched as far as Sissy could see. But Gertie, standing on the shingle, her broad face wincing and her hand shielding her eyes from the glare, pointed to the far distance – a stone gable nestling in a puffy breath of trees.

'See,' she said triumphantly, glad to have found a landmark, 'that's the Bronskis' place.'

Bronski is the landlord, for whom Papa works.

But Sissy would not look towards the destination of Gertie's pointed finger. What she longed for was an unmarked horizon, where land and sky would melt into one another in an unbroken skein, and an ocean wide and endless as the summer sky.

She is fascinated by water; she wants to know what is going on underneath. In the long lilac evenings swarms of midges and flies hang suspended over the river like a twitching cloud. She squirms her toes in the oily mud. Beneath its glittery, thrashing surface there is a teeming underworld of sluggish earth and slimy stones, a city of gloating toads, worms steadfastly burrowing. She peers constantly at the reflections in the rain barrel in the yard. The face she sees there belongs to a vampire who lives at the bottom trapped in a porthole world. Vampires, Papa has told her, are babies who were drowned without having first been baptised. They grow to the age of seven in water, whereupon they take on human form. When Sissy splashes the surface with her hand the face of the vampire breaks into a thousand shimmering ripples. She worries that in the night the vampire might rise from the barrel and stalk the house. She follows Gertie into the yard on winter mornings, watching as she breaks the ice on the top of the barrel. Sissy always checks to see that the vampire is down below, safely locked in the frozen underworld.

Maria shook her awake. She could not believe that she had slept and missed so much of the journey. The cart slid across the slimy cobbles. The horse neighed in fright. Sissy had never seen such a crowd; they could barely move for the throng. The street was lined with stalls piled high with food. Peddlers proffered baskets of loaves and bagels. There was the yeasty smell of baking, the pungency of caraway seed. More baskets of plums and cherries sat on trestle tables glistening from the recent rain. There were tubs of smoked herrings, brown beans and hot peas, barrels of gherkins and sauerkraut. The noise was deafening as the traders and stallholders shrieked their unholy litanies, followed by the dull thud of brass weights on scales. Urchins ran along beside the wagon, pulling faces and trying to clamber aboard.

'Oy!' Papa shouted, and they fell away as he brandished his whip.

Behind them a skinny boy was driving a gaggle of geese. A water carrier crucified by two pails wove his way through the marketplace. In a dark entrance to a courtyard Sissy spied a cow tethered to a wall and a woman ferociously beating a carpet as if it were a naughty child. Strange men with beads and locks and long gabardine coats hurried along the street, gripping bundles of books. Little boys, wearing velveteen caps and fringed vests, trailed after them. Tendrils of hair hung by their cheeks.

'Jews,' Maria hissed.

Felix helps Papa to unload the wagon. He is a strong boy, nine years old but already bursting out of the trousers Mother made him only a few months ago. They flap around his mid-calf. The soles are rising from his boots and make a funny slapping sound, like a dog lapping water greedily. Sissy watches as he hefts a sack of potatoes and cabbages and sets them on the ground. He swings a pair of geese, followed by the sad, scrawny, plucked bodies of chickens whose necks Mother has wrung. Sissy knows the sound from the yard. That awful scurrying, the choking screams when Mother gets her hands on them, the quick snap as she breaks their tiny bones. Now they seem to shiver on the cold cobbles, though Sissy knows this is impossible. They are dead, aren't they?

Finally Felix clambers into a corner of the cart and fetches Mother's basket of eggs. Carefully he moves to the edge, eyeing the eggs warily. His tongue inches between his teeth in concentration. Suddenly he slips on a wet cabbage leaf and he tumbles off the cart. The eggs fly as if Felix has done a masterful juggling trick. They land one by one with a whiplike crack and succulent splat. Several dogs rush from nowhere, hungry, lean creatures with mangy backs and spindly legs, jostling with one another as they feast noisily. Felix squats on the ground, rubbing his chafed shins and whimpering. Papa rains blows on his head.

'Simpleton,' he roars. He turns and appeals to the two girls standing in the scattered mess of yolks and whites. 'Would God not grant me a normal son?'

It is the first time Sissy realises that Felix is not like other boys.

On the way home, Papa sang into the night, streamers of bawdy songs. Maria and Sissy had sat in a dark corner of the inn for what seemed like hours while Papa haggled and argued with several other men. Felix was banished to the street, where he had to tend to the horse and watch the cart.

'All you're fit for,' Papa growled.

It was smelly inside the inn, the grainy ferment of ale and the burning of tallow, but at least it was warm and one of the serving girls had given them some bread and pickle.

Maria hid a crust in her pocket for Felix. When they finally left they found Felix huddled close to the horse for warmth. It was a clear, cold night.

'You,' Papa ordered, 'in the back. With the girls.'

Every so often he would break off his song and remembering the eggs he would turn around to scowl at Felix. His temper was quick to rise and slow to diminish; he would labour to keep his rage fuelled. Sometimes Sissy believed it was what kept him warm. No matter how cold the weather, Papa always sweated. It oozed from him, fumy and sweet.

'Your mother, boy, will not thank you,' he said to Felix, as they rolled into the yard. He lifted a sleepy Sissy off the cart and planted her on the frostbitten ground. And he gave Felix another clip across the ear as they entered the eerily dark and silent house.

'Where's your mother?' Papa asks absently as he moves around the unlit, abandoned kitchen. It looks as if Mother has run out of the house leaving everything just so. There are some glowing embers in the stove; the table is scattered with the tacky leavings of dough as if she were interrupted by a knock at the door and had gone to investigate with floured hands. Maria runs into the bedroom.

'Papa, Papa,' they hear her excited voice call.

'What is it now?' Papa replies exasperatedly. It is as if his children are too much for him and every cry is a demand.

'Come, come quickly!'

Papa is not going anywhere. He has pulled off his damp boots and sits sprawled by the stove, half-heartedly trying to stoke life from the flaky ash.

'The eggs . . .' he begins again his litany of lament, 'the bloody eggs.'

Felix hovers by the door, nursing his burning ear.

'Mr Schanzkowski!'

The face of a gold-toothed woman appears in the

doorway. Her face, bathed in the flickering glow of a candle she holds gingerly in a small hand, has a dwarfish look. She beams triumphantly at Papa. Sissy is afraid of the midwife, the gold terror of her smile.

'Yes, what is it?' Papa answers wearily.

He does not even look up, or register the strange voice in his house.

'You have a son!' she proclaims.

'Don't I know it!' He casts a surly eye on Felix.

'No,' the midwife insists, 'you have another son.'

BABY! SISSY BELIEVED he was a charmed child. Born magically of the fecund splattering of eggs and Papa's desperate prayer in the foetid marketplace. What power he must have! Sissy watched avidly as the infant suckled at Mother's breast. She had climbed up on the high, ruined bed, the twisted mess of bloody sheets and sweated blankets. The dark room, lit only by a candle sputtering on the low sill, had the warm whiff of the stable and the sour milky odour of Mother's cheesy sweat. Baby had a mop of dark hair. His tiny claw was puckered as if his skin were too loose for him. He had an old, wizened face. Surprised wrinkles creased his angry-looking forehead. Sissy sensed his great newness, the sheer strangeness of him. If she pressed up close enough to him she thought she might get a whiff of where he had so recently come from, as when Papa came home, smelling of smoke and spirits, his coat soaked with faraway rain, his boots bearing the dead leaves of distant places. But Baby had come from somewhere even darker and more mysterious, the deep pulp of Mother's innards.

Papa stood in the doorway, stooped under the lintel, looking, as always, as if he was too big for their dim and cluttered house. Gertie, large and attentive, mopped Mother's brow. She had always seemed to Sissy like another mother with her big-boned, capable frame, her amiable dexterity. She poured steaming water into a basin by the bedside. It smelt of burnt onion, which the midwife had ordered to hasten the delivery.

'A difficult birth, Mr Schanzkowski,' the midwife was saying, 'a long, hard labour . . .'

A look passed between her and Papa, of warning.

'I had to send Gertie to ask Father Kosinski to open the door of the church and expose the Holy Sacrament.'

Mother smiled dazedly. She looked small in the bed, her soaked hair and her beaded skin luminous in the candle-light. The midwife lifted the child and carefully moved with the swaddled bundle towards Papa.

'Your son, Mr Schanzkowski, do you wish to hold him?'

Papa waved his hands in the air deflectively, but the midwife held Baby aloft like an extravagant gift. He hitched up his trousers and sighed and took the child into his large embrace. Sissy watched a look of baffled and luxuriant pride steal over his features. His face broke into a wide, embarrassed beam.

'Where's Felix?' Mother asked.

A cloud descended. Papa scowled.

'I don't want him in here. He might cast a spell on my fine, healthy son,' he said.

'He's not bewitched, Josef,' Mother said wearily. 'He's just slow.'

Maria had warned her that Papa would thrash them.

'It's the tradition,' she said.

It happened the day Baby had his first bath. The midwife dipped him in the bread trough so, she said, he 'would grow like dough'. She added mugwort and thyme to the water to make him strong. Baby had made a good start. He was born on a Tuesday, the best day for boys.

'Not like poor Felix,' Maria said, 'born on a Friday, and a Good Friday what's more. No one will ever marry him. But who would have Felix anyway?'

When the midwife washed Baby he cried and kicked,

213

which meant that though he would have a temper he would thrive and grow. When the bathing was done the midwife lifted Baby out of the trough and held him out for Mother and Papa to kiss. Sissy envied Baby that kiss, Papa's lips noisily smacking the infant's damp head. She stole a glance at Felix who stood behind her. His lower lip trembled. Sissy turned away. If Papa saw tears he would see red. But luckily he was too busy carrying the bath water away to spill it on the threshold to give Baby a lucky future.

'This is it,' Maria said to her under her breath, as he returned with the empty trough and a switch in his hand.

The midwife put Baby on Mother's bed and Papa lifted the switch and struck the pillow once, calling out to the bright child, 'Obey your father and your mother.'

The harsh tone must have frightened Baby and he set up a high, aggravated wail that continued while first Felix, and then Maria, were motioned to come forward and bend over. Papa clattered them several times each on the back of the legs and the rump with the thorny stick. Sissy thought he would halt at her, that he would never strike her, not knowingly, not when she had done nothing. But he crooked his finger at her when the other two were done and he whacked her briskly on the calves.

'So you will never forget,' he said when the deed was done and the children had straightened up, their legs and buttocks smarting. 'Obedience is meant to hurt.'

For days Papa is in high good humour. He whistles around the house or sings jovially in the yard. He has a strong voice; it carries in the crisp, silent mornings. The first snowfall of the winter has lodged in high-mounded drifts around the house, looming at the windows. A pearly luminescence leaks into the darkest corners. Sissy follows in the wake of Papa's breezy cheer, sinking into his large snowy footsteps, which criss-cross the yard to and from the byre and then to the store. This is Papa's domain, a wooden lean-to at the gable end of the house. The ceiling sags where the timbers have rotted. Grandfather Schanzkowski died in the old iron bedstead abandoned in the corner. Maria says the store is haunted. But Sissy likes its feeling of ghostly possibility accompanied by the scratch and scurry of mice.

Here Papa stores his tools and fashions stick dolls for the girls out of driftwood. He will spend weeks building a milking stool or a clumsy chair or the crude dresser in the kitchen, a rough and tender object much like himself. She tiptoes into the sawdusty room. Sissy loves its air of random splendour, the kiss-curl shavings, the broken pieces of furniture. Plaits of onions hang from the rafters. Old flour bags lie folded in a pile which Mother will bleach in the spring. Her jars of pickled gherkins stand in serried rows. Apples and plums seethe in their sugared juices. Papa is busy whittling at a small piece of elder, humming and talking to himself as if he is conversing with frightened ghosts. She hides behind a large chest, trying to still her breathing. If she is quiet she knows he will let her stay. Papa's humming comes to an abrupt halt.

'Sissy?' he calls out. 'Is that you?'

She peers through the legs of an upturned chair.

'This is no place for a little girl.'

'Please,' she begs, 'let me stay, I'll be good.'

She is desperate to savour the backwash of his happiness.

'Imagine, Sissy,' he says, throwing his arm up and gesturing to his kingdom of junk, 'one day all of this will belong to Baby! I have a son, Princess, a son and heir.'

Princess and Baby uttered in one breath. Even Papa saw them as a pair. The two most favoured. She knew the feel of Baby's downy skin as well as she knew her own, the silken rise of his cheeks brushed by his lovely lashes, the swaddled warmth of him, his gritty breath against her cheek, the plump perfection of his feet. She liked to watch him in the cradle as he burrowed into his deep, dreamless sleep; she envied the sated contentment of his slumber. She loved the noises he made, gurgles coated with frothy bubbles, a crooning babble punctuated with high, delighted shrieks, his arched glee when she swung a spoon or a glass bead in front of him. He loved anything shiny; he would make for it with a dimpled hand.

'Another magpie,' Mother said, 'just like you.'

When Mother allowed her to take him outside, Sissy would lift him up and point to his reflection in the mossy depths of the rain barrel.

'Who's that in there? Why is Baby in the barrel?'

And Baby would scream with terrified joy as if she had made magic.

The thaw begins. Mother is churched. It is the first time she has been in the village since Baby was born. She wears her Sunday best, a coat the colour of charcoal with a fleecy astrakhan collar, the one she calls her Poznan coat. The stove is fully ablaze as they leave and Gertie, fearing a fire in the house while they are out, removes some embers in a shovel and carries them out into the yard.

'No,' Papa shouts, 'you little fool. Never carry fire out of the house. It will make the cows go dry. And it makes women barren.'

He eyes Mother.

'Didn't you hear the midwife, Josef?' she says. 'Baby will be my last.'

Gertie will walk with her the two miles to the church. Mother is not allowed inside. She must kneel in the doorway while Father Kosinski prays over her. He will hold a candle as he prays and she will touch it. Then she will follow him around the altar, holding onto his stole so that Baby will have a lucky hand. Then she must go to the midwife and fall three times at her feet, kiss her hands and thank her for her trouble. The midwife will sprinkle her with holy water. And then, only then, will Mother be clean.

Baby has become Walter. Gertie and Papa brought him to be christened the week after he was born. Mother dressed him in the christening robe, fetched from the chest in the store. It smelled of camphor. Baby looked like a princeling in it.

'Made from the best lace,' Mother said. 'All of our family were baptised in this.'

'All the high and mighty Dulskis, you mean,' Papa said.

'I cannot deny my roots.' There was a quiet steeliness in Mother's voice that was often a prelude to an argument.

'These are your roots now, Countess,' Papa said as they stood in the kitchen. There were unwashed pots on the stove, globs of mud on the flagstones.

'Give me my son,' he said, taking Baby roughly from her and planting her in Gertie's arms. 'Come on, girl, let's turn this child into a Christian.'

Sissy was sent to school that year, in place of Felix.

'What good will book learning do him?' Papa had asked.

Unwittingly Papa had done Felix a favour. He had been bullied by the village boys. His cowed acquiescence seemed to infuriate them. They drove him from the schoolyard with stones; they smashed his slate. Mother had sat with him late into the night poring over the German alphabet, but it was no good. Like his father's contempt, it was a mystery to him.

The school was in the village, which stood at a crossroads, four miles from the forests which gave it its name. The white timbered houses petered out, swiftly falling away into dilapidation as if the effort of standing tall had exhausted them. The mill alone stood proud, the village's only battlement, its wheel tirelessly churning the waters of the Slupia. In summer the village's two lonely streets would billow with choking dust, in winter the churning of carts and horses turned it into a mire. The one-roomed schoolhouse, ochre on the outside, deep brown within, had a high-beamed ceiling and long windows, through which the spire of the church could be glimpsed. Framed by a lozenge of blue, this view was one of two fixed points in the schoolroom. The other was the portrait of Kaiser Wilhelm behind the teacher's podium. The church and the king were keeping their eyes on the children of Kashubia. Or so it seemed to Sissy.

Sissy was good at school, cleverer than Maria, despite the six years between them. She had to crook her arm around her slate to stop Maria copying her subtractions. She was a wizard at calculation. Maria struggled with reading and spelling. When asked a question in class she would babble and stammer, casting around desperately as if the answer might come floating down from the ceiling on a scroll. Sissy could not bear the terrible tension of it. The schoolmistress, Miss Tupalska, would peer over her spectacles and rap the high teacher's desk with her cane and bark, '*Mach ein Ende, Schanzkowska. Mach ein Ende*!' Sissy would whisper the answer or scribble it on her slate, but so great was Maria's panic that she could neither see nor hear. And despite her poor eyesight, Miss Tupalska could detect prompts or cheating at a hundred paces. Even when her back was turned – when she was writing on the board or stooping to replenish the pot-bellied stove – she would pause in mid-task and holler, 'Franziska Schanzkowska!' And Sissy would have to slope to the back of the schoolroom and stand for the rest of the day until just before going home when she would get the quick whip of Miss Tupalska's cane.

All through the winter the children wore their coats and gloves in the classroom, which became a fuggy mist of damp clothes and shoe leather thawing by the low glow of the fire. The abused room with its pitted desks, its scored floorboards, its weeping windows and the roar of the stove at full throttle was what Sissy imagined a great factory in the city might be like. And she loved it. They learned by rote, no trouble to Sissy, who had once chanted the names of her brothers and sisters into a glorious mnemonic hymn. She was determined to memorise all she could. By the summer she could rattle off the names of all the German kaisers.

Meanwhile Felix sprouted, as if in defiance. His little boy's body grew alarmingly, grew soft, that is. His chest swelled and drooped; he had little breasts which Maria teased him about.

'Look, look,' she would shriek, dancing around him as he chopped wood in the yard stripped to the waist, poking at the little rolls of fat at his hips.

He would swat her away angrily. His face too seemed like a baby's, soft, quivering. Sissy imagined him in a carriage with a frilled bonnet like a foolish, full-grown infant. He glared at them both from a sullen, hurt distance, but he said nothing. Only Mother kept faith with him. Sissy came upon them in the kitchen one afternoon during haymaking. Hot from the fields, she rushed across the yard but something, perhaps the weight of the silent house, stopped her calling out as she pushed open the door. Sun streamed into the mottled room. Mother was bent over, crushing her engorged breast between squat fingers. But Baby was not in her arms. Instead Felix knelt at her knee, his mouth sucking at her bruised areola, as he drank milk her body had made for Baby. He fed greedily, gazing up at Mother, drugged and adoring while she stroked his close-cropped head and crooned to him. Neither of them saw Sissy standing in the shadows. Slowly she backed away, the cry of greeting dying on her lips. She did not tell anyone what she had seen. It seemed to her too sacred and forbidden.

SISSY'S GRANDMOTHER HAD been well born.

'God spare us from Poland's curse,' Papa would sneer, 'the minor nobility.'

The Dulskis owned a large house on Franziskanska Street in Poznan, to which Mother had been brought to visit as a child.

'Your great-grandmother Dulska,' Mother would say, pulling a grimace, 'she was a grim old bird.'

Mother would fall into reminiscence during the slow, measured rituals of laundry. The boiling of Papa's shirts, the folding of the sheets. Sissy loved the courtly dance they made of it; the gay beginning with an acre of bleached hessian between them, the respectful touching of fingertips as the corners of the sheets were matched, and then Mother's coy retreat with a stole of white on her arm.

'I had to take my boots off in case I soiled her rugs,' she would say, giggling. Sissy tried to imagine her mother as a giddy eight-year-old called Bella, and failed. Bella would be left on the corner of Franziskanska Street and pointed in the direction of the Dulski house. She had to visit her grandmother alone. Her mother had been disowned for marrying beneath her station. After the marriage, mother and daughter were never to see one another again. But after Bella's birth, Grandmother Dulska sent the christening robe with a message that she would like to see her granddaughter. Once a year Bella, dressed in her best outfit made up of offcuts from the tailor's shop, would have an audience with her grandmother.

'There was a footman to open the door and servants to take my bonnet and when I met Grandmother Dulska I had been warned to curtsy,' Mother went on.

'Like royalty?' Sissy asked.

'More like the parlourmaid,' Mother said ruefully.

'And then?'

'Tea would be brought in on a silver tray with a tall pot with a spout like the neck of a swan.' She laughed gaily. 'And Grandmother Dulska would point to the pastries and say to the maid, "The child will have one of these." She always called me "the child", if she called me anything at all.'

Her grandmother would enquire after Bella's schooling, correct her low German, or speak about her own troubles – a bad knee, the inclement weather. She never mentioned her daughter, and certainly never her son-in-law, the lowly tailor with whom her daughter had eloped. Little Bella knew the rules and yet she would try to smuggle information through to Grandmother Dulska – how her mother had sewn her dress specially for the occasion or garnered the ribbons for her hair from an old dress of her own. She thought her grandmother would approve of such artful thriftiness. If she did, the old woman never pretended. She greeted the little girl's prattle with a baleful silence and when the visit was terminated – sometimes in the middle of one of Bella's gabbled passages – she would rap on the floor with her cane and the footman would appear to show her out. Grandmother Dulska permitted the child to brush her cheek with her lips.

'She smelled of perfumed dust,' Mother said, wrinkling her nose.

Outside on Franziskanska Street, Bella's mother, who would have spent the hour shivering on a park bench or pacing up and down out of sight of the house, would hurry towards her.

'Well?' she would demand.

Bella never knew what her mother expected – some sign, some chink in Grandmother Dulska's armour, a sliver of forgiveness. But Bella would only shrug her shoulders and hand over a couple of coins the footman always slipped to her on the way out.

Sissy loved to hear this story. She pressed her nose up against the glass of its lost splendour. She felt a special connection with the Dulski house on the street with a name so close to her own. (Years later she was to discover that the street was named for the neighbouring Franciscan monastery.) She tried to imagine the wide promenades of Poznan her mother described, the black-plumed soldiers – it was a garrison town – flags fluttering from the fortress and gala evenings, where well-born young women like her grandmother might have made a match. Mother, at least, had known it even if it was from behind the counter of Tailor Kurowski's shop. In the early days the shop was packed with customers who had come, not to order suits, but to see how the mighty had fallen and to gawp at Eva Dulska, the tailor's new wife. Sissy looked around their sad, cramped house and for the first time felt the impoverished constriction of it. Eva Dulska's wilful foolishness had brought them to this. And all that was left of that other life were remnants – the christening robe, Mother's Sunday coat and the wall clock in the kitchen.

'Maybe we could go to Poznan some day? Back to Great-Grandma's house?'

'Sissy, love,' Mother replied, 'let's not get carried away.'

Mother had a fear of being carried away. Perhaps because her own mother had been so entirely carried away. Her parents had met when Eva had entered his shop to order a waistcoat for her father. Stefan Kurowski emerged from the darkness of the back workroom, a tall, dark-eyed young man, hair in tight drills, though even then, at

222

twenty-two, it was already receding. In his hand (he was left-handed, which made him clumsy with sharp instruments and uneven as a tailor) he had a pair of large pinking shears. He was irritated by the peremptory tinkle of the bell at the front of the shop which had broken his concentration at a delicate juncture in the cutting of a collar and reveres. His father was supposed to look after the customers but was nowhere to be seen. Stefan had several pins clamped between his lips, which made it impossible to speak. He need not have worried. The young lady did all the talking. A bright, glossy-haired beauty, seventeen years old, who spoke disarmingly all in a rush but with the briskness of her class, almost as if she were talking to herself.

'It's for my father,' she was saying, fingering a leather pelt that lay, naked-looking, on the counter. 'We want it as a surprise for his birthday so we thought you would have his measurements. He always comes here, so we – that's my mother and I – she'll be along presently, thought we might order something very special for him. Brocade, perhaps? Mother doesn't agree, says it's too extravagant. But I don't see the harm in extravagance, do you? I mean, he's not a young man any more, and soon he might be dead . . .' She laughed, a gay whinny. 'Oh, what a thing to say! You'll think me indiscreet, worse, heartless. It's not that I wish him dead, not at all. God forbid, but life is short and we should grasp our happiness while we can, don't you think?'

She stopped for air, or for an answer.

Stefan opened his mouth and a tiny shower of silver came out. He'd forgotten about the pins . . .

Papa allows Sissy to wind Grandma's clock into the new year of 1903. She has learned to tell the time from it, the big hand for the minutes, the little hand for the hours. It always seems the wrong way round to her.

'It is a job for the man of the house,' Papa says, 'but till Walter comes of age you can do it, Princess.'

Felix is crouched by the stove, feeding wood into the roaring porthole. Even as Papa lifts Sissy in his arms, she realises that one mistake is enough to make. One mistake like Felix's and she too might be abandoned. Papa opens the clock's octagonal glass door and produces from his pocket a brass key.

'Here.'

He points to the slot at the bottom of the face just over the seven. Sissy grasps the warm key and clicks it in. Then she begins to twist it. It always resists. It is as if time is weight, pushing against her like a gale trapped behind a flimsy door.

'Gently, gently,' Papa admonishes, 'three times to the right. That's all. Otherwise you'll overwind it. And it is a family heirloom, isn't that right, Mother?'

Sissy wondered how her grandmother had managed to smuggle it out of the house on Franziskanska Street. It did not seem the sort of thing you would bring on a honeymoon with a tailor.

'Your grandma knew it was in for repairs and persuaded the watchmaker she was collecting it for her father,' Mother explained. 'The watchmaker knew nothing of her scandalous match and handed the clock over. It wasn't his place to question. He told her that the pendulum had stuck, but he had oiled all of the clock's works and it would run for a lifetime. And it has!'

'But why?' Sissy persisted.

'She wanted her mother's time,' Mother said. 'Dulski time.'

'Such fancies,' Papa mutters as he swings Sissy to the floor. Below, in his bassinet, Baby holds his little fist up as if saluting his father.

'That's my soldier,' Papa says, 'a glorious patriot for Poland.'

It is Mother's turn to shake her head.

'How can he fight for something that doesn't exist?'

They live in a place that doesn't exist. Each day Sissy walks through what Papa calls Poland – the track across the fields with its aisle of green in the centre, the waving summer fields of corn, the woods of tall umbrella pines, the needle-brown carpet underfoot. It is called Poland, but it is not written down. Even the village, Borowy Las, has become something else – the sign above the schoolhouse now reads Borowihlas, as if someone has waved a German wand over it. When she tries to find the village on the schoolroom globe it is not there.

'It's a one-horse town, Sissy,' Mother tells her, 'you won't find it on any map. It's too small.'

Sissy locates Poznan and Gdansk, but they are not themselves; on the map they are Posen and Danzig. She has heard of Lodz, but that belongs to Russia. She fingers the globe carefully, searching for Poland. Finally in desperation she asks Miss Tupalska.

'Poland is a dream, my dear,' she says mockingly. 'What do we sing every day before class?'

'God save the emperor,' Sissy replies.

'Precisely! You are a little Prussian girl living in the German empire. And that's thanks to the kaiser.' She points fondly at the portrait of the emperor.

Sissy finds herself living on Dulski time in the German Reich.

A man starts calling for Gertie. Sissy is amazed. Plain, stolid Gertie with flour under her fingernails and bad teeth. His name is Theo. His father is the blacksmith in the village, a small, elderly man with bandy legs and a crooked smile. She and Maria spy on the courting couple sitting in the kitchen. They make a funny pair. Theo, neat and small-boned, with a large wreck of a nose and deep-set eyes the colour of mud, and Gertie, large and loyal and ill at ease with love. He moves gingerly in the house, clutching his cap; he has a nervous twitch in his eye. When he calls shyly at the door Mother treats him with a fond indulgence as if, Sissy thinks, he is a fool. He is sweet and bashful in Gertie's company. When he is with her he acts like a man who cannot believe his own luck. He paws her affectionately on the hand; he gazes at her doe-eyed while she clatters about, a meal bucket on her arm or elbow-deep in potato peelings.

'Bit of a frog prince, if you ask me,' says Maria, who at thirteen has developed an appraising eye where boys are concerned. She spends summer evenings loitering near the mill-wheel, where village boys go dipping. In bed at night she speculates constantly about them in a half-mocking way. There is a roll-call of names which Sissy knows by heart – Leszch, Wladek, Piotr.

Gertie's stout capability so at odds with her age – she is eighteen – gives way under Theo's devotion to something softer. Sissy fears for her. Softness in the Schanzkowski family is something to be hidden.

'Probably a gold-digger,' Papa mutters when the match-maker arrives with a flower in his buttonhole and his coat bulging with a bottle of vodka. Mother releases a bitter, silvery laugh.

'Gold?' she queries. 'What gold?'

Three weeks before the wedding the peddler makes his yearly visit. He is a bearded man, tall but stooped from many years of pushing his wares ahead of him in a handcart. He has come from Lodz, where the Russians are. He might as well have come from the other side of the world. Polish on his tongue sounds strange, foreign almost, as if the words stick in his throat. Mother invites him in and feeds him while he unpacks lengths of cotton and serge. The peddler's cart stands for many hours in the Schanzkowski yard, its shafts pointed skywards, as Mother debates the merits of his merchandise. She must choose a year's worth from him, enough to make trousers for Papa, a shirt for Felix, shawls for the girls, a sailor suit for Walter. He carries in his boxes and fishes out his treasures. Sissy fingers the pouches of needles, the blue-rimmed enamel plates, the shiny lacquered boxes. Papa arrives home to a kitchen adrift with swathes of cloth. He does not approve of the peddler; he is Jewish and Jews, he says, would rob you blind. But today he is merry. A man in the village who owes him money has coughed up and his pockets jangle.

'Pick something, Princess,' he says.

'Josef,' Mother warns.

'Really, Papa! Can I?'

A gift, something for nothing, is a rare thing, especially from Papa.

'Anything you want.'

'Josef,' Mother says again, 'you mustn't favour Sissy over the others.'

'Hush, woman,' he says and scowls at her.

She chose a matryoska doll. She had never seen a doll like it. She knew only Papa's stick creatures, but this doll was round and fat and painted.

'Look,' said the peddler, holding the doll in his small, nimble fingers. He was as proud of his wares as if they were his children. 'You can open her up and inside – look – another doll lives.'

Sissy opened it excitedly four times until the last doll, which was no more than a miniature wooden egg.

'What will you call her, Princess?' Papa asked.

'Them,' Sissy insisted, 'each one has to have a name.'

'Olga, Tatiana, Maria and Anastasia,' the peddler intoned, 'the Russian grand duchesses.'

Sissy tried them out.

'And this one', the peddler said, pointing to the smallest, 'can be the Tsarevich Alexei, the boy who will rule Russia.'

Sissy dances with Papa in the yard. The wedding band plays a mazurka. It is Gertie's day. She is garlanded, fat with pride, but Sissy will remember only this, dancing with her father. She tries to follow the shuffle of his dusty boots as they reel about in the tumbleweed. In the summer-streaked night his dripping shirt tails have a white, dishevelled splendour. And then he swings her high and the world falls away, the wheezing band fades, the halo of trees spin, the sky overhead like the furred blush of a ripe peach. She is in Papa's arms; she will not forget.

WITH GERTIE GONE, Maria is taken out of school to help Mother in the kitchen and Sissy is given the yard work. In the mornings she must milk the cow before school. The skies are leaden with snow-fat clouds. A wind howls at the gable, pouncing as she turns the corner on her way to the cowshed, then whistles through the clumps of weeds that have grown up around the rusting mangle. The house seems hunkered down, vainly trying to escape the bitter wind. The track made by feet going from the house to the byre is peppered with hoar frost. The cow bellows, anguished and mournful. She slaps its rump and sets to work in the dark. Her fingers pull on the cow's swollen, fleshy teat, her head rests on its russet flank. She has to cajole and croon before the cow will yield up a full pail. She goes to school with the smell of stable in her hair and the curdled spurts of cow's milk on her skirts.

Now that he is weaned, Walter sleeps with the girls, sharing the small room off the kitchen with Sissy, while Maria gets Gertie's old cot. He is a golden-haired child, the dark mop at birth has been replaced by flaxen kiss-curls, and now that he is tottering uncertainly around the house his fat baby limbs have become sturdy and strong. Sissy may be the cleverest of the Schanzkowskis, but Walter is the most cherished. She sees the blamelessness of his milk teeth, the limpid innocence of his blue gaze, the startling softness of unblemished skin. But she cannot stifle the constriction in her throat when Papa halts at the doorway on his way to bed and leans over Walter, fetching his outflung arm and placing it reverently under the blanket or fingering stray strands of his dream-soaked hair. Once she must have been gazed upon with such love. She turns towards the wall and pretends to be asleep. She cannot bear to watch. A picture dances on her closed lids; Papa and her, alone together, travelling towards the horizon, propelled by the dream of the distance. To Poznan, Berlin, Gdansk. Anywhere but here.

It is Baby's third birthday. ('Not Baby,' Papa roars, 'the child's name is Walter, he's been babied too long. Too many bloody women in this house.') It is All Souls' Eve. Mother is baking pancakes in the kitchen, which later they will eat with fruit and honey. A pot of cooked barley bubbles on the stove, fruit of the recent harvest. At twilight they will sit at the table with an extra place set for the dead. The doors and windows will be thrown open and they will pile the dead person's plate with peas and barley gruel.

'What dead people do we know?' Sissy asks, as Mother rolls out the floury dough and saves a little knob for Baby, which she will bake in the oven separately.

'There are generations of the dead, Sissy, since time began . . .'

'But we don't know them, do we?'

'We know dead people. Grandfather Schanzkowski, you remember him, don't you?'

Sissy has a vague memory of a leathery purse of a face and a smell of tobacco.

'And there's the first Mrs Schanzkowska, we set the place for her too.'

Sissy feels a soft turnover of shock. Mother pounds the dough.

'The first? Aren't you the first?'

'Oh no,' Mother says softly. 'Papa was married before, but she died in childbirth. With Maria. The labour went on for days and the midwife did not know there were twins. She was frail, poor creature, it was too much for her. Only Maria survived, her baby brother was stillborn.'

'So Maria is not my sister?'

'Your half-sister, and Gertie too.'

'And Valerian? Felix?'

'You and Felix and Walter,' Mother says, rubbing Sissy's cheek with a floury knuckle, 'you are *my* children.'

Sissy pondered on this new knowledge, this sudden doubling up. It was simple, Mother said, two families had become one, but to Sissy it seemed that one had become two. She pestered Mother with questions, but while she had been happy to talk about Grandmother Dulska, she would not even utter the first Mrs Schanzkowska's name in the house.

'Your father was left with three young children. He could not afford to grieve for long. The Schanzkowskis were distant cousins of ours and he came to Poznan. I was,' she said softly, blushing, 'of a certain age. It was a lucky match.'

'And what about her?'

'Poor woman!'

'Did you know her?' Sissy asked.

'No, I didn't ... but I know her now, I have her life.'

The notion of the other Mrs Schanzkowska made Sissy thrillingly uneasy. Her mother was living a life that did not belong to her. When she looked around the house she wondered what things here belonged to the other Mrs Schanzkowska. The rolling pin, the enamel bin for maize, the smoky-blue china platter on the dresser, cracked and sewn together. Had these been part of *her* dowry? Sissy mentally collected these items as if they were shiny trinkets. Like a curious magpie she pecked over them as if together they might conjure up the ghost mother. She even examined the clothes her mother wore. Could these too have been inherited? Sissy noticed how her blouses strained at the bosom and her skirts creased at the hips as though they had been made for a smaller, slighter, more fragile woman. When she entered the kitchen, she could sense another presence hovering and, in the yard, a shadowy wife scattering feed for the chickens. Sissy studied Papa in the belief that she might catch a glimpse, if she caught him unawares, of the life he had lived with the mother that was not hers. It made him seem like an impostor, somehow, as if he had been fooling her, nursing a secret other life within. One thing she was glad of. At least her mother was intact, still flesh and blood, and not some vague and sickly ghost. The discovery made their inside world seem vast with possibility. Their house harboured other lives, interrupted, unlived. The air was thick with spirits; the sudden silences that descended were theirs. If Sissy listened hard, she was convinced that they would speak to her.

At seven she is a strong, pretty girl, dark hair to her waist, a moon-shaped face, eyes the colour of pale slate. She has reached the age of reason. She must confess her sins to Father Kosinski. She must enter the confessional and whisper her secrets to the dark. Martha Borkowska shakes her round, fleshy face and knits her brow. Her ginger hair frizzes in the damp. She is a worrier, a biter of fingernails.

'I don't know what they mean by sins,' she complains as they sit in the pew in the Lenten church. The statues are swathed in purple. 'I have nothing to tell. Do you, Sissy?'

But Sissy has dozens of crimes to choose from, her urgent longings to escape, her greediness to have Papa to herself, her reluctant envy of Walter, her complete lack of innocence. How can she confess to never having been innocent?

All Saints' Day 1904 was mild and damp. Sissy loved this

day, when they trooped to the graveyard carrying candles and bundles of dried flowers. In the early afternoon the small cemetery behind the church was filled with villagers pulling weeds and sweeping off the headstones. Papa traced around the inscription on the Schanzkowski grave with his fingertips, loosening a year's worth of grit and dust which had lodged there, while Mother placed bunches of lavender in jars around the plot and Maria lit the dozens of candles they had brought from the house. Sissy was left in charge of Baby – he thought the flickering flames were butterflies that he could catch in his little fist. For the first time Sissy was able to read the carved lettering on the tombstone. There was Grandfather Schanzkowski, old man of distant memory, then Grandmother who had died before Sissy was born, and there, too, was the first Mrs Schanzkowska, Elena, her life etched in stone, 1857–1890. So it was true then, Sissy thought. As daylight faded they gathered round the grave and prayed for the dear departed. Papa left soon afterwards – there would be revelry in the village – and Mother returned to the house. But Sissy wanted to stay and because Baby fretted when Mother tried to take him home, he stayed too. Once distracted from the candles, he played on the swept path near the grave where he counted pebbles seriously. Sissy savoured the vigilant glow in the church-yard where thousands of candles would be left to burn through the night and the shrouded figures of the living moved about with a slow solemnity. Maria spied Wladek Dudowski, a lanky boy she had been mooning over. Sissy could not understand what attraction such boys could have with their gapped grins and dung-covered boots and their sudden outbursts of raucous laughter. When she passed them gathered in the schoolyard or roaming in gangs through the pastures, she would look the other way. Unlike Maria, she did not want to excite their attention. They would nudge one another as she passed, whistling and mocking, and laughing their loud, mysterious guffaws.

They did not talk but rather shoved one another and scuffled lazily, or stood broodingly kicking the dust.

'Don't tell Papa,' Maria admonished as she and Wladek hurried away into the gloom, leaving Sissy alone with Baby.

Some of the villagers had brought comets to light their way to the graveyard. These were metal cans filled with the leavings of the stove. They left a faintly charred smell in the air and rusty embers in their wake. Sissy inhaled the perfumed dusk – smoky, leaf-rotted. Surrounded by liquid pools of candlelight and the low murmur of prayer, she felt a palpable vastness as if the familiar churchyard was pitched at the edge of the world and beyond the silhouetted tombstones, the quivering light and the grey autumnal mist there was only a sublime emptiness. She thought of Elena Schanzkowska, imagining her in that space, moving furtively through the crowds, a distraught young woman, robbed of her life, clamouring to come back, to reclaim. Sissy shivered. Martha Borkowska bounced up and broke the mood.

'Let's go into the village,' Martha said brightly.

Suddenly Sissy was keen to go. The candles and the garlands and the uttered prayers were summoning up unhappy ghosts. She looked around for Baby.

'Baby,' she yelled, panic rising like a gorge in her throat.

She hunted high and low among the crowd, praying softly to herself, half-admonition, half-threat. Find him, God, please find him. She thought of the river that ran behind the village, the lake not half a mile away, the well, where a little child could slip in and be swallowed by the silent deep.

'Baby!' she screamed.

She ran from headstone to headstone, peering between the men's stout legs and the pious hunch of women for a glimpse of gold, or a flash of fair flesh. But he was nowhere to be seen. She had lost him; he was gone.

'Baby,' she sobbed.

She too was lost. Papa would kill her.

Hours later they found Baby asleep among sacks of flour in a storehouse behind the grocer's shop. Felix discovered him, doggedly scouring every backyard and craggy alleyway in the village. Sissy had sent Martha back to the house for help, knowing that she could not face Papa, while she tramped through the wet fields down by the river calling Walter's name out into the night. She did not dare to look at the water, afraid of what she might find. She thought of running away, but the darkness frightened her. When Papa arrived, he strode through the village, raging and howling, catching men and women alike by their lapels and shouting at them, spittle flying, 'Have you seen my son?'

He had not killed Sissy, but he had struck her, a sharp blow across the cheek. Her face smarted for days, out of shame, not hurt. She saw in his eyes the contempt he had reserved for Felix. Mother gathered the drowsy child into her arms and nuzzled into his damp hair.

'We have Walter back,' she said, 'that's all that matters.'

It was as if she had killed Baby, or at least meant him harm. Papa decided that Walter should not sleep in the girls' room any more. He was put in the settle bed in the kitchen instead, where, Papa said, he would be safe – this accompanied by a darting glare at Sissy. He ruled that she should never be alone with Baby in case she put a spell on him with her evil eye. He ordered Walter to cover his teeth when Sissy was in the room – she was an ill-wisher now. It made Baby nervous of her. He whimpered if she came close, sensing some danger from her. She was not allowed to pick him up or touch him. If he started crying, Mother or Maria would be motioned to quieten him. She missed his touch, the tickling warmth of his breath in the bed beside her.

'Papa will forget', Mother said to her, 'in time, but for now we must do what he says.'

But Sissy knew that while he might forget, he would never forgive.

In the spring Papa takes Walter out on his Sunday expeditions. They go to the river or gather wild mushrooms.

'A boy must learn to hunt and fish,' he declares.

Sissy prepares food for them and watches as they set off through the poppied fields, father and son. The little boy trots after him, carrying a satchel with bread, white cheese and cured ham. Felix is not included in these trips either, although his nature is more suited to the long waiting and the hushed stillness required of the hunter. Felix is, above all, patient. It is his patience that most infuriates Papa, who takes it as a sign of cunning on Felix's part, an elaborate plotting that might somehow undo him. After years of exclusion Felix does not seem to mind. But Sissy does. She tries desperately to appease. She polishes Papa's boots. She gathers herbs to bathe his feet in. She runs to greet him when he returns, but he swats her away as if she were a farmyard dog. She waits at night to hear his foot on the threshold and peers through the crack of the open door to the kitchen as he wanders around grumbling to himself. She feels like the first Mrs Schanzkowska, slight and insubstantial.

'Go to bed,' Papa says wearily, without even looking up, 'go to bed.'

She is no longer his Princess.

THESE ARE THE years of banishment. Sissy, hungry for redemption, turns to God. Daily, after school, she visits the deserted church. She likes the solemnity of its silence, punctured only by the hissing of candles. She does not light one for herself. She knows that what she would ask God for is not worthy; she wants things to be as they were. To undo Walter, to have Papa love her again, her alone. She tries to unravel the spool of time back, back to when Walter wasn't born, but she finds it hard to imagine such a time, let alone remember it. It is the only time her memory fails her.

She sits in the front pew and gazes up, as she used to at the sky, and is awed by its lofty height. Used to the low eaves at home, living crushed up against the roof, this airy openness feels like freedom. At first it is not God who draws her in, but this, the notion of lightness and escape. Of being at one moment, kneeling, small and singular in a dwarfed pew, and in another winging about in the thin, mote-flecked realm of the heavens. It makes her dizzy and appalled; it feels illicit, this solitary, exotic joy. And if she feels a real presence it is the first Mrs Schanzkowska's. She sees her in the blank eyes of the stone Virgin staring upward, appealing to the heavens. Her baby son rests in the bloodied glow of the sanctuary lamp. Her voice is buried in the susurrus of Sissy's urgent prayers. She, too, must have come here, uttering imprecations in the cowed silence. Her tentative absence gives Sissy comfort. She draws solace from the mothering silence. She thinks it must be God working in mysterious ways, granting her compensation. And she repays him with her prayers, dogged entreaties to keep Baby safe and well, to spare Mother and Papa, to protect Felix. And it soothes her as once the roll-call of siblings did, or the recitation of the kaisers. Memory and repetition, these will save her.

Mother takes it as a good sign and is relieved. When Mrs Borkowska, mother of Martha, stops her on Slupia Street on a fine blue Sunday in May, it is not to croon over five-year-old Walter, the apple of his father's eye, it is to commend Sissy's piety, the long hours spent at the altar. Mother blushes with a quiet pride. She has always thought Sissy strange, a complicated, covert child. Used to Felix's slow docility, she found her second-born difficult and demanding. Sissy cried for months and would not wean. She clawed at the breast, scrabbling with her fingers as if no amount of milk would satisfy her. Bella blanched at such appetite and felt it somehow unseemly. And later even Sissy's cleverness seemed less than wholesome. Her eagerness to learn – how she pestered to be taught the time or to learn her alphabet – seemed like more of the same avidity. A girl could be too clever and it mightn't do her any favours.

Bella Kurowska had been sent to Countess Zamoyska's School of Domestic Economy in Zakopane in the hope that it would aid her in being matched quickly, although her fellow pupils assumed that being the daughter of a tailor she was training to go into domestic service. There was no point in telling them that she was related to the Dulskis of Poznan. And though the long hours in the kitchen, dairy and laundry, the cutting out and making of clothes, the courses in practical book-keeping and the Bible-reading classes had prepared her to run a Christian household, they had been no help in securing her a match. No amount of education could wipe out the sins of her mother. In the end it was not her skills in Christian husbandry that had won her hand in marriage at the age of twenty-eight, but cousin Josef's need for a mother for his orphaned children.

Secretly, Bella preferred Sissy's elder sister. She might not be Maria's mother, but the girl's capriciousness was, at least, familiar. Bella might fear reckless impulse but she understood it. How could she not, being the fruit of it herself? But Sissy she distrusted. Right from the start. From the moment she fell pregnant with Sissy, she was subject to extraordinary cravings. She did not tell her husband that in the third month she ate fish, expressly forbidden for a woman in hope in case the child would swim in luxury or immorality. She does not hold now with all her husband's superstitions, but then she was keen to please him. When Josef was away she asked Felix to fetch her some herring she had pickled and hidden in the store. The taste remains with her, salty and tart. It reminds her of Sissy's temperament.

Maria and Sissy paint the eggs together for the last time in 1908. Martha Borkowska and her sisters join them. It is Holy Thursday, the weak, pale light of spring draining from the evening sky as they set to in the kitchen. Maria is almost eighteen, fine-boned, slender and pretty, like her mother, Sissy suspects, a living token of the first Mrs Schanzkowska. She still feels the presence of the first mother in the house, perhaps because she has so completely inherited the first Mrs Schanzkowska's place, ghosting around the farm and the fields, banished and alone. The girls gather the eggs from the henhouse and lay them out on the kitchen table. Sissy coats each egg with wax, then draws a design on its shell with a needle. The parts of the egg not covered with wax will take the colour when they are dipped. Maria has spent all day mixing the colours, boiling up roots and herbs on the stove and pouring them

into small dishes. There is orange from the infusion of
crocuses, black from a brew of elder bark, light green from
moss collected from the shaded underside of stones. Each
time an egg is dipped in colour, a fresh design must be
traced on the waxy eggshell. Sissy loves the minute care
needed to draw the patterns of leaves and flowers on the
egg's surface. It is at such odds with the rest of their lives,
this delicate refinement lavished on something as fragile as
eggshell. The eggs retreat with each dipping, under the
velvety soot of blue and the bold impertinence of corngold,
until they are no longer recognisable as the mud-spattered,
straw-flecked offerings of the henhouse. They will sit in a
bowl on the table all through the penitent fasting of Good
Friday and the vigilant worship of Holy Saturday until
Easter Sunday, when they will be given away as gifts. Were
it left to Sissy, she would never part with them. She would
keep them for the rest of the year, sitting in the bowl, little
prisms of polished beauty.

Maria has already decided who will get her favourite.

'This one', she says, picking one with a dove motif from
the pile, 'is for Wladek.'

Four years on, Wladek Dudowski is still on Maria's
mind. She meets him secretly when her chores are done. In
her solitary rambles, Sissy has seen them necking in the
barn, or kissing in a secret spot down by the river they
think no one else knows about.

'It certainly is not, my girl,' Mother interrupts, 'that
would mean that we welcome his attentions. You may, but
your father doesn't.'

Wladek is a farm labourer, worth only his hire. His
father has no land of his own, and has nothing to offer a
bride.

'You be careful,' Mother warns. 'If Papa gets wind of
your carryings-on with Wladek, it's the high road for you.'

On Holy Saturday Sissy brings a basket of food to the
church to be blessed. This is her job, as the youngest girl in
the household. Mother has prepared bread, sausage, salt,

vinegar and eggs cooked in onion sauce. On Easter Sunday, Papa eats the first blessed egg, peeling back the orange-stained shell with his fingers. He pops it whole into his mouth. Sissy feels a tremor of connection.

Sissy returns to the house one evening, barefoot and hot, and finds the place in uproar. After the dense silent heat of the church, the sunsoaked yard seems harsh and glaring. Wladek Dudowski, hands hanging by his side, stands in the centre of the yard. Papa has him by the throat, his shirt knotted in a bunch between whitening knuckles. In his other hand he holds a stick. Mother's hens scurry heedlessly about, pecking at the dust. Maria is sobbing by the door, her face streaked with dirty tears. Mother is standing in front of her, trying to shield her from Papa's ire.

'The lad meant no harm,' she is saying.

The rain barrel shimmers.

'I'll be the judge of that,' Papa bellows.

He looks old and bruised beside the younger man.

'I came across them in the barn. He has had his way with her, he has disgraced her, and the honour of this family.'

Sissy sidles in behind the gate, hoping not to be noticed. Papa looks up and is momentarily distracted.

'Ah, Sissy,' he says softly.

For a moment she is bathed in his benign gaze. She waits for him to say something more, but it is just absent-mindedness. He turns back to the task in hand.

'Come here,' he roars at Maria, who is rubbing her streaked face with her apron. Mother prods her forward and she moves out of the shadow of the house into an oblong of hard light. She squints, blinded by the sun. Papa catches her by her hair and yanks her towards him so that she is within spitting distance of Wladek. Big and rough as he is, the boy's hands are trembling. Papa stands between them for all the world like a priest joining them in holy matrimony, here in the glare of the afternoon sun, with the chickens and the rain barrel and Mother's heat-wilted geraniums on the sills as witnesses. To Sissy their pretty pink blooms look too garishly eager; the yard seems to throb with an unseemly fever. At times like these, pregnant with imminence, she imagines it is the anger of the first Mrs Schanzkowska that she senses, railing against the indignities piled upon her lost children. But, Sissy knows, only she recognises such signs.

There is a crash of skulls, the sickening thud of flesh and bone colliding as Papa smashes Wladek's and Maria's heads together.

'Imbeciles!' he bellows.

Once, twice, three times. Mother screams at him to stop. Maria falls in a faint and Papa, ignoring her, turns on Wladek with the stick, raining blows across his head and chest with a whistling thwack that draws blood through the stuff of his shirt. Wladek sinks to the dirt, his hands vainly trying to protect his head as he cowers at Papa's feet. Mother is on all fours, trying to drag the lifeless Maria away. Sissy is rooted to the spot. She is horrified, but she cannot look away. She is mesmerised to see such magnificent violence, Papa standing like an enraged beast in the sunlight while Wladek limps bloodily away. Sissy has never seen such passion. Papa looks at her again and smiles a foolish, drunken kind of smile.

'At least I don't need to worry about where you've been,' he says, 'my little holy one.'

Maria's love token, the painted dove egg, rolls away into a dusty corner of the yard.

A position is found for Maria in Poznan. Mother writes a begging letter to Aunt Irena, a Dulski relative. She will help, Mother says with a determined certainty. A helpful Dulski relative seems a contradiction in terms; whatever Mother has got from them has always been by stealth. And this is no different. The letter Mother writes makes no reference to Maria's unfortunate circumstances.

Martha Borkowska skips into the yard the following morning, brimming with the news.

'What's going to happen to her?' she asks Sissy excitedly.

Maria is still in bed, nursing a black eye and a gashed forehead. Sissy shrugs. What's going to happen has already happened, or so she thinks. It is only Martha's appetite for gossip that alerts her.

'She'll never be matched now. No one will have her, not even poor Wladek.'

Sissy cannot find it in her heart to even pity Wladek. She has got what she has wished for most fervently. She has got her Papa back. Nothing else matters.

Maria will be accommodated on the lowest rung of household service. She will be a pantry maid, but, Mother says, if she works hard and applies herself, who knows what advancement she could make. She is pretty, after all, Mother says, eyeing her meaningfully.

The bruise on her face is still yellow when Felix takes the cart out to drive her to Bydgoszcz; from there she will take a train to Poznan, where her new employers will meet her. A sister in the outside world! In Great-Grandma Dulska's city. Under other circumstances, Sissy would have envied Maria the chance. But watching her drive away into the dusk, bruised, tearful and shamed, Sissy knows there is no cause for celebration. Maria is venturing out into the world without her father's blessing.

COME SEPTEMBER THE pig is killed. Sissy is kept home from school. Papa sends her to the gate to look out for Kazek Wolski, the man from the village who will oversee the killing. He is a heavy, rough-looking man, with a red, jowled face crowned by a thin covering of stubble. Sissy has never seen a pig killed – Mother usually hunted the young ones away when Kazek came. But now that Maria has gone, Sissy is not considered young any more.

Mother has moved the kitchen table out into the yard and has spent the morning sharpening knives. Sissy will never forget that sound, the dry, grating bite of steel on steel, the glinting danger of blades. She loiters in the kitchen, fingering the familiar globes of cups as Kazek and Papa go about their grisly business in the yard. Even before they reach the outhouse, the sound of their shuffling footsteps alerts the chosen pig and it sets up a fearsome squealing. It dashes for the open door and finds itself cornered in the yard. The noise is deafening, the animal's shrill, panicky shrieks as the men close in on it, weakened by a day's fasting and its own sweaty fear. Kazek guffaws triumphantly above the squealing din and Sissy covers her ears, not knowing which she finds more upsetting, the pig's cries or Kazek's snorting laughter. Even when they finally catch the pig the squealing continues as they lash it to the kitchen table with ropes. Mother, who has been watching the spectacle in the yard, calls out to Sissy. She cowers,

244

hoping that if she cannot be found they will go ahead without her. It is not even that she likes the pigs. They are always hungry, gnawing away at the piggery door, snouting for food. They are the fat, greedy kings of the farmyard and yet, when they are let out, they roll themselves in the muck and live in their own dirt. She has seen animals killed before – Mother's poor chickens and geese – but this is different. It is the premeditation of it; Kazek Wolski brought from the village and the ritualistic glee he takes in his trade. The pig is fattened up purposely and there is the entrapment, the brute force of its killing. Both Papa and Kazek downed a shot of vodka before taking on the hysterical creature, as if they were preparing for battle.

'Sissy!' Papa roars. 'Get yourself out here.'

She steps gingerly outside. Russet crackle of leaves underfoot and the pungency of smoke. Her eyes smart. A fire smoulders in the centre of the yard, on which a vat of water steams. The smoke swoons softly in the air, drifting over Papa and Kazek as they pore over the pig splayed on the table, its twitching limbs stuck out as it shits hotly. Mother hands Sissy a large basin and orders her to crouch on one side of the table. Kazek lifts the knife and with one deft slice he slashes the pig just below its flabby, cloth-like ear. The sharpened knife slides easily through the pig's quivering, blubbery flesh. Savage and wounded, the pig screams, its cries rending the air. Sissy shuts her eyes tightly as a great rush of blood, thick and hot, spurts into the basin she holds. But she cannot shut out the noise, the yelping, pleading, ear-splitting screams. Her stomach heaves as the blood leaves a clotted trail on her apron and snags in her hair. For fifteen minutes she sits in the stench of slaughter, her eyes fixed on the spattered dust at her feet until Kazek puts the animal out of its misery and plunges it through the heart. A fresh gorge of blood is released, but at least it is quiet now; the silence so shocking it almost hurts. Even the blink of her eyelids sounds monstrous.

After that day schooling is over for Sissy. Someone has decided. Mother, Papa? Walter takes her place at the village school. He is tall now, as high as her elbow, and summers in the fields have made him nut-brown and hardy. He is no longer a baby; she has missed his babyhood. He does not like her to fuss over him. She finds it hard to stop herself. But she has to smuggle embraces from him – ruffling his corn-coloured hair in passing, buttoning him into his coat, knotting the laces on his boots, or taking his small rough hand in hers as she walks him as far as the shrine in the mornings.

'Pay attention now, won't you,' she urges him. 'Be a good boy and learn all you can.'

Walter pulls a face.

'I hate school,' he says, 'learning useless things.'

He is a bright boy, but he has no time for books. Sissy envies him his unwanted schooling. She steals his books when he is in bed; she reads voraciously. Imperial history, the great march of monarchies.

She cannot understand her love for Walter, accompanied as it is by a dangerous undertow. The feel of him reassures her, the lovely swell of his cheek, the bony bravery of his small, scarred knees, his grey gaze. Touching him will keep her safe. She waves after him fondly. The countryside murmurs about her. Leaves shiver. There is the plangent call of birdsong. Walter hardly gives her a backward glance, turned as he is towards the outside world while she stands fixed. Fixed and filled with a seething tide of something close to hatred, so strong she feels that she could do him harm. She tries to shake the feeling off, but it clings to her. She turns back towards the house. There are sheets to be washed and apples to be collected from the orchard. She retreats into the darkness of the house, her head full of pickling and sewing and jam-making. Useful things.

She cooks and cleans. She sows potatoes. She sets

cabbages and beets and radishes. She soaks the dirty
clothes, then boils them in layers sprinkled with wood ash
so the lye will percolate. She hawks the laundry to the river
and scrubs until her fingers are raw. She helps Mother to
cure the ham. They brew kvass from stale bread for the
thirsty work of the summer months. She and Mother sweat
through several seasons in the dark kitchen with the door
and windows tightly shut. Sissy feels she will never remove
the grime of earth from underneath her fingernails or the
smell of smoke from the tiny roots of her hair. But there
are rewards. Papa, returning home to such industry, is
mellow. She serves him in the evenings – potatoes and
bacon pieces fried in lard, or dumplings in beet soup. She is
a good cook. Even Mother notices her light hand with
pastry.

'Lovely stuff,' Papa says as he pushes back his chair from
the table and belches approvingly.

But certain things are forever lost. She can no longer
touch him. An attempted embrace would be lethal. A kiss
would be an outrage. She is too old for that now. She is
twelve years of age and feels already spent.

Papa gave the house a fresh coat of lime. It was as dazzling
as an unexpected snowfall. Sissy saw it as a celebration, a
fresh start. But if she had wormed her way back into the
heart of the family, Felix still remained stranded outside.
He slept now in the store, as if this was where he belonged,
amid broken furniture and wood shavings and food saved
up for the lean times before harvest. It was warm and evil-
smelling in there, like a furry cave. In the summers he took
the horse grazing at night and slept wherever the grass was
lush, giving the horse a long tether. He would take Papa's
gun and go out hunting in the fields, killing rabbits and
birds which he cooked over a brazier in the yard. It made
Felix seem like some benign predator who tramped out in

the dawn and went about some vital business of survival. Mother worried about him. When he was a child she had known how to care for him, but now that he was grown, she viewed him with a fearful eye. She knew how to deal with Papa, how to humour and appease him, but Felix was a different matter. She was scared now to be alone with him. Sissy was the only one to approach Felix, but she did it cautiously as if he were a wild animal who must not be frightened by sudden movements. She watched him carefully, not because she was afraid of him, but to view his extravagant bereavement. Felix had fallen in love.

Johanna Grabowska was a girl from the village. Sissy remembered her from the schoolroom, though she was several years older. She had a mane of grape-coloured hair and pale, plump skin. Her hands were like small peaches. Felix had nursed his infatuation with her from afar, following her home from the schoolhouse, haunting the fields near her father's house. Johanna had been flattered, not by Felix's attention, but by the attention of anyone. She was a kind-hearted girl and so she greeted him daily with a coy, teasing kind of smile. And Felix, mistaking this for encouragement, had decided to make a declaration. Merely that. When she started to back off he took her roughly in his arms and shook her, to make her see, he insisted afterwards, to make her see. But she had extricated herself from his insistent clutches and ran screaming to her father, saying Felix Schanzkowski had tried to force himself upon her. He was a madman, she said, and should be locked up. Poor Felix, Sissy thought. He had been told often enough that he was a dolt, but no one had warned him that dull-wittedness precluded him from love.

In the old days Papa would have cornered Felix and thrashed him as he had often done before, as much out of disappointment over what he was not as for anything he might have done. But Felix was a strong fifteen-year-old. He had inherited his father's build, if not his temperament, and his slowness had schooled him in defending himself with his fists. His mind might be dull, but he was quick on his feet and as alert as the small animals he so efficiently murdered.

'The boy's touched,' Papa said to Mr Grabowski, whom he confronted in the yard. 'If he were normal he would have had his way with her. There's no damage done, is there? You just tell your Johanna to stay away from him. Egging him on, like that.'

Mr Grabowski, a small, timid man with a sharp nose and shrewd eyes, had been expecting at least a show of remorse.

'I'm warning you, Schanzkowski,' he said, wagging a thin finger at Papa, who towered bullishly over him, 'if anything like this happens again ... on your head be it. He's *your* son.'

'Yes, yes, yes,' Papa agreed wearily, 'he's my son.' He looked accusingly at Mother.

After Mr Grabowski left, he turned on her.

'You talk to him,' he ordered, 'it's a woman's job.'

Mother did not talk to Felix; nobody did. They left him to his solitary grief. In the evenings Sissy would sometimes sit with him in the murky confines of his lair. He wept copiously. He avoided her gaze. Sissy knew why. Everywhere he went now there was taunting, the sly asides if he went into the village, every woman giving him a wide berth. He had acquired danger, though when Sissy saw him thus, the loud sniffling, the large childish tears as he rocked back and forth, she wondered what any woman could possibly fear from him. She was fascinated by his decline. This, she thought, truly was madness. It was as if this was Felix's destination from the moment he had betrayed himself in front of Papa all those years ago. He could not hide his weakness then; now he seemed to glory in it. He had become what Papa had always suspected he was – a dumb, braying beast who could not control his urges.

'Johanna,' he would bleat, 'Johanna, my Johanna.'

As if he had been reduced to living and breathing her name.

Sissy tried to tell him how unworthy Johanna was of his stricken passion, but if he heard he took no notice. Johanna, too, was stupid, but in a different way from Felix. She was a silly girl, giddy with the power of her own body, her capacity to madden. Sissy envied her effusive good looks, her startling hair. But what Felix had thought of as a vague dreaminess was simple heedlessness; Johanna did not know what to do with herself. If I had those looks, Sissy thought to herself, I could slay men.

There is a cry in the middle of the night. Sissy wakes out of a dreamless sleep to a sound like the silvery caw of a gull. It comes from the settle bed close to the hearth, where Walter sleeps. Sissy tiptoes into the kitchen. She does not know why she is being so quiet. From the other room she can hear the sharp growl of Papa's snores. Walter is sitting up in bed, his face blemished by night shadows.

'What is it,' she asks him, 'a bad dream?'

He nods sadly.

She sits next to him on the tormented bed. He curls in close to her. Gratefully she puts her arm around his shivering shoulders and draws him in. She presses her lips to the crown of his head. She remembers a time when she could have felt the flutter of his fontanelle there. Now it is covered over by matted hair.

'There, there. Tell Sissy all about it.'

He is being pursued, by whom he cannot say, through the orchard and down the ferny path to the river. It is dark and he is running, running for his life. Behind him, an older, stronger set of footsteps is gaining on him. There are the sounds of snapping twigs as his pursuer pounds after him. If he makes it to the river he will be all right. The water will kill the smell of his fear, salty and piercing in his own nostrils, and will shake off the pursuer. He reaches the river and wades in, but suddenly he loses his footing and is propelled downwards by some force above. He can see a thrashing on the surface, but it is not of his own making. Something is holding him down, some heavy weight of stone which bears down on his chest. His lungs are bursting; he opens his mouth ... and comes to, aghast, swallowing great mouthfuls of air. The sheets are soaked.

The dream recurs. It is the only secret Sissy shares with Walter. In those midnight hours in the mulberry gloom of the kitchen, she is allowed to baby him, to caress his fingers or brush his temple with her fingertips and croon softly to him. She often sits with him long after he has sunk restlessly back into sleep. Only then can she glimpse the baby that he once was. She has seen his soul; she has counted his milk teeth. Slumber irons out the hardnesses of rough wind on his cheeks and the boyish swagger which marks his waking hours. His gentle, easy breathing obliterates the raucous hollers of war cries, the urgent physicality of boyish play. Only his fists are clenched, as if in readiness for the next schoolyard scrap, or the next night demon.

A year has gone by and there is no word of Maria. Apart from a short note at the start griping about how hard the work was, how her hands were ruined from the bleach, how cramped their quarters were, there has been no news of her. Sissy is disappointed. She misses Maria, her presence around the house, her gleeful chatter, her knowing air. She was Sissy's signpost. Where Maria went, Sissy might follow. She feels the solitude of being the only girl in the house now (she does not count Mother; Mother was never a girl). When Maria left she had thought of her as an extension out there in the great world. Maria's presence in Poznan had given Sissy a foothold there; now she is adrift and Sissy has no way of placing her. Mother's letters to Maria are returned. She frets. She has always had a soft spot for Maria. A relative dispatched to the house where she worked is told that she has left, under a cloud.

'Surprise, surprise,' Papa says.

'Maybe she's found a better position,' Mother says.

'On her back,' Papa says, 'more than likely.'

Sissy marvels at Papa's unrelenting absolutism. He has large feelings, she knows. Passion and rage battle within him. But he cannot deal in lesser currencies, the small change of gentleness, the mere coinage of sentiment. These he treats as irritations, trifling, female. When the farmyard cat produces a litter of six kittens he fetches a sack from the store and throws the scraggy bundles of fur into it. Sissy can still hear the furious scrabblings as he lifts the writhing bag and plunges it into the rain barrel. But Papa does not hear their wretched squealing nor even Walter's pleas to save them. He had stayed up all night to watch them being born. He carried the runt of the litter around in the crook of his arm for days. Sissy will not forget the look on Papa's face as he drowns the kittens. Flinty, insouciant. He is deaf to all wheedling. He is all power and no mercy.

HER BLOOD CAME in the spring of her thirteenth year. She woke to find her nightshirt soaked and a stickiness between her legs where the blood had dried, leaving a rusty stain. She thought she was having a baby. She had seen the cow calving, lying ruined and almost dead in the byre as Papa dragged forth a slimy young one, blood to his elbow. She remembered watching as the calf, half-mad it seemed to her, staggered to its spindly legs and fell about in the blood of its own making. Now it was happening to her, the bad fruit of her secret longing. She lay quite still, hoping that she had woken from a dream and when she looked again there would be no blood, no shame. But no, the ruinous blood was everywhere. She must have crushed the baby to death with the weight of her sleep so that all that was left were these clotted remains. She leaped out of bed, pulled off the sheets and bundled them together with her nightshirt. She dressed quickly, the sour, fecund smell of stale blood in her nostrils. Whatever she had done she must hide the evidence. She tiptoed out of the room and through the kitchen, her soiled bundle under her arm. Alarm and guilt came over her in waves, making her skin prickle and her mouth dry. She must not be discovered. She knew what happened to young girls who had babies.

The year before last Julianna Sikorska, already big with child, had had her head shaved and been led through the village in a halter. She had been made to stand for hours in the blistering heat of a midsummer's day as young boys and men gathered and taunted her. Some of them spat at her. Sissy had not properly understood then what Julianna's crime was, and Mother had hurried her on when she had tried to ask. But despite the starkness of Julianna's public humiliation, she walked proudly down Slupia Street with her fat, healthy, bastard son, and all those selfsame villagers with their switches and spittle could do was to fall back with a kind of awe at her brassiness. She might have been a fallen woman, but she had somehow triumphed. When the child was weaned she had gone to Berlin to work, leaving the infant with her parents. It was unlikely that she would ever return to Borowy Las. But no one would forget the name of Julianna Sikorska.

Sissy opened the latch door into the yard. A glowering dawn greeted her; the frantic clamour of birdsong invaded the sleeping house.

'Sissy?'

A sleepy murmur from Walter.

'Shush,' she said, 'go back to sleep.'

'It's blood,' he cried. 'Mother, Papa, Sissy's hurt, she's bleeding.'

She stood paralysed by the door, willing him to stop.

'Sissy's hurt.' He was yelling now.

A floorboard creaked. Papa trod heavily into the kitchen.

'What is it, Walter? What's wrong?' Sleep snagged in his throat.

He did not even see Sissy. She looked at them, father and son, locked in their bartering, complicit gaze, a look that locked her out. But for once, she was glad of it. It gave her a chance to escape. Papa must never discover her secret. She darted out into the yard and made for the river. She plunged the sheets and nightshirt into the eddying waters. She squeezed and squeezed until she had throttled the lifeblood out of them.

*

She set her face against it. She would not let it happen. She feared that once she had started she would bleed continuously and be confined to bed like some delicate, thin-blooded royal. The full moon of her childhood was eclipsed. Mother tried to explain when she discovered Sissy sitting on a sawn stump in the orchard, guardian of her sheets spread to dry on the bushes. This, Mother said, pointing to the ghosts of blood on the sheets, this happened to all women. This would *make* her a woman.

'I will not,' Sissy said.

'But, Sissy,' Mother said, 'you can't simply refuse. You have no choice in this.'

All is changed by the spilling of blood. She has always thought of herself as solid, arms, legs, skin, hair. Now there is a hollow, a blank at her centre. She does not like to think about this newly opened inner chamber. It makes her dizzy – but it is not the pleasant giddiness of contemplating the vastness of the sky or the domed loftiness of the church. This is an unhinged airiness that comes from within. When she goes outside she is afraid she might be picked up by a puff of wind and whisked away. The ground is no longer solid beneath her. And when the pain comes it is as if the earth is tugging at her innards, pulling at the pit of her belly, heavy as stone, draining her power away between her legs. Mother says she has gained her womanhood. Sissy feels as if she is being robbed.

As soon as she saw the carpet of hair falling on the floor Sissy was sorry. She had caught the thick braid of hair and chopped it with one downward swipe of the kitchen knife. She attacked the rest of it with scissors, gapping the front and sides until she looked like a piebald boy. Some of the hair, which curled now at her feet, had been with her since babyhood. Mother came upon her in the scullery, scissors clenched in her fingers. For a moment she thought the girl had been attacked; her immediate unspoken fear was – Felix. Then she realised the damage was self-inflicted. She approached Sissy as she might a cornered animal.

'Sissy, what have you done?'

Sissy dropped the scissors on the flagstones, and stared down at the feathery pile at her feet. Mother drew her close. She could not remember the last time her mother had embraced her. It made her feel weak and grateful all at once.

'The neighbours will think we have lice in the house,' Mother said as she fingered Sissy's shorn head. 'You'll have to wear a cap now like an old married woman.' She cupped her hand around Sissy's gapped crown and tried to smooth out the cruel handiwork.

'What possessed you, child, to do such a thing?'

Sissy shrugged miserably. She did not know, in truth, what had possessed her. A mood had overtaken her, like a shift in the weather, a wind suddenly rising up and tormenting the leaves of the trees, a shiver of birds' wings, a cloud stealing over the sun. It was a new sensation, quite different to the vague and dreamy longings which had afflicted her before. They had made her lethargic; this gave her a ferocious energy. She had an urge to destroy, to break things. A kind of bile rose up in her throat and she had to act. She had tried to dispel it by applying herself to household tasks. She took over from Mother the job of wringing the necks of the chickens. She crushed beets for the pigs, enough for a week, beating them to a sodden pulp. She took the axe and chopped logs mercilessly in the yard. The flail of the axe and the thwack of stone against wood made her feel powerful and dangerous, but her arms ached from the effort. But nothing satisfied her enough. She wanted to do damage. She fingered the braids of her hair, which hung at her waist like the useless tail of a donkey. This, she thought, I could destroy. What use was her hair to her, or to anybody? And the next moment the knife was in her hand and the braid was lying dead on the floor.

Felix wept when he saw her. He unwound her severed plait and laid the strands on the table reverently. Kneeling, he gathered up her shorn locks and cupped them in his palm as if they were spilled gold. He pressed his lips to her lost hair, as if grieving for her vanished childhood. Only Felix understood, there on his knees, gaping at her with a dumb, brotherly bewilderment. Papa shoved him aside.

'Who did this to you?' he demanded.

'She did it herself,' Mother explained.

Sissy expected a blow, but instead a shadow of sorrow crossed his features.

'Your hair,' Papa said, 'your lovely hair.'

The tone of lament softened her. She felt the ancient familiar love for him well up in her, the devotion that was as natural to her as breathing. Then she realised she had hurt him, and the thought strangely pleased her.

'She looks as if she's been punished,' he said to Mother.

'Punished for what?'

'I don't know,' he said. 'What has she done?'

'You look ugly,' Walter said, 'ugly and mad.' He tittered and Papa joined in. His own shrill laughter and Papa's rumbling guffaw egged the child on. 'They should lock you up. You and Felix. Soft in the head, both of you.'

Papa spluttered into a fresh bout of laughter.

'Oh yes,' Sissy said. 'And who wakes up in the middle of the night crying for his mother like an infant.'

'That's enough, Sissy,' Mother said.

But it wasn't. Her blood was up now.

'Who's so afraid of the water that he wets the bed?'

The laughter halted abruptly. Walter, eyes downward, refused to look at Papa. Sissy trembled with a sense of victory; she savoured the triumph of betrayal. Finally she had outdone the boy child. But Papa merely reached out his hand and placed it on Walter's head.

'If the boy's afraid of water,' he announced, 'then we must teach him to swim!'

She watched them, unseen. It tantalised her, father and son in the river, skin on skin. Papa standing naked in waist-high water, holding Walter at arm's length as he drew him along, the boy kicking and thrashing noisily. Papa urged and remonstrated.

'No, Walter, no . . . like this!'

She was familiar with this spot on the river with its apron of shingle. She had scrubbed clothes there and laid sheets out to dry on its smooth platform of rocks. She had paddled in the shallows and once or twice she had immersed herself, fully clothed, on summery days when the meadows sizzled with heat. Papa plunged head down into the water, gliding along with a side stroke which sent out eddying ripples around him. His head, sleek as an otter's, rose and fell with an elegant ease as if he had found his true element. His work-coarsened body marked by the high tide of seasons – his arms brown to the elbows, his sun-beaten face – looked pale and newborn in the water. Then suddenly he rose out of the water in a fountain of spray and plucked Walter, shivering at the edge, and threw him high into the air. Walter shrieked in delight as Papa caught him deftly and the sun formed an arced halo of glistening light around father and much-beloved son. Sissy retreated into the undergrowth.

TIME IS RUNNING out for Sissy. A dowry is being saved for her. Mother has put aside two large pots and a pair of sheets which would have gone to Maria had she stayed. The next calf to be born will be given to Sissy's betrothed. She is fifteen and should be looking around, Mother says. It won't be long before the matchmaker will arrive at the door. A clever girl like her should have no trouble, she declares brightly. With her own history, Bella does not want her daughter left on the shelf. The memory of the long wait for Josef Schanzkowski still makes her burn with humiliation. She determines that her only daughter will not suffer likewise. She tries not to dwell on Sissy's strangeness, her quick temper, her haughty indifference to young men, her rage at the playful drenchings with buckets of water that boys indulged in on Easter Monday, her refusal to join in on the St John's Eve festivities in the village. *She* would not stand with a gaggle of girls on the water's edge pushing forth whitethorn wreaths alight with candles out onto the millpond and watch while the village boys rowed out to fetch them. She did not want anyone making a claim on her. Still, Mother counters, it is time to use her charms, the wiles of womanhood. Sissy knows nothing of them and does not want to know. She remembers Maria's little tricks of flirtation; even Gertie, blessed with a love match, had known how to hold out, when to retreat and when to surrender. But what good was it to know these things

259

when she did not want the reward that would go with them?

Covertly, Sissy observes her mother. Once, she too had been a young woman, though the girl in her had long since been killed off. Now she was sad, dejected, indomitable in her small rebellions, but defeated by a life of servitude and appeasement. How easy it would be to eclipse her mother, her tired beauty, her cracked skin and her hair faded to the colour of ashes. Sissy might be plain and ungainly, but she was young and untried. Her flesh at least was innocent. It was the only thing she had left to offer Papa.

She waited up for him one Saturday night, steering Mother towards bed when midnight struck on the wall clock and there was no sign of him.

'You'll lock the door, won't you, when he comes in, and don't let him here with the lamp burning, he's inclined to nod off.'

'Yes, Mother, I know.'

Sissy wondered how her mother could forget that she knew the ritual of these late nights. She, too, had spent many years lying vigilantly awake in the darkness, waiting for Papa to come home. Then it was with a mixture of delight and dread she waited: now it was with helpless desire. As a child she had never known what adult drama might ensue in the small hours of the morning – raised voices, often a litany of her mother's grievances countered by Papa's grumpy justifications. And there were not always rows. She had watched once behind the half-open door as Papa, creeping up soundlessly behind her mother, had kissed her with a rough passion on her bared neck. An expression flickered across Mother's face, as if she were in delicate pain. Then she shook him off.

'Hush, Josef, the children,' she hissed, casting an eye anxiously towards the children's room as Sissy melted back into the darkness.

Once her mother had gone to bed, Sissy dressed her hair with a bridal wreath. She had plucked darnel, daisies and white clover, and threaded them through with a red ribbon she had found in her dowry chest. She wore an old nightgown of Mother's, low in the front for nursing. She wrapped a shawl around the bare knobs of her shoulders where she had pushed back the gown. The sky was still streaked with ebbing brightness, the moon a pale shadow chasing the sun. Walter, in the cot by the stove, unfurled himself into abandoned sleep.

Sissy heard Papa singing long before he arrived, his voice ragged in the tumult of the summer's night – the throaty rumble of toads, the throbbing pulse of crickets. But it reached Sissy like a song of courtship. A field of bristling goose pimples rose on her forearms. Beneath the startling white of her gown, she could feel her nipples harden. She tried to moisten her lips as she willed herself to be still, not to betray herself to him too soon. The door scraped open and Papa stood silhouetted against the smoke-coloured night, stamping his feet noisily on the threshold as if it were the depths of winter and he were shaking snow off his boots.

'Elena?' he whispered incredulously.

The sight of his daughter standing barefoot in the half-light, her hands kneading her breasts, her lips parted, her eyes closed, made him think of his first wife. As if the years had suddenly fallen away, or history had been peeled back and he had stepped into an impassioned version of his past. Then he checked himself – drink was making him see things.

Sissy had not been able to wait. As soon as he had met her gaze, she thought the touch on her breasts was his and the seeping moisture between her thighs had come from his hand. He stepped towards her; she reached out, clinging to him fiercely, her fingernails digging into his fleshy arms, her lips crushed against the craggy skin of his breast bone as she came with a wrenching cry. Suddenly he seemed to wake from her assault, sinking his lips against her mouth, his tongue burrowing in, vainly trying to retrieve the trailing streamers of her ardour. But all that was left was the sharp windfall of her desire.

Walter stirred and opened a sticky eye. Papa froze, then pushed Sissy aside as he moved quickly to the settle bed. The child had only time to see the silhouettes of father and sister against the dying glow of the fire before sleep clawed him back into its clutches. He smiled drowsily as he fell.

A fury, hard and despising, gripped Sissy's heart. Was she never to have what she wanted? Papa turned his back on her.

For the first and only time in his life, Josef Schanzkowski felt the scalding of shame.

She was up early. She had slept little; some restless power awoken in her she could not quench. She was stoking the stove when Papa came in from the yard. He avoided her eye.

'Did Sissy look after you last night? We saved pork and dumplings but you didn't eat,' Mother said.

'Oh yes,' he replied, 'she looked after me all right.'

He turned his back and doused his face in the enamel basin by the door.

'Water,' he called.

Sissy heaved one of the pots from the stove and brought it over to where Papa had already begun to shave. She poured the water awkwardly. Hot splashes seared his soiled vest.

'Dammit, girl,' he shouted, 'careful!'

'I knew I should have stayed up,' Mother prattled. 'Sissy just has no idea . . .'

He took out his cut-throat and began to shave.

'I had no appetite,' he bayed.

Sissy's eyes blazed and she almost shouted 'liar!' Josef Schanzkowski hid behind a lather of white.

Walter bounded in. 'Papa! Papa!'

'Is the house on fire?' Mother asked petulantly.

'Leave the boy alone,' Papa said, tamping his wet chin with his discarded shirt.

'Are we going to the river?' Walter asked excitedly. 'You promised!'

'Make holy the Sabbath day,' Mother intoned.

Papa scowled at her.

'Take Sissy with you,' Papa said. 'Wasn't she a great one for the church?'

He spoke of her as if she weren't there.

'Please, Papa, can we go?' Walter pleaded, wrapping his arms around Papa's waist and nuzzling into his side. Sissy looked away.

'Yes, son, yes. We'll leave these women to their idle prayers.' He shot a look of scorn at Sissy. 'Ask God to send Sissy a husband. It's high time she was off our hands.'

In the afternoon Sissy went out into the fields. The parched stubble spoke of months without rain. The world had a bleached-out look. The blue sky was rinsed and brittle, the half-shorn meadows looked pale and penitent. She wandered through a field of sunflowers. They gathered round her, their black hearts glowering. They eclipsed her, towering at her shoulders. She felt protected by the darkness at their centre. It matched her own. The clammy heat made her lethargic, as if the passion of the previous night had seeped away into her father's mouth. She blushed to think of it, the spot on her cheek where he had scalded her with his stubble, his rough breath misting at her ear, his smell, sweet and stale. She touched her ear, her cheek, her mouth in a prayerful benediction, to ensure that she had not dreamed it up. The whorl of ear, the svelte of cheek, the fleshy cushion of her mouth, these could not lie. Witnesses all, no matter how Papa might try to deny it. To escape from the merciless sun she climbed into the barn and lay among the bales of just gathered hay. Here, purblind and hectic with lust, she fell into a troubled sleep.

She is three again, lying in the warm rustle of hay. It is the first full, fat year of the century. It is the life before Walter. She is innocent again. If she sleeps on, no harm will come to her. She can roam for ever in the sun-soaked days of childhood, the baby of the family, her father's little Princess. The ghost of that little girl is already turning away, waving sadly as if from a great distance. She is still waiting. Waiting for her mother to emerge from the house, a woman calling for her last-born in the busy heat of haymaking, waiting for Papa to unravel the straw-flecked nest of her hair while Grandmother's wall clock ticks in waltz time. It is not too late to go back, Sissy. Open the flimsy door. Turn the hands back . . . before the spilling of blood, the breaking of eggs. Go back!

I am woken by the drumbeat of rain, the curdled sleep of years in my mouth. I float in the murky, louring sky, surveying what was once my kingdom. I see the sodden track, the dreeping house, the spattered yard. I ruled here once, this man my husband, my children ran among the dogweed, supplanted now by impostors and their ragged mother, who bears the name that I once had.

I am Elena Schanzkowska. Wronged woman. Sensed only by the middle child, the strange, bewitched one. She it was who felt my presence in the kitchen, my hand on the oven door, my spirit in the throbbing summer light of the yard and in the cemetery on the day of the dead. She who made hymns of my children's names to join these worlds together, hers and mine. But what's mine is mine. Valerian, Gertruda and Maria, and the unnamed one who stole my life from me before I was ready to go. All mine. Now that they are scattered, who is there to honour me? Not Josef, certainly. He banished me before I was even cold. He struck Valerian for weeping at the sight of me stretched out upon my birth bed, deathbed, a pfennig on each eyelid. My first-born, my roguish, playful son. Usurped, disowned. Gone to a distant place where I hold no sway. Does he even remember me? Perhaps only as a faint image, a tender, melancholy icon. Gertruda did, but she was scolded for it. Scolded too when she burned the bread or scorched the sheets or couldn't quell the little one's cries. Maria, poor motherless mite. I saw myself in her, her fancies, her hunting out of love, but she too was driven off.

I was not two years dead when he brought another woman in. To my place at the hearth. He did not once weep for me, nor for our lost infant son, drowned in the womb. The stupid midwife who would not listen when I told her there was a second child within. A boy! A boy who might have suckled at my breast, a boy whose tiny toes had drummed a tattoo inside my belly. Instead she boiled up onions and untied the knotted bedclothes. The doors of the church were flung wide open to ease the delivery. But all her superstition could not save me. If she had put her ear close to my lips I could have told her there was another child within, but who listens to a woman mad with hours of labour? And where was Josef? Out, away. He never was a man to stand a woman's pain. He would not tell that new woman my name, although she heard it in the village. It's better, he said, that I do not speak it. He knew that if he did a doorway would be opened, a doorway that would let me back in. And in the end he called me forth himself. Desire forced him to speak my name. Elena!

Now I speak for two, for myself and for my son, who cannot speak for himself. He is the vampire in the barrel. The dead child I brought into this world who is trapped here. I could go, melt away peacefully, but there is no passage out for him unless I make it. So I have waited, hovering like a change of mood, a shimmer on the lake, a shiver in the trees.

Some would call us spirits. Call us what you will, it is we who disturb the commonplace solemnity of the world because we cannot bear its complacent bulk, its solid satisfaction with the particular. We are imprisoned by the places that have imprisoned us. When humans look up into the night sky it is not just the vastness of the universe they feel, but us, the unhappily dead who crowd the hours of darkness. But do not think that we are benign. We take our sorrows with us. Remember, what I was, I am. A woman scorned.

The sky opens. Large, fat drops at first, hesitant as a child's sulky tears, then a downpour. Summer storm. I am running over sodden earth and greedy grass. Ahead the great smoke-coloured clouds gather like swathes of ruffled cloth. The trees feel me pass. I see the creased frown of their barks, their arms in leafy semaphore, passing the urgent secret on from one to the other, warning birds to scatter. I reach the angry river.

There is a boy waist-high in water, a boy who could have been mine, but mine was buried in a field without the blessing of water. I do not even know where. Josef did it in the dark as if I had committed a crime by smuggling a dead child into the world. A swaddled corpse, a child knotted into birth clothes in an unmarked grave. This boy is standing in the fast-swelling water, his back to me, glistening. He is lost in some watery dream, while all about him the trees swirl and the clouds rail in a magnificent temper. By the river's edge there are stepping stones, large flat ones on which we used to beat the laundry. They are worn smooth from bleach and lye and the silky brush of bare feet. I slip into the shallows and place a hand on this boy's damp crown. The feathery touch alerts him. He turns his head.

'Sissy?' he cries.

I grab him by the hair and plunge him under. Face down into the boiling spume. I hold him there. He struggles, arms thrashing, but his feet have lost their purchase. He does not

266

surrender easily. It takes all my strength to hold him under. He must be totally immersed. This is a baptism for my son so he can be released. A baptism of desire.

A voice calls.

'Walter, Walter!'

Josef's voice, I let go of the child's sodden locks and he floats off, a pale, bloated thing just visible amidst the foaming water. I rise slowly and wade back to the river bank. I make for the brushy undergrowth and sink into its thorny shelter. From here I see Josef stumble towards the edge. He contemplates the bundle of clothes his son has left, weighted down by a small stone. Oh, the puny defences of the world.

'Walter?' he calls again above the racket of the trees and the whipping, angry rain.

He looks up and down the tormented river. He knows then. He stands, his head flung back, bellowing.

'Walter.'

I watch him and am pleased.

Sissy stumbles back the sodden track away from the roar of the river, blinded by the rain, her skirts heavy, the rag-tails of her hair weeping. The shelter of the house is all she thinks of, the harbour of hearth, the dull ache of the familiar. The rain batters her as she pushes back the dipping arms of bushes, the thrashing stalks of sunflowers, her arms scraped by thorns, her clothes snagging in raging branches. She turns into the muddy yard. Mother's geranium pots have crashed from the sills and roll about, the petals strewn in the pools the rain has made. She lifts the latch on the kitchen door and falls inside, leaning against the door to shut out the rage without. Mother rises from the hearth.

'Sissy?'

'The river,' she splutters.

'Look at you,' Mother says, 'you're drowned.'

'The river,' she repeats.

'What about the river?'
'The river has taken Walter.'

The body was not recovered for three days. It was driven
downstream by the high winds and the tempestuous flood
until it came to rest in a nest of fallen branches ten miles
away, a ghastly fruit of the storm. Sissy sat up for two
nights with Mother as the men searched for him. Gertie,
big with her third child, came home, though her belly was
like an insult. When Mother raised her head what she could
see was a young, happy woman, blooming, five months
gone. Papa sank into a stupor, for once not drink induced.
He had not been prepared for Mother's anger.

'How could you?' she yelled, pummelling him with her
fists and clawing at his face.

'How could you have left him alone? The river was in
flood and you left him alone, a little boy.'

Papa shielded his face with his hands and said nothing.
Sissy had never seen him silent, beaten like this. But what
could he have said? Everything Mother accused him of was
true. His fecklessness, his sodden tempers had been clear to
all but not to him. In those days and nights of waiting he
seemed to shrink. His cruel inattention of many years was
magnified by this one incident. He had abandoned his son,
his bright silvery piece of a son. Mother railed against him.
She roared at him in his absence – the bastard, the bastard!
She spat if he came near.

'You killed him,' she said, 'as surely as if you had driven
a knife through his heart!'

Sissy was mesmerised by the torrent of anger that came
spilling from Mother's lips. She who had always seemed so
resigned, so defeated, was now breathing fire. Sissy was so
persuaded by Mother's grief that even she believed it was
Papa who had stood on that slippery rock and with both
hands pushed his son under and held him there, thrashing
and gasping, throttling the life out of him. Only he would

have the strength to do such a thing. Sissy was only a girl, after all, prone to weaknesses and fits of fancy and hysterical love. *She* could not have done it. She did not have the power.

The doors and the windows are ajar. Every cupboard and box in the house is opened wide. Walter is laid out on a trestle in the kitchen in his sailor suit. There is a slight smile on his lips, a sure sign, Mrs Borkowska says, that he is already in heaven. When Sissy bends to kiss him goodbye she is sure he will still be wet, but he is dry and cold as a stone. She thinks of when he came, all raw and angry, and the gravity and silence of his going. He has returned to the distant place from whence he came. His boots are put in the coffin beside him and the comb Mother used to part his hair. Sissy places a painted egg by his side. Papa halts the pendulum of Grandmother's clock. Time stands still.

Culpeper, Virginia, November 1983

HIGHWAY PATROLMAN FREDERICK (Foxy) Browne lazily dismounts and lifts off his globe of black. The radio on his bike crackles loudly. A station wagon is pulled up on the hard shoulder, an old model, listing to one side. Smoke is billowing from the open hood. The road is deserted, black top as far as the eye can see snaking through the leafy countryside, though the town is only five miles away. These folks may not know how close at hand help is. Foxy whips off his sunglasses and latches them onto the mouth of his top pocket. Automatically he produces his little notepad. Misdemeanours are on his mind. He strolls up to the rear of the steaming car. He peers in through the driver's window, which is rolled down half-way. Keys in the ignition, but no driver. An old dame is sitting in the passenger seat. She has a thatch of white hair and the flat, pursed leer of someone who has forgotten to put in her dentures. She is wearing what appears to be a man's overcoat over a hospital gown of some description. Her blue-veined bare legs are thrust into a pair of furry slippers. In the back a blue wheelchair is folded, spokes glinting in the sun.

'Ma'am,' Foxy says, stooping at the open window and leaning his elbow on the roof of the car. 'Are you alone?'

She stares at him vacantly. Lights on, he thinks, nobody home.

'Officer!'

Foxy turns to find a burly, crew-cut man standing next to him. His fleshy face sports two sharp points – a large nose and the jutting precision of a widow's peak. He is in shirt sleeves, an egg-stained necktie is slung loose over his chest. He has a soiled, dishevelled air.

'Is everything all right here, sir?' Foxy asks.

'No, Officer, the radiator, I think . . .' Another billow of hissing steam emanates from the engine, as if to endorse the driver's diagnosis.

'Well, sir, I can radio back for help. A patrol car could take you back to Culpeper. You', he hesitates, 'and your mother.'

'My wife, Officer, actually.'

Foxy blushes to his rusty roots.

'Begging your pardon, ma'am,' Foxy says, tipping his forelock rather than meet the driver's eye. 'And where are you folk heading to?'

'Home,' the old dame says thickly.

'And where might that be?'

'Charlottesville,' the man replies.

Foxy twigs immediately. The pair from University Circle, their house a pigsty by all accounts. The subject of several contentious court cases taken out by the long-suffering neighbours. The woman, the wife, is some eccentric European, thinks she's royalty. Foxy has heard the stories. He knows too that the old lady has been reported missing from a hospital in Charlottesville. There's been an APB out on them. The husband kidnapped her. Climbed a ladder to the second floor and literally carried her off. Like some god-damned fairy tale. They've been on the loose for three days, like a latter-day Bonnie and Clyde (thankfully unarmed, Foxy notes, as he pats his own holster reassuringly), careering round the county on a geriatric spree in a battered automobile that fits the description of the clapped-out vehicle perched on the camber. They've been spotted at a gas station in Petersburg, at a diner in Fredericksburg, a drive-in theatre in Richmond. And judging by the state of the interior, they've been sleeping in the car.

'Mr Manahan,' Foxy starts.

'How did you know?' Manahan interjects.

'You have committed an illegal act. Kidnapping is a felony.'

'Listen, Officer, I had to do that. My wife', he says *sotto voce*, though the old bird seems hardly to register their conversation, 'has a fear of being locked up. They put her in an asylum when she was a young woman, and the truth is she never recovered. They broke her spirit there. When she was committed to that institution, it brought all those awful memories flooding back. I couldn't have that.'

He pauses then and sighs.

'Are you a married man, Officer?' Manahan asks.

Foxy nods assertively. 'Yessir.'

Foxy Browne is newly married and diverted by the novelty of his nuptial state. He thinks of Janice, her peachy skin, her candyfloss hair, the baby-dollness of her.

'Well, then,' Manahan says, clapping Foxy on the shoulder, 'you know what it's like to be separated from your beloved.'

Reluctantly Foxy suspends his mild reverie.

'We'll have to take you in, sir.'

'You don't understand,' Manahan says.

'She's a sick woman, sir, she should be in the hospital.'

'The car,' Manahan counters.

'I can call for a patrol car.'

'No, you don't understand. My wife could not consent to travel in a police car. She'll have to be towed.'

Foxy is not sure if Manahan means his car, or his wife.

'Hey, lady,' Foxy says, hoping a slangy casual approach will defuse the situation. 'Are you game for getting out?'

The little woman, scarecrow figure, scarecrow hair, looks scared herself.

'I have done nothing wrong,' she says.

Foxy radios in for help. The old lady sits grimly in the passenger seat while Manahan, face framed in the open window, pleads and cajoles and gesticulates at her.

'It's the uniform,' Manahan explains, 'maybe if you kept out of sight?'

Foxy loiters behind the car, trying to look invisible, as Manahan gently opens the door.

'They haven't come for you, Princess, it's all right, everything's going to be all right.'

The old dear swings her scraggy, mottled legs slowly out onto the tarmac.

'Now, Officer,' Manahan confides, man to man, 'when she gets out she'll expect to be treated with respect.'

'Sure,' Foxy says.

'Real respect, I mean,' Manahan reprimands him.

'Oh yeh?'

Just then two Culpeper patrol cars appear, slewing to a halt, lights flashing. A lot of manpower, Foxy thinks, for one little old lady.

'You'll have to kiss her hand,' the old guy is saying.

'Do what?' Foxy guffaws in disbelief.

'She's a grand duchess, Grand Duchess Anastasia Nikolayevna,' Manahan hisses.

'And what does that make you?' Foxy asks loudly as Manahan, struggling, is bundled into the back of one police car and his wife, unprotesting, is led to another. 'The King? Ain't you heard, pal? The King is dead.'

Note

Anastasia Manahan died on 12 February 1984 in Charlottesville, Virginia. Franziska Schanzkowska disappeared in Berlin in early 1920. Officially, her fate remains unknown.

Poland was partitioned three times during the eighteenth century and was divided between Prussia, Austria and Russia. After the formation of the German Reich in 1871, the part of Poland where Franziska Schanzkowska grew up was under German rule.

For clarity's sake, I have not used the diminutive and intimate form for first names, commonly employed in Polish and Russian. For place names in Poland, I have chosen modern Polish versions, though many of these would have been Germanified in the period in question.

Acknowledgements

For their loyalty and support, thanks to David Cutler, Orla Murphy, Margaret Mulvihill, Joanne Carroll, Marian Fitzgibbon and Rosemary Boran. For their practical help and advice, thanks to Nancy Quinlan, Jann Tchak, Krystoff Schramm, Marian Nowakowsky, Beata Kozak, Thomas Überhoff, Gwynn Baylis and Séamus Martin. A special word of thanks must go to the Lannan Foundation for a literature award which recognised my previous work and aided in the writing of this book.

I read a great deal of work, both fiction and non-fiction, in the preparation of this book but the following titles were invaluable:
Song, Dance and Customs of Peasant Poland, by Sula Benet (AMS Press, New York, 1951); *Victory Must Be Ours (Germany in the Great War 1914–18),* by Laurence Moyer (Leo Cooper, London, 1995); *Munition Lasses,* by A.K. Foxwell (Hodder and Stoughton, 1917); *The Female Malady: Women, Madness and English Culture, 1830–1980,* by Elaine Showalter (Virago, 1987); *Reading Berlin, 1900,* by Peter Fritzsche (Harvard University Press, 1998); *Anastasia: The Life of Anna Anderson,* by Peter Kurth (Pimlico, 1995); *The Last Empress: The Life and Times of Alexandra Feodorovna, Tsarina of Russia,* by Greg King (Citadel Press, New York, 1996); *Fabergé Eggs: Masterpieces from Czarist Russia,* by Susanna Pfeffer (Hugh Lauter Levin Associates, Inc, 1990)